All That I Am

Jeanne Whitmee

ROBERT HALE · LONDON

ISBN 0 7090 7535 9

Robert Hale Limited
Clerkenwell House
Clerkenwell Green
London EC1R 0HT

2 4 6 8 10 9 7 5 3 1

Typeset in 11/13 Sabon by
Derek Doyle & Associates, Liverpool.
Printed in Great Britain by
St Edmundsbury Press, Bury St Edmunds, Suffolk.
Bound by Woolnough Bookbinding Limited.

CHAPTER ONE

Eastmere, 1919

Only one passenger stepped down from the train when it stopped at Eastmere station, and as Abigail walked across the footbridge and stood on the up-line platform looking round her at the familiar scene, she was overwhelmed by a sudden feeling of nostalgia. It was six years since she and her father had left; six long years during which she had grown from a sixteen-year-old schoolgirl into a young woman, yet as she stood here, with the steam swirling about her and the shouts of the porters ringing in her ears, it might have been yesterday.

She watched as the baskets of produce piled high on to the platform were loaded on to the train by perspiring porters; early spring flowers, potatoes and cabbages; carrots and parsnips. Later in the year it would be luscious ripe strawberries, apples and juicy plums. Eastmere was clearly still one of the country's main fruit and vegetable producers. Nothing had changed despite four years of war.

She picked up her valise and walked out into the station yard, giving up her ticket at the barrier as she went. In the yard the farm wagons were lined up, the horses snorting and exhaling plumes of steamy breath into the cold air. Men stamped their feet to warm them as they waited their turn to discharge their loads. Abigail stared at them incredulously. It seemed that the four years that had robbed the nation of the flower of its young manhood and taken her beloved father from her had changed the daily life here in Eastmere hardly at all.

'Miss Abigail!'

She turned at the sound of a voice calling her name and saw a tall young man walking hesitantly towards her. He stopped and pulled off his cap respectfully, his face flushing with embarrassment as he looked at the fashionably dressed young lady who stood before him. He cleared his throat.

'Er – it *is* Miss Abigail – Miss Banks, ain't it?'

'Yes, it is.' Abigail peered at the youth closely. 'Why, it's *Teddy*,' she said. 'Teddy Johnson!'

The lad's blush deepened. 'Ted, miss,' he said proudly. 'No one ain't called me Teddy since I was a kid.'

'I'm so sorry. But the last time I saw you, you were just a little boy.' Abigail held out her hand. 'It's very good to see you again, Ted.'

'Likewise, miss, I'm sure.' He surreptitiously wiped his hand down the side of his trousers before he put it into hers. 'Ma sent me to meet you off the train,' he said. 'She said to carry your bags. She's really made up about you coming back.'

Ashford's Yard, where the Johnson family lived, was just a short walk from the station. Adjacent to James's timber yard, it cut through from the riverside to the market-place, a narrow, winding street paved with cobblestones down the centre of which ran a channel carrying domestic effluence directly into the river. Abigail saw with dismay, as they made their way down the street of mean little terraced cottages, that little had changed here either since the days when her father and his friend, Theo James, had worked so hard to try to improve living conditions for the working folk of Eastmere.

At number seventeen they stopped, and Ted took Abigail's valise from his shoulder and pushed open the door. It gave directly into the Johnsons' main living-room. To the left, the cast-iron range that provided warmth and cooked their food sat in its alcove in the chimney breast. On the floor were the rag mats that Maggie had made from clippings of old clothes. The high mantel was draped with dark-red chenille edged with bobbles, and on it were Maggie's cherished and much-pawned brass candlesticks. In the centre of the room was the deal table at which the family ate, also covered by a chenille cloth in the middle of which stood an oil lamp with a glass chimney. On either side of the fireplace were high-backed chairs with worn and faded cushions, and against the wall stood an ancient sofa stuffed with horsehair and covered in slippery, unreceptive leather cloth.

As Ted put down Abigail's valise, the door opposite opened and Maggie came bustling in. Her sleeves were rolled to the elbows, and her face was red and moist with exertion.

'Miss Abigail! I'm right pleased to see you.' She wiped her hands on the sacking apron she wore before holding them out. 'You'll have to excuse me. It's wash day. I thought I'd get it done before you came, but bless me if you haven't beat me to it.' She took both of Abigail's hands and looked at her admiringly. 'Well, well! Who'd have thought it, eh? Our Miss Abigail back in Eastmere after all this time!' She ran her eyes over Abigail's attire. 'My, my! Quite the fashionable young London lady now, ain't you? Just wait till my Sarah sees that coat and frock!'

Abigail laughed and threw her arms around Maggie's plump figure, hugging her warmly. 'Oh, Maggie, it's so good to see you. You haven't changed at all.' She looked around her. 'And neither has this place.'

Maggie shook her head wryly. 'No, it ain't, more's the pity. Now . . .' She nodded to Ted. 'Don't stand there gawping, Ted. Take Miss Abigail's bag upstairs.' As Ted disappeared through the door that gave on to the steep staircase, Maggie turned to Abigail. 'I hope you won't mind sharing with Sarah and me. I've put up another bed. It's a bit of a squash but we'll manage. The boys have the other room.'

'Not at all. It's very good of you to offer to put me up, Maggie,' Abigail said. 'It won't be for long, I'm sure. And of course I'll pay you.'

'Well, you're welcome to stay just as long as you need to,' Maggie said. 'I don't like taking anything from you, but I won't pretend that a bit of help with the housekeeping won't come amiss.'

At the top of the steep, narrow staircase two doors faced each other across a small square of landing. Maggie pushed open the one on the right. The window of the tiny bedroom looked down into the small paved yard at the back of the house, which was festooned at the moment with Maggie's washing. Beyond the yard ran a narrow passage at the end of which, Abigail remembered, were the communal privies shared by all the occupants of the street. It was the one feature of her stay at Ashford's Yard that she looked forward to least.

The iron-framed double bed that Maggie and her daughter, Sarah, shared was pushed against the wall to make room for the truckle-bed provided for Abigail. The only other furniture was a chest of drawers, on top of which stood a damp-spotted mirror, a basin and ewer.

'There's no room for a proper washstand,' Maggie explained apologetically, 'so we make do as best we can. Any time you want a bath, I can put up a screen for you to have one in the scullery downstairs. We always heat up the water in the copper every Friday night. Me and Sarah go first, the boys after, but from now on I'll see to it that you have first go.'

'You're not to go to any trouble for me,' Abigail told her. 'I really appreciate being able to stay here till I get myself organized.'

When Abigail had unpacked as many of her things as there was room for, she went downstairs and joined Maggie, who was waiting with a freshly brewed pot of tea and a plate of home-made bread spread with margarine.

'I always cook our meal when I get back from Prospect House. We like to eat together when the lads get back from the yard,' she explained. 'I hope this'll tide you over for now.'

'Of course. Just do as you always do,' Abigail said. 'I don't want you to change anything.' She sat down and accepted the cup of strong tea Maggie poured for her, noticing that the older woman was using her treasured willow-pattern china, something normally kept for high days and holidays.

'Now, I want to hear all about what's been happening,' she said, taking an appreciative sip. 'The family first, of course. Are they all working now?'

Maggie nodded proudly. 'All except Ted. The other two boys, Patrick and Jim, work in the timber yard. Sarah did really well at school. Her teacher wanted her to go on to the grammar school; kept on at me, he did. He even said he'd apply for a scholarship for her.' Maggie shook her head. 'I'd have liked the girl to have had her chance, but I just couldn't afford it. It's hard enough to manage as it is, without keeping her on at school for another three years. Still, she's done well for herself. Got herself a job as assistant in Mr Hudson's chemist's shop. Besides, I daresay she'll be married and settled in a few years' time. Pretty as a picture she is, if I do say it myself.'

'So – it's just Ted, then?'

'Ted was offered the chance to work for Mr Gathercole, the blacksmith,' Maggie told her. 'But he's always had his heart set on gardening. Mr Brown, the head gardener at Lord Branford's, has promised to take him on as an apprentice soon. Poor Harry Jarvis, the under gardener, was killed at Passchendaele, God rest him. So Ted's looking forward to that. He starts after Easter, and meantime he does a few odd jobs – earns the odd shilling here and there. 'Course, he won't earn much for a while, but if he works hard and does well he could even rise to be head gardener one of these days.' Maggie laughed. 'Least, that's what he keeps telling me.'

'He's still your baby, then, Maggie?'

Maggie's eyes grew misty. 'He's always been a bit special, since I lost my poor little Arthur. And he wouldn't be here at all if it hadn't been for your dear pa,' she said. 'Best doctor Eastmere ever had – taking my Teddy's tonsils out right here, on this very table, when them doctors wouldn't let him use the hospital.' She shook her grey head. 'That's a night I shan't forget in a hurry – that an' the typhoid. I reckon if it hadn't been for your dear pa showin' me how to go on to keep the infection down, we'd all've been wiped out instead of just my Albert and baby Arthur.' She looked at Abigail. 'Things have

9

been so much better for us here in Ashford's Yard since your pa got the piped water put on for us, though I reckon that was the cause of him being hounded out.' She shook her head. 'The Town Council were dead set on putting up that statue of Councillor Briggs in the market place. It was like pulling teeth, making them spend the money on the likes of us instead. It was only Doctor Banks telling 'em there'd be more epidemics if our conditions weren't improved, and that next time they'd likely spread to other parts of the town.' She smiled wryly. 'That made 'em sit up and take notice.' She laid a hand on Abigail's arm. 'You must miss your pa sorely,' she said softly. 'Terrible, him being killed in the last year of the war like that.'

Abigail nodded. 'I do miss him, Maggie. I think I always will. It's really for him that I've come back to Eastmere.'

The older woman frowned, uncomprehending. 'For him – how do you mean?'

'I want to try to finish what he began,' Abigail said. 'But time enough for that later. First, I intend to start up my own business.'

Maggie's eyes widened. 'You? A young woman alone? What kind of business?'

'Father taught me a lot about photography. As you know, it was always a hobby of his. Since I left school, I've been apprenticed to a large photography studio in London. Now I mean to start up on my own.'

'Here, in Eastmere?'

'Yes. Well, there isn't a photography studio here, is there?'

'Not as I know of, no,' Maggie said doubtfully. For the life of her she couldn't see anyone but rich folk shelling out good money for things like photographs, but she didn't say so.

'Well, as soon as I can find suitable premises I intend to open one,' Abigail went on. 'I thought if I could find a shop to let – preferably one with living accommodation above, I'd set up on my own.' She pushed her empty cup back towards Maggie. 'But that's enough about me. Pour me another cup and tell me more about life here in Eastmere. Were there many local men lost in the war?'

Maggie sighed. 'Bless you, yes, my love. Six good lads from here in Ashford's Yard never came back. What with the war and the typhoid in '13, it left a good many widows and grieving mothers. I was so thankful my boys were too young, though my Patrick was all for volunteering till I talked him out of it. Them recruiting sergeants were a wily lot, then there were all them posters and the songs. Patrick was all for going. But he was only a lad, barely seventeen, and I couldn't bear to lose another one.'

'And you still work at Prospect House?' Abigail asked.

'I'm cook there now, though they've got a good girl who can finish off and serve up, so I get home early. It suits me well.'

'I've lost touch with Sophie,' Abigail said. 'She used to write regularly, but she stopped about a year ago. Is she all right?'

Maggie's eyes clouded. 'You'll have heard, of course, that her poor father died.'

Abigail nodded. 'Yes. She wrote and told me. I wrote back, but after that I heard nothing.'

'So you didn't know she was married?'

'*Married* – Sophie?' Abigail shook her head. 'No! When was this?'

'Very shortly before her father died. To a Mr Edwin Dean. Not from round here, mind. A stranger to the town.'

'So, what's he like?'

Maggie drew down the corners of her mouth in the familiar disapproving way that Abigail remembered so well. 'Handsome as they come, I'll give him that. And charm the birds off the trees with his soft talk. But handsome is as handsome does, I always say. Still, it's not my place to judge.' Maggie rose to her feet and began to clear the tea things. 'All I know is that my Miss Sophie isn't the happy girl she used to be. I should know.' She looked up with moist eyes. 'Nursed her from a baby, didn't I? Just like one of my own.' She reached out a work-roughened hand to cover Abigail's. 'Just as you are, dear. I can't tell you how good it is to see you sitting there, large as life. Seems like only yesterday you used to come to Prospect House to have your lessons with Miss Sophie. Two poor motherless little lambs.'

Abigail laughed. 'You always did your best to mother us, didn't you? Making sure we wore those awful flannel petticoats, and refusing to let us out to play in the snow.'

Maggie nodded. 'That were because of Sophie's delicate condition. A sickly child, she always was. Took real bad with the bronchitis every winter.' She sighed. 'And there's another thing I daresay you don't know . . .' She swallowed hard and looked up at Abigail. 'Six months ago, she had a baby, a little girl. The prettiest little thing you ever saw.' She shook her head. 'My poor lamb very near died giving birth, and then after all she went through the babe never thrived, bless her little heart. Just faded away.'

'She died? Sophie's baby died?' Abigail asked, aghast.

Maggie nodded. 'At just six weeks. And my poor Miss Sophie hasn't been the same since.'

'Oh, poor Sophie. I must go and see her,' Abigail said. 'I'll go tomorrow.'

When Maggie had left to prepare the evening meal at Prospect House, Abigail went for a walk round the town. As she picked her way along the cobblestones of Ashford's Yard, she received many a stare. A tall slender figure dressed in the latest London fashion, a saucy little feathered hat fitting closely over her newly cut dark hair, she looked like a peacock among sparrows.

As she emerged into the market-place, Abigail stood for a moment to look around her. All the same shops were there. Mr Harris, the butcher, with his joints of beef and pork displayed in the window, and poultry and rabbits hung up outside. Samson's, the grocers, next door, where you could stand outside and sniff the appetizing aromas of ground coffee and ripe cheese. Miss Phipps still presided over her little sweet-shop, the window filled to bursting with jars of tempting dolly mixtures, liquorice bootlaces and trays of home-made treacle toffee. In every way that Abigail could see, nothing had changed.

It was market day, and the aisles between the three rows of

stalls piled high with fresh produce were thronged with people. She wandered among them, looking for familiar faces, memories of her childhood flooding back.

Doctor George Banks and his small daughter had come to Eastmere in 1911. Doctor George, as he quickly became known, was the town's first 'panel' doctor, appointed by the Government in accordance with Lloyd George's controversial National Insurance Act. With his jovial kindliness and his re-assuring manner, he quickly became popular with the local people, especially the poor. However, the other doctors in the town did not share their enthusiasm. Already violently opposed to the new act, they saw Doctor Banks as an upstart and an interloper, threatening their very livelihoods by snatch-ing patients from under their noses. They refused him access to the cottage hospital, and made life difficult for him in as many ways as they could.

Apart from his patients, who adored him, Doctor George had only one good friend in Eastmere. Theo James was one of the town's most prosperous businessmen. He owned and ran a timber yard and a fleet of barges on the banks of the River Nene. In common with George, Theo was also a widower with a young daughter. Desperately protective of her, Theo engaged a tutor so that Sophie could be taught at home. But the child was lonely without other children to play with, and when Theo knew that George was having trouble finding a suitable school for Abigail he suggested that the two little girls shared their lessons. The girls' health and wellbeing was presided over by Maggie Johnson, who had nursed and cared for Sophie ever since her mother died.

As Abigail wandered from stall to stall, she remembered the fun that she and Sophie used to have, playing hide and seek in the large garden at Prospect House; romping with Sophie's little dog, Pixie; climbing the trees, much to Maggie's disap-proval, and stealing the luscious raspberries and gooseberries from under the gardener's nose. Thinking back, Abigail real-ized that she had been the instigator of most of the mischief they got up to. She had been the most terrible tomboy, forever

13

hitching up her skirts and getting her knees grazed and her clothes torn and muddied, much to Maggie's consternation.

Moving away from the market, she turned into Cray Street and looked into the window of Mr Hudson's chemist's shop, where Beecham's Pills and Anzora hair-restorer jostled for importance alongside Phulnana face powders and Icilma vanishing cream. She wondered if Mr Hudson would mind if she stepped inside for a moment to see Sarah. The last time she had seen Maggie's only daughter, the girl had been a skinny little scrap aged ten. She wondered if she would even recognize her now.

The shop was empty, and Sarah stood behind the counter, a white overall covering her dress. Maggie had been right, she was as pretty as a picture with her red-gold hair and green eyes. Her complexion was smooth and creamy, and it occurred to Abigail that she was the perfect advertisement for the face creams and powders that Mr Hudson sold, except that she clearly had no need of them. Abigail stepped up to the counter and smiled.

'Hello, Sarah. Remember me?'

For a moment Sarah stared at her, then her face relaxed into a smile of recognition. 'Oh! It's Miss Abigail, isn't it?'

'We've both grown up, Sarah,' Abigail said. 'It's been a long time. You look wonderful.'

'Not as wonderful as you,' Sarah said, looking enviously at the smart navy two-piece with the new low-cut waistline and floating red scarf. 'You'd never get an outfit like that round here.'

'All made out of my old things,' Abigail told her. 'I haven't got money for expensive clothes, so I alter and make do.'

Sarah looked impressed. 'You'll have to teach me how to do it. You've had your hair cut, too. Ma won't let me have mine off.' She raised a hand to the gleaming mass that she wore secured neatly into a chignon.

'I don't blame her,' Abigail said. 'Your hair is glorious. You know what they say – a woman's crowning glory. Mine's as straight as a poker and just plain old brown. It was always falling down and getting in the way. I was glad to get rid of it. I wouldn't if it had been like yours, though.'

Sarah pulled a face. 'I still want to have it cut. After all, it's good enough for Mary Pickford.' She leaned across the counter eagerly. 'We get the moving pictures here every Saturday night in the Institute Hall. But I suppose that must sound really countrified to you. I bet in London you get the latest films every night. Can't think why you wanted to come back here. I mean to go to London to work as soon as Ma will let me. I can't wait to get away from Eastmere.'

'Oh, I don't know. It's not so bad,' Abigail said.

Sarah's lip curled. 'What, in Ashford's Yard? It's bad enough now, but you want to wait till summer, when it gets hot. The stink from that gully is enough to poison you. It's a disgrace. After your pa got them to put the piped water in, they promised to do something about the drains.' She shrugged her slim shoulders. 'Some hopes. We're still waiting.'

'Maybe they'll pull it down soon,' Abigail said hopefully. 'Build some new houses, with proper plumbing and drains.'

Sarah shrugged. 'Pigs might fly, you mean. Ma says that's what your father had in mind, and he would have got them to do it, too, if they hadn't have hounded him out . . .' She blushed. 'Sorry, Miss Abigail.'

'That's all right, Sarah. And it's true. Father and Mr James tried hard to get Ashford's Yard rebuilt. I'm sure it will happen one of these days, now that the war is over. Just you wait and see.'

Sarah pulled a face. 'No offence, Miss Abigail, but I hope I'm long gone from here before then.'

Abigail smiled. 'Well, we'll see. And please drop the "Miss", won't you? Abigail will do, or Abby. That's what my friends call me.'

Sarah smiled. 'I'm really pleased you've come back, Mi – er – Abby. I reckon you'll brighten this old place up a treat.'

'Well, I promise I'll try to, Sarah. You and I are going to have a lot to talk about. I'll be relying on you to fill in all the gaps since I've been away.'

15

'That won't take long,' Sarah said wryly. 'Nothing ever happens here.' She grinned mischievously. 'But maybe it will, now that you're back!'

A customer came into the shop and Abigail turned to leave. 'I'd better go and let you get on. See you later, Sarah,' she said.

Maggie got back from Prospect House at half-past seven and went into the scullery to prepare the meal with the help of Sarah and Abigail. The two older boys, seventeen-year-old Jim and eighteen-year-old Patrick, arrived from the timber yard soon after, and by eight o'clock all six of them sat down to the evening meal of meat and potato pie and cabbage. Like Ted, Jim blushed furiously every time Abigail looked at him, but Patrick eyed her boldly. To him, she was like some exotic butterfly, descended on a dung-heap. He couldn't imagine why she should want to return to Eastmere at all, much less to Ashford's Yard, and when his mother took the used plates out to the scullery he seized the opportunity to voice his suspicions, in no uncertain terms.

'What's it feel like to be living in the slums, then, Miss Banks?' he asked.

Sarah frowned at him. '*Pat*! What a thing to say to Abby. She don't think of us in that way.'

Patrick's eyebrows shot up. 'Oh! Abby, is it? What's up – decided to see how the other half lives, is that it? Not often we have a real live lady stayin' with us. I suppose we should be honoured – you condescending to slum it here with us after living the high life in London!' Patrick rose from the table and stood leaning against the chimney breast, eyeing Abigail cynically. 'Anyway, our Sarah, she looks as if she's well able to speak up for herself, so why don't you let *her* answer?'

'I'm here because I intend to start up in business,' Abigail told him. 'And your mother has very generously offered to put me up until I'm settled. I shall be paying my way.'

'Huh! Glad to hear it!' He laughed. 'Going into business, is it? Well, good luck to you! I reckon you'll have about as much luck with Eastmere folk as your pa did! Him with his mouthing off about better homes for the workers. All talk, wasn't it?'

'*Patrick*!' Maggie had come back into the room, bearing the pudding, a massive jam roly-poly that had been steaming in the copper all afternoon. She slammed it down on the table and regarded her eldest son with a withering look. 'Just you apologize to Miss Abigail this minute. She's a guest in this house, and you'll treat her with the respect she deserves. And don't let me hear you speak ill of Doctor Banks. He was the kindest man as ever lived.'

'Just airing my opinion,' Patrick said. 'We're all entitled to that, ain't we?'

'Not in this house you're not,' Maggie told him. 'Not if it means talking to folk like that. I brought you up to have proper manners, so just you mind them if you want to go on living here.' She began to cut generous slices of pudding and pass them round the table. 'Come and get your pudding, and watch that tongue of yours. It'll get you hanged one of these days.'

But Patrick, his face red with anger, reached his cap down from the peg by the door and rammed it on over his thick coppery hair. 'I've had enough, thanks. The air in here is too refined for the likes of me. I'm going out.' The next moment, the door slammed and he was gone.

Abigail looked at Maggie. 'I'm sorry. I'm afraid he doesn't want me here.'

'Take no notice of him,' Sarah said, her green eyes flashing. 'He's always in a bad mood. *We* want you here, don't we, lads?' She looked hopefully at her brothers, who nodded, red-faced, staring hard at their plates.

Maggie shook her head. 'He's been like this ever since he got in with that hot-headed lot from work, always on about trade unions – more money and better working conditions. One week they're all for a strike, the next it's a revolution they're hell-bent on. It'll all end in tears, I tell him. If he's not careful, he'll end up in prison. But does he listen? Does he heck!' She patted Abigail's hand. 'Don't you take on about what he said about your pa. He knows nothing about it. He was only a lad when it happened. Just let it go in one ear and out the other,

17

love. That's what we do.' She passed Abigail a plate of pudding. 'By the way, I told Mrs Dean – Sophie – that you were back. I took the liberty of telling her you'd go and see her tomorrow. She was so excited.' She bit her lip. 'I did do right, didn't I? I reckon a sight of you is just what she needs at this moment.'

Abigail nodded. 'Of course you did right, Maggie. I'm looking forward to seeing Sophie.'

But as she ate Maggie's superbly sticky and substantial pudding, Abigail couldn't shrug off the stinging hurt of Patrick's remarks. *Mouthing off about better homes – all talk wasn't it?* Only she knew how sincere and dedicated her father had been in wanting to better the lives of the poor. Could she really do anything to bring about the change he had worked for? Clearly it wasn't going to be easy. Now she saw that she would have to fight prejudice and mistrust from Patrick and others like him, as well as those in authority. But she promised herself that she would do it, if it was the last thing she ever did. Patrick's scathing cynicism had served only to strengthen her resolve. Now she was more determined than ever.

Later that night, Abigail sat by the dying fire, writing a letter to her aunt. Sarah, Maggie and the boys had already gone up to bed, and she planned to join them as soon as she had finished her letter. She was just sealing the envelope when the door opened and Patrick came in. He didn't see her at first, sitting quietly in the corner, and she cleared her throat, making him start and spin round in the act of hanging up his cap.

'God almighty! You made me jump.'

'I'm sorry. I was just writing to my aunt to tell her I'd arrived safely.'

'We turn in early here,' he said stiffly. 'Working folks have to get up early in the morning.'

'I shan't disturb anyone,' she said. 'At least, no more than you will.' Abigail stood up, smoothing down her skirt. 'Patrick, you seem to have formed the wrong idea about me. My family are working-class too, you know. There's nothing of the high and mighty lady about me. I've worked ever since father and I left Eastmere. My father worked very hard in a poor practice in the East End of London after we left here. You've no idea what poverty is like until you've been there. We lived with my Aunt Jessica in Hackney, who is a widow and has to work for her living at dressmaking.'

'You're breaking my heart,' Patrick said cynically.

Abigail ignored him. 'And then there was the war. Do you think it was a picnic, living in London during the bombing?' she challenged him. 'My father joined up and was later killed. Gothas and Zeppelins pounded the East End, both day and night. Hundreds of people were killed and injured, and others lost their homes and the few possessions they had. But we all had to carry on. No one gave up working because of the raids. That's courage! You didn't know there was a war on, here in Eastmere!'

'Yeah – well . . .' Patrick couldn't meet the steady brown gaze.

'I came here because I wanted to try to carry on the work my father had to abandon,' she went on. 'It's something I've wanted to do ever since I can remember. I thought I'd at least have the support of the people I want to help. People like you.'

His eyes came up to meet hers. 'We're all right on our own,' he said stubbornly. 'We can help ourselves.'

'It looks like it, doesn't it? This place hasn't changed at all since we left it. The drains still overflow, and the sewerage is non-existent. Do you remember the typhoid outbreak that took your father and baby brother? Well, if something isn't done it's only a matter of time before there's another.'

'Think I don't know that?' he shouted at her, his colour rising. 'Do you really believe I want my ma and sister to have to live like this? It's what makes me so angry. What can we do, when we have to work all the hours God sends for a pittance? When the war ended, they talked about a country for heroes to live in, and what have we got?'

'At least you have a job,' Abigail retorted 'You should see the poor ex-servicemen begging on the streets of London, some of them without limbs they lost in the fighting. Selling matches and bootlaces to make a few coppers.'

Patrick had the grace to look shamefaced. 'All right. I wanted to go and fight, too. I would have, if I'd been older. As it was, Ma threatened to tell them I was underage.' He shook his head. 'What the hell can the likes of us do about it?'

'It's up to us,' Abigail told him. 'We each have to do what we can in the best way we're able.'

'You're right. Some of the lads and me are trying to get better wages,' he told her.

'Your mother told me. She worries that you'll get into trouble. Being violent and making trouble isn't the way, Patrick.'

'Then you'd better tell me what is, 'cause I'll tell you one thing: they sure as hell don't listen unless someone gives them a kick up the . . .' He cleared his throat. 'Till someone makes 'em sit up and listen.'

For a long moment they stood looking at each other. Suddenly Abigail saw that he was right. To get anything done you had to get yourself noticed. You had to make such a fuss that opinions were changed and hands were forced.

For Patrick's part, he was noticing for the first time how bright her eyes were when she was roused. Maybe he had got the wrong idea about her. Time would tell. Words were cheap enough, he told himself. And after all, she was only a woman.

CHAPTER TWO

Prospect House stood on the opposite side of the river to James's timber yard; an elegant Georgian town house built by Theo James's grandfather for his young bride in 1798. Marcus James had inherited the yard from his own father, added the fleet of barges and built the business into a flourishing concern. His study had been at the front of the house on the second floor, where he could see the river from the window and keep a watch on all that went on. Theo had inherited both house and business in 1895, and Sophie, who had been born at Prospect House, inherited it on her father's death.

As Abigail walked up the front steps and rang the bell, she reflected that there could hardly have been a greater contrast between the grand three-storeyed Georgian villa and the mean little cottage in Ashford's Yard.

Theo had loved his home and had installed every comfort in it. Over the years he had added every modern convenience, having what had once been his father's study converted into a bathroom in 1900 for his young wife. It was one of the first in the town, and greatly envied. As a little girl, Abigail had often enjoyed the luxury of taking a bath in the enormous bathtub, so large that it was possible for a child to take one whole swimming stroke.

The front door was opened by a young girl in the black and white uniform of a parlour maid. The girl took her coat and hat, and ushered her into the morning-room, where Sophie rose from her chair by the window, coming to greet Abigail with outstretched hands.

'Abby! It's been such a long time. Oh, it's so good to see you.' There were tears in her eyes as she embraced her friend, and Abigail tried hard to conceal her dismay at how ill she looked. Always delicate-looking, with her blonde hair and fine-boned features, Sophie was now almost ethereal, her skin nearly transparent and her violet blue eyes dull and listless. As Abigail held her close, the other girl's body felt bird-like; so fragile that it might easily break.

'Come and sit down,' Sophie invited. 'I love to sit here in the mornings and watch the birds in the garden. We put out nuts, and sometimes a squirrel comes down from the cedar tree and feeds. Jenny will bring us some coffee soon. You'd like coffee?'

'That would be very nice.' Abigail saw that two spots of hectic colour had appeared in Sophie's cheeks.

'Why did you stop writing to me, Sophie?' she asked reproachfully.

The other girl bit her lip. 'Dear Abby, always straight to the point.'

'I had to hear from Maggie that you were married,' Abigail said. 'Don't you remember how we each promised to be the other's bridesmaid when the time came to be married?'

Sophie sighed. 'I know. And I'm sorry. You know you're my oldest and best friend. I never meant to neglect you, but Papa was so very ill. He wanted Edwin and I to be married while he still had the strength to attend the wedding, but he was too ill to withstand any kind of festive occasion. It was very quiet – just a simple ceremony at the church and a meal here at home afterwards with just the three of us. No guests at all.'

'But you didn't even write and tell me about it,' Abigail admonished. 'I would have liked to send you a present – my love and good wishes.'

Sophie reached out a slender white hand to cover hers. 'Please forgive me, Abby. I know you have had your sadness, too. Your dear father – Maggie told me – so awful for you.'

Abigail nodded. 'I miss him terribly. As you know, we lived

with Father's sister in London, and Aunt Jessica was a great comfort to me. Now that the war is over, she has gone to live with a distant cousin in Hastings. They have opened a guest-house there.'

'And you have come back to Eastmere.'

'That's right, though not only for that reason.' She smiled and paused as the maid entered with the tray bearing delicate bone china cups and a silver coffee-pot. As the girl withdrew, Abby said, 'So – here we are again, Sophie, you and I. We have so much news to catch up with. So – tell me all yours.'

Sophie bent over the task of pouring coffee as she began. 'Edwin and I have been married just thirteen months,' she said haltingly. 'It should have been a happy time – the happiest year of my life. But I'm afraid it has been full of sorrow, which is partly why I stopped writing to you. I had nothing to tell that would have pleased you.'

'Maggie told me about the baby,' Abigail said softly. 'I'm so sorry, dear.'

Sophie nodded, her eyes filling with tears again. 'She was so sweet, Abby, my little Jane Louise. Such a little angel, and so very dear. Yet it wasn't to be. And the worst of it is that the doctor says I'll never have another.'

'Perhaps he's wrong,' Abigail said, but the other girl shook her head.

'No. There's no doubt. When little Jane was born, I almost died. Doctor Maybury says another birth would probably kill me.' She raised her eyes to meet Abigail's. 'Sometimes – I have to confess that sometimes I wish I *had* died, Abby. I really . . .'

'*Sophie!*' Abigail stopped her words with a shake of her head. 'Don't ever let me hear you say such a thing! This isn't like you. Maggie told me you were depressed, but I never thought to see you like this. Tell me about your husband. Tell me about Edwin. He must surely be a comfort to you.'

But if Abigail had expected a mention of Sophie's husband to bring a smile to her face, she was wrong. The other girl sighed.

'Edwin is handsome and charming,' she said. 'Everything

one could ask for in a husband. It's me who is lacking. I let him down.'

Abigail frowned. 'How can you possibly have let him down?'

'I'm afraid I irritate him,' Sophie said. 'He gets tired of my sadness and my – my long face.'

'Tired of your sadness? But surely he should be the one to comfort you! It was his child, too.'

'I know, but Edwin is so busy. He has so much to occupy him – the business and his – other interests. When he comes home in the evenings, he expects a wife who is witty and amusing. But how can I be those things when I have nothing but these four walls to look at all day long? And memories that haunt me.'

'Doesn't he see that you need taking out of yourself?' Abigail tried hard to conceal her anger. What kind of man would be so insensitive as to abandon his wife at such a tragic time – to expect her to be witty and amusing when she had lost her father and her child within one year? 'Well,' she said firmly, 'I'm back in Eastmere now, and I have such plans, Sophie. And you can help me, if you will.'

Sophie looked up, a spark of interest bringing back some of the old vitality to her eyes. 'What plans, Abby? How could I help you?'

Abigail leaned forward, her face alight with enthusiasm. 'Do you remember how Father loved his photography?'

'I do. I still have the likeness he took of you and me when we were children.'

'Well, he taught me how to take photographs as soon as I was old enough, and when I left school I went as an apprentice to a photographer in London; quite a grand one. He used to be commissioned to photograph society ladies, débutantes in all their finery and so on. Sometimes we went on assignments to court balls, and to country houses when there was a hunt ball or a shoot. We took serious photographs, too, of the bombing and ruined houses during the war, and the poor ex-servicemen on the streets.'

'Oh, Abby, what an exciting life you've had! And how brave

you are. You make me feel quite guilty and inadequate. But why didn't you stay there?'

'Because I wanted to have a studio of my own,' Abigail confided. 'And I wanted to come back here to Eastmere for another reason. Can you keep a secret, Sophie?'

'Of course. I promise.' Sophie's eyes were shining now. 'Do tell me.'

'I intend to finish what Father and your papa started.'

Sophie's eyes widened. 'Are you talking about the slum clearance?' she asked.

'Yes. When I was going through Father's things after he was killed, I found the plans that he and your father drew up between them; for improving Ashford's Yard. They were wonderful plans, Sophie, and they would make such a difference to the lives of the people who live there. I want to see them put to use. I haven't been able to get the idea out of my head. That's why I came back.'

Sophie's eyes were wide. 'That dreadful Ashford's Yard. I don't know how people can bear to live there. Wouldn't they be happier living in the country, Abby?'

'Perhaps they would. But they need to live close to their work. I want to try to get better conditions for them.'

'But how could you do all that, Abby, just you on your own? Surely it isn't possible?'

Abigail regarded her friend thoughtfully. 'Sophie, did your father leave the timber yard to you?'

Sophie shook her head. 'No, to Edwin. I could never have managed it, could I? I'm not nearly clever enough.'

'But you still have an interest in it. Could you talk to your husband on behalf of the people of Ashford's Yard? Try to make him see that he'd get more out of his workers if he helped them?'

Sophie looked doubtful. 'I don't think he would listen to me, Abby.'

'You see, the land Ashford's Yard stands on belongs to the timber yard,' Abigail went on. 'But the houses belong to an unknown landlord – Father guessed that it was someone with influence on the Town Council, which is why he found it impossible to get planning permission. The houses would have to be purchased before they could be pulled down, but of course the Council would have to put in the drainage and sewerage. Things could well have changed by now, though. Ownership might have been passed on. It would be well worth another try.'

Sophie was beginning to look worried and confused, so Abigail decided not to pursue the subject for the moment. 'Anyway, that's for the future,' she said. 'First, I want to establish my photographic studio, because I have to earn my living. I'm going to need all the help I can get. So – will you help me?'

'*Me?*' Sophie shook her head incredulously. 'I don't see what I could do.'

'You can do a lot. I know there isn't a photographer here in Eastmere, and there must be people who would patronize me – people you must know, Sophie. People who give grand parties and hold functions; who have young daughters and sons getting married. A memento of a family occasion – family groups.'

Sophie looked doubtful. 'Well, yes, I suppose I do, although since my illness I haven't been interested in social life of any kind. But you are right. People have to engage a photographer from Norwich or Peterborough when there are weddings or special occasions. Edwin and I didn't even have a photograph to mark the day, our wedding being such a quiet affair.' She frowned. 'But would that kind of work be enough to support you – pay the rent and so on?'

'Oh, I intend to offer my services to the local newspaper, too,' Abigail said. 'But in the meantime, do you think you could give me an introduction or recommend me to some of your acquaintances?'

'I could do better than that,' Sophie said, her eyes bright. 'I could give a dinner party, here at Prospect House. Edwin has been urging me to give one for months. I could invite people who might be potential clients.'

'That would be marvellous, Sophie, but I don't want you to

go to a lot of trouble and tire yourself out on my account.'

'It's no trouble – the least I can do for my oldest friend, and as I said, Edwin will be delighted.' Sophie suddenly looked worried. 'Abby, do you think it's wise to involve yourself with Ashford's Yard? Surely it could do you more harm than good, and won't you be too busy?'

'I'm hoping that somehow it will all tie in,' Abigail told her. 'But that's something for the future. First things first.' She glanced at the clock and got up. 'Now I must go and let you have your lunch.'

Sophie rose from her chair, looking thoughtful. 'Abby – I wish you'd written to say you were coming. You could have stayed here, with us. I hate to think of you at Ashford's Yard. I know Maggie is a dear, but it must be dreadfully cramped and it can't be very comfortable for you.'

Abigail shook her head. 'Don't worry about it. Maggie does her best, bless her. She's kindness itself and keeps everything as clean as a new pin. And you forget, Father and I lived in circumstances that were not much better when we came to Eastmere. Besides, I need to experience life at Ashford's Yard for myself if I'm to gather all the evidence I shall need.'

Sophie shook her head. 'You're so brave. You always did have more courage than me.' She rang for the maid to bring Abigail's coat and hat, then walked to the door with her. 'I'll talk to Edwin tonight and arrange something,' she said. 'But in the meantime I'll make a list.' She hugged Abigail warmly. 'Oh Abby, I'm *so* glad you're home. I've got something to look forward to now. I'm, so happy we're friends again and that you've forgiven me.' She looked up anxiously. 'You *have* forgiven me, haven't you?'

Abigail laughed. 'Of course I have, you goose! And don't worry,' she smiled mischievously, 'I intend to see that you make up for your neglect.' She paused on the doorstep, frowning as she suddenly remembered something her friend had said earlier. 'Sophie, did I hear you say that Doctor Maybury attended you?'

'That's right.'

'He's still practising, then?'

'Yes.' Sophie's face cleared. 'Oh, not the Doctor Maybury that you knew. This is his nephew, William. He took over the practice when his uncle retired.' She smiled. 'He's very different from his uncle, I can assure you.'

'I'm glad to hear it,' Abigail said wryly. She kissed her friend. 'Goodbye for now, then. We'll be in touch again soon.'

Sophie stood at the door and watched wistfully as Abigail strode across the road towards the bridge, admiring the proud straight back and the determined set of her shoulders. It was so good to see those shining brown eyes and hear that ringing laugh again. Somehow, this morning, she felt as though the icy chill of sadness and despair had thawed to reveal tiny green shoots of hope. Having Abigail here in Eastmere again, she felt she had a purpose in life once more.

Abigail walked round the town in the spring sunshine, familiarizing herself anew with the shops and the half-forgotten landmarks. In a street behind the market-place, she saw a sign above the side door next to a cobbler's shop. It read:

EASTMERE CHRONICLE
Editor, Andrew Naylor
Offices above

On a sudden impulse, she opened the door and began to ascend the dusty staircase.

At the top of the stairs, a woman with her hair dressed in plaited 'earphones' sat behind a tall black typewriter, busily clacking away. She looked up over her spectacles.

'Yes? Can I help you?'

'I'd like to see Mr Naylor, please,' Abigail said.

'Do you have an appointment?'

'No. But I know he'll want to see me.'

The woman took off her spectacles and met Abigail's dark brown eyes with a challenging stare. She was used to protecting her boss from unwelcome time-wasters. 'If you're looking

28

for work, I can save your time by telling you that we're fully staffed,' she said icily.

Abigail drew herself up to her full height. 'I am not looking for a job,' she said. 'I'm here to offer a specialized service.'

'And what *service* might that be?' the woman asked, a look of cynical disbelief curling her lip.

'That is something I intend to discuss with Mr Naylor,' Abigail said firmly. 'And I'm sure it is an opportunity he will not want to miss. So, could you please tell him that I would like to speak to him?'

The woman hesitated for a moment, hoping to freeze Abigail out with the look she reserved for such occasions, but the brown eyes that looked steadily back into hers clearly had no intention of backing down. At last she sighed and rose reluctantly from behind the desk.

'Oh, very well then,' she said curtly. 'I'll see if he's free, but I warn you, he's an extremely busy man. You'd better tell me your name.'

'Abigail Banks.'

'Right. Wait there.' The woman disappeared through a door to her right, reappearing after a moment or two with an expression of acute disapproval on her face. 'Mr Naylor will see you now,' she said. Lowering her voice, she added, 'But I should warn you, he gives short shrift to time-wasters.'

'I'll bear it in mind,' Abigail replied drily. She crossed the office and went in through the door indicated, the lift of her chin belying the quaking feeling in her stomach.

The office was full of pipe smoke, fragrant and, to Abigail, nostalgically reminiscent of her father. Behind the desk sat a man of about thirty wearing a brown tweed suit. He had dark wavy hair and a neatly trimmed moustache. He looked up at Abigail with amused grey eyes, taking the pipe from between his teeth.

'Miss Abigail Banks, I presume.'

His twinkling smile laid Abigail's fears to rest.

'That's right. I'm sorry to take up your time, Mr Naylor, and I promise not to waste more than is necessary.'

He burst out laughing. 'Oh dear! Our Miss Audley has been

terrorizing you. I recognize the terminology. She guards me like a bulldog. She's a gem really, and not nearly as fierce as she'd like you to think.' He tapped his pipe out into an ashtray and leaned across the desk. 'Do have a seat, Miss Banks. And tell me how I can help you.'

Abigail sat down and attempted to look relaxed. 'I'm here to offer you my services as a photographer, Mr Naylor,' she said, coming straight to the point.

Andrew Naylor's eyebrows shot up. 'A photographer, is it?'

'Yes. But perhaps you already have a resident photographer?'

'No. Not a resident one, as it happens.' He cleared his throat. 'Forgive me for being personal, Miss Banks, but have you worked for a newspaper before? You seem very young to have the kind of experience necessary.'

'My father was a keen amateur photographer. He taught me as a child. Later I became apprenticed to Jeremy Cusak of Cusak Studios in Kensington.'

'*The* Jeremy Cusak?'

'Yes. Do you know him?' Abigail asked.

'I know his work. He's one of the most talented men in his field.'

'I have a testimonial from Mr Cusak,' Abigail said, reaching into her handbag. She found the envelope and handed it to him. He opened it and read the letter carefully. At last he folded it and put it back in its envelope.

'Very impressive. Cusak obviously thinks very highly of your work.' He handed the letter back to her and reached for his tobacco pouch, refilling his pipe thoughtfully. 'So, if you worked for the Cusak Studios in Kensington, what are you doing here in Eastmere? By the tone of that letter you had an assured future in London.'

Abigail swallowed. 'I spent a lot of time in Eastmere as a child,' she told him. 'My father was a doctor in the town. I – have friends here, and I wanted to come back after my father was killed.'

'A doctor, you say?' His eyes suddenly lightened. 'Ah! Would that be Doctor George Banks – the panel doctor who was accused of malpractice just before the war?'

Abigail flushed. 'There was no truth in the accusations,' she said hotly. 'He was completely innocent, and in the end they had no choice but to exonerate him. The other doctors hated him because of the work he did with the poor, and he was a thorn in the flesh of the Town Council because he tried tirelessly to clear the slum areas . . .' Andrew Naylor stopped her with a wave of his hand.

'Please, Miss Banks. I apologize. I didn't mean to speak so bluntly. It was long before my time, of course, but I've read about your father's case in back numbers of the *Chronicle*. It caused quite a furore at the time, and it is a case I happen to be extremely interested in.' He sat back in his chair, applying a match to his pipe and puffing on it. 'With the war, things have had to change, course. The old order and all that. Most doctors were obliged to give in eventually, as I'm sure you know. Most now have their list of panel patients as well as their private ones. Your father was something of a pioneer. It's sad that he died before he was able to achieve his ideal.' He looked up at her enquiringly. 'The war, was it?'

She nodded. 'He was a captain in the RAMC – killed on the Somme when the first aid post he was working in received a direct hit. He was awarded a posthumous military medal,' she added proudly.

Naylor nodded. 'I was there, too. Hell on earth.' He thrust out one stiff leg from behind the desk. 'Caught a packet myself. Left me with a gammy leg. Lucky to be alive, though.' He sighed. 'Right, Miss Banks, to get back to the point. You're offering us your services. You have a studio here in Eastmere?'

'Not yet, but soon, I hope,' she told him confidently. 'When I can find suitable premises. I need somewhere with living accommodation, too. I'm staying with a friend at the moment.'

'What about equipment? I take it you have your own.'

'Of course. Everything that was my father's, and some more up-to-date items that I bought from Mr Cusak.'

Andrew Naylor rubbed his chin thoughtfully. 'And you're looking for premises – something in the centre of town – with a good position – a window for displaying your work?'

'That's what I have in mind, ideally. A studio and somewhere to use as a darkroom – always supposing it isn't too expensive, that is. Plus simple accommodation above. A couple of rooms would do.'

'I'll keep a look out for something for you, Miss Banks. Meantime, would you like to show me some of your work?'

'Yes, of course.' Abigail felt her heart lift with excitement. 'I have a portfolio, but I had to leave it at the left luggage at the station, along with all my equipment. There's no room where I'm staying, you see. I could collect it and bring it round for you to see – tomorrow, if you like.'

'Photographic equipment is valuable and easily damaged. You'd better have a porter bring everything round here,' he said. 'You can store it here at the office for the time being, if that would suit you. Better than leaving it at the "left luggage".'

'Thank you, Mr Naylor. That's very kind of you. I'll arrange it right away.'

He smiled, touched by her enthusiasm. 'Right, then. I'll see you tomorrow morning. Shall we say about eleven o'clock?'

'Eleven o'clock. I won't be late.'

'And you never know,' he said, with a twinkle, 'if we play our cards right, Miss Audley might even make us some coffee. Good day, Miss Banks.' He rose to shake her hand. 'And thank you for calling.'

Abigail felt she was walking on air as she made her way back to Ashford's Yard. Already she had made an auspicious start. Sophie had promised her a dinner party. With luck, that would give her some contacts. Andrew Naylor had not actually offered her any work yet, but she was sure he would when he saw her portfolio. She had taken some very good pictures in London, both landscapes and portraits; also of some of the damage caused in Zeppelin raids during the war, and harrowing pictures of the homeless. She was quite proud of her collection. Even Mr Cusak had praised her. She could hardly wait for tomorrow.

She called at the railway station and arranged for the boxes containing her equipment and portfolio to be delivered to the *Chronicle* offices first thing in the morning, then she went back to Ashford's Yard and set about preparing the vegetables for the evening meal.

When Maggie got home from Prospect House, she already knew all about the dinner party.

'Miss Sophie is full of plans,' she said. 'She's already made a list as long as your arm. We'll have to get help in. A really grand affair she's got in mind for you.'

'Oh dear!' Abigail felt slightly guilty. 'I never meant her to go to so much trouble,' she said. 'I hope it won't cause you a lot of extra work, Maggie.'

Maggie chuckled. 'Don't you worry your head about that,' she said. 'The family will have to manage without me for one night. I'm to stay late. And I'm to get something extra in my wages.'

But Abigail did worry. Sophie hadn't even had time to ask her husband if he was willing to give a dinner party for her. After all, he was the head of the household and would, presumably, be paying for it all. Abigail was a complete stranger to him. He might object. From what she had learned of him from Sophie, he sounded impatient and insensitive. She must try to think of a way to repay the favour. She did not intend to begin her business by owing favours to strangers.

She was helping Maggie and Sarah with the washing-up later when the idea came to her. Sophie had said that they had no pictorial record of their wedding day. Perhaps they would like a photograph? Sophie was sure to have her wedding dress still. She would suggest it to her friend the very next time she saw her.

When the work was done and the two older boys had gone out, Abigail, Maggie, Sarah and young Ted sat by the range. Maggie took up her knitting and the girls chatted. Ever since Sarah had met Abigail again she was somewhat in awe of the elder girl. Now she watched her as they sat by the fire, admiring the luminous brown eyes, the firm set of her chin and the proud way she held her head. She wasn't exactly beautiful, she told herself; and yet there was something irresistibly attractive about her.

'Tell us about your pa, Abby,' she said. 'I can't remember much about that time. Tell us about what he tried to do, and what happened to make you leave Eastmere.'

Maggie looked up with concern. 'Miss Abby don't want to talk about them days,' she admonished her daughter. 'I'm sure thinking about it must pain her.'

'No. I'd like Sarah to know,' Abigail said. 'Father came to Eastmere as one of the first panel doctors when Mr Lloyd George's National Insurance Act was first passed. It meant that for the first time poorer people could afford to have medical treatment without getting into debt, and Father was quite excited about it. But almost as soon as we arrived here it was made clear that Father wasn't welcome in the town. The other doctors saw him as a threat to their livelihoods.'

'Can't think why!' Maggie put in wryly. 'I'm sure none of them ever made a fortune out of treating the likes of us. If we got poorly, most of us used to doctor ourselves or send for old Ma Pringle down the end of the yard in them days. She did all the layin's out and the confinements. Doctors was a luxury we couldn't afford.'

'The local doctors made it very difficult for Father to treat people at all,' Abigail went on. 'They denied him the use of the cottage hospital, and even persuaded the local pharmacies to refuse to make up his prescriptions, forcing him to be his own dispenser.'

'So you had no friends,' Sarah said.

'Oh, we had plenty of friends,' Abigail smiled.

'That they did,' Maggie added stoutly. 'The plain folk of this town loved Doctor Banks for the good he did. And if he'd been allowed to stay on, he'd have done a lot more.'

'Ma told us that he and Mr James, Miss Sophie's pa, tried to get Ashford's Yard knocked down,' Sarah said.

'Yes, they did. They drew up plans for a smart new estate of houses. You see, most of Mr James's workers lived in Ashford's

Yard, and he knew how much they suffered, always ailing with the ague, bad chests and gastric troubles. Father saw that it was all down to the living conditions here. No clean water supply, just that old communal pump; no proper drains or sewerage system; all the effluent from the privies going straight into the river; the houses were damp, and Mr James was tired of trying to get the landlord to repair places that were virtually falling down. In winter, the fetid fog rising from the river caused bronchial troubles, and in summer germs from the festering gully out there in the back lane made people sick, especially the children, who had nowhere else to play.'

'It's not much better now.' Sarah shuddered. 'I remember when we used to sail paper boats in that gully, and all those horrible bilious attacks we used to get. Makes me feel sick just thinking about it.'

'Mr James was willing to pay for the building of the new houses himself,' Abigail went on. 'But, of course, the Council would have had to put in the drains, water supply and sanitation.'

'And they didn't want to do it?' Sarah asked.

Abigail shook her head. 'No one would tell him who owned these houses. The Council wouldn't even listen – not until the typhoid epidemic. So many people died, a lot of them Mr James's workers and their families. But even then it was only when Father warned the authorities that another epidemic would probably not be confined to Ashford's Yard but could spread through the town, that they actually paid any attention.'

'Doctor Banks got the *Chronicle* to print photographs of the yard,' Maggie put in. 'Took them himself, he did. I remember him coming round here with his camera. I remember the headline in the paper, too. "Slum riverside yard a disgrace to the twentieth century", it said.' She chuckled. 'Oh, lor'! That done it good and proper – knocked some of them high and mighty councillors in their posh houses right off their perches. It was after that we got the piped water. It wasn't as much as he wanted, but it was better than nothing.' She sighed. 'But soon after that the doctor left, and then the war started.'

'That's right.' Abigail was silent for a moment, remembering the price her father had to pay for this meagre and grudging success. 'A few weeks later, Father was accused of – of malpractice,' she said. 'The local doctors got together and reported him to the General Medical Council. They tried to get him struck off.'

Sarah gasped. 'No! What did they say he did?'

'Never you mind about that,' Maggie interrupted sternly. She shot Abigail a look which clearly said 'Enough is enough', and she shook her head at her daughter. 'You ask far too many questions for your own good, my girl. You'll upset Miss Abby with your nosin' and ferretin'.' She rolled up her knitting and stuck the needles into the ball of wool with an air of finality. 'Anyway, I think it's high time you was in your bed. I'll make the cocoa.'

It was a relief to Abigail not to have to go into detail about the disgraceful accusations made against her father, particularly in front of Sarah and Ted. A young, unmarried woman in the town had suffered a miscarriage. Doctor Banks had been called out to the girl, who was haemorrhaging badly. Later, the case had come to the attention of Doctor Maybury, who had accused Doctor Banks of procuring an illegal abortion. Banks was on the point of being struck off when the girl's mother had come to his defence, admitting that she herself might have unwittingly caused the miscarriage.

'Here, drink this up. It'll help you to sleep.' Maggie put the mug of cocoa into Abigail's hands, and her face was full of compassion as she looked into her eyes and saw the pain of remembrance that darkened them. 'And you two drink up and get off to bed,' she instructed her two offspring, 'or you'll never get up for work in the morning.'

When Sarah and Ted had said their goodnights and retired, Maggie looked at Abigail. 'You didn't mind me stopping you, did you?'

Abigail shook her head. 'It wasn't a story for them to hear. It isn't something I like to dwell on myself. It was brave of that woman to come forward as she did. She could have found herself in deep trouble.'

Maggie snorted derisively. 'Lucky to get away with it, if you ask me. Her own daughter, too. Ginnie Metcalf had done a good few of them so-called operations, as she referred to them. And that wasn't the only one that had gone amiss. Your dear pa saved that girl's life, as he had a few others, and I reckon Ginnie knew what she owed him. That's why her conscience pricked her.'

'Well, Father was saved the humiliation of being struck off, so I'm grateful to her for that,' Abigail said. She smothered a yawn. 'I think I'd better follow Sarah up to bed,' she said. 'Today has been busy, and if I'm lucky tomorrow will be even busier. Goodnight, Maggie.'

'Goodnight, dear. I'll be up directly when I've damped down the fire and washed these mugs.'

As Abigail climbed the narrow staircase, she wondered where Patrick was and what he was doing. They had not spoken again since their conversation the previous night, and he had been silent at the evening meal, refusing to meet her eyes across the table. No doubt he was drinking with his cronies in one of the dockside public houses – plotting how to get the better of their employer.

At the top of the stairs she paused, frowning. What kind of employer was Edwin Dean, she wondered? Theo James must have trusted him implicitly to leave his beloved daughter and the business he had worked so hard to build in his hands. Yet from what Abigail had learned of him today, Sophie's husband didn't sound like the kind of man to tolerate rebelliousness kindly, nor to negotiate wage rises with angry men such as Patrick Johnson and his militant workmates. He'd be more likely to dismiss them out of hand, with no references.

Sarah was already asleep, and so Abigail undressed quickly and slipped into bed. On the edge of sleep her thoughts were about the next day and the coming interview with Andrew Naylor of the *Chronicle*. So much depended on it.

It was much later that she was wakened by the sound of

footfalls on the steep uncarpeted staircase. Patrick was home, then, she told herself, turning over. As she slipped back into sleep, she heard the church clock strike two.

CHAPTER THREE

Abigail climbed the dusty stairs to the office of the *Eastmere Chronicle* the following morning, a mixture of excitement and apprehension making her heart beat faster. Entering the office, she found the formidable Miss Audley no less welcoming than she had been the previous day.

'Good morning,' Abigail said briskly. 'Mr Naylor is expecting me. It's Miss Banks.'

'Yes, Miss Banks. Mr Naylor is in his office attending to his post at present.' The secretary rose from her desk and, peering at the fob watch she wore pinned to her blouse, she said reproachfully, 'Actually, you are three minutes early, but if you will take a seat I will inform him that you have arrived.'

Abigail perched on the one and only available chair, a hard and somewhat wobbly bentwood, and watched the ramrod back of Miss Audley disappear through the door to the adjoining office. A moment later she emerged, her mouth a tight line of disapproval.

'You may go through now,' she said, holding the door grudgingly.

'Thank you.' Abigail walked past her into the office.

Andrew Naylor looked up from his morning post and smiled, taking his pipe from his mouth.

'Ah – nice to see you, Miss Banks,' he said. 'So prompt, too.' He indicated the chair opposite with the stem of his pipe. 'Do have a seat.'

When she was seated he pushed aside the pile of envelopes

on his blotter to make room for Abigail's portfolio which he drew out from beside the desk.

'You'll be relieved to know that your equipment arrived safely from the station first thing this morning. I hope you don't mind, but I've already taken the liberty of having a look at some of your work,' he said.

'Not at all.' Abigail held her breath.

'Of course, you don't need me to tell you that you've produced some first-rate work,' Andrew went on. 'Far too good for a run-of-the-mill rag like the *Chronicle* or a one-horse town like Eastmere.' He leaned back in his chair. 'In fact, I wonder if you realize that you're throwing your talent away. You're wasted here. You could be earning good money back in London, especially with a testimonial from Jeremy Cusak.'

'Is this a nice way of telling me you can't offer me any work, Mr Naylor?' Abigail asked, meeting his eyes with her direct brown gaze.

'Far from it!' Andrew's lips twitched at her directness. 'When you know me a little better, Miss Banks, you'll realize that what I say is what I mean. But, at the same time, I feel that you're a single-minded young woman with a mission, and that you're not going to be deterred by some small-town hack like me. As for employing you, I'm afraid that my budget doesn't stretch to a full-time photographer. I only wish it did, but if you'd really like to do some freelance work for us, I'd be pleased to offer you what assignments we do have. In fact, I'd be delighted.' He grinned. 'I happen to know when I'm on to a good thing. Particularly at the kind of fees the *Chronicle* could offer, which are far below what you're worth.'

Abigail felt her heart lift. 'I'd love to work for you on a free-lance basis, Mr Naylor. And believe me, you'd be doing me a favour, too. You see, all I really need is something to get my work known locally and to provide me with a little money until I get on my feet.' She added hurriedly, 'Oh, not that I'd let you down once I've got enough work of my own. Quite the contrary.'

40

He smiled. 'I realize that. I think I can recognize integrity when I see it. Right then, let's get down to business and discuss terms, shall we? But first, I seem to remember promising you coffee made by the fair hands of none other than our Miss Audley.' He got up from his chair, and Abigail saw with dismay that he walked with a painful limp.

She half rose. 'Oh, please – it's quite all right. I mean – can I . . . ?'

He turned to look at her. 'Let's start as we mean to go on, shall we – keeping our promises to each other? Coffee I promised, and coffee you shall have.' He opened the door and called out, 'I'll take my coffee now, Miss Audley, if you don't mind. And will you make it two cups, please?' As he resumed his seat again, he smiled at Abigail. 'By the way, this looks worse than it actually is.' He tapped his stiff leg. 'From the knee down, it's best English oak.'

By the time Sybil Audley came in ten minutes later, with the tray of coffee, Abigail had agreed to the terms of employment Andrew offered.

He looked up at his secretary with a smile. 'Miss Banks has agreed to work for the *Chronicle* as freelance photographer,' he said. 'I'm sure you'll want to join with me in welcoming her, Miss Audley.'

Sybil put down the tray and straightened her back. 'I'm sure that will be most agreeable,' she said stiffly. Turning her attention to Abigail, she added, 'And you can be assured of my cooperation at all times, Miss Banks.'

Abigail stood up and offered her hand to the older woman. 'Thank you, Miss Audley. I appreciate that.' She cleared her throat and added, 'And I hope we can be friends as well as colleagues.'

The corners of Sybil's mouth lifted slightly in a semblance of a smile, and her pale cheeks coloured slightly as she said, 'Indeed, Miss Banks. I hope so, too.'

When she had withdrawn, Andrew smiled. 'That was very diplomatic of you.'

'I can see that being on the right side of all the Miss Audleys in Eastmere is essential, if I'm going to get on here,' Abigail said.

He laughed and picked up his coffee-cup. 'You may well have hit the nail on the head.' He took a biscuit from the plate on the tray and dipped it thoughtfully into his coffee. 'And it looks very much as though you've made a positive start in that direction. We don't get Garibaldi biscuits every day of the week!'

Over coffee they discussed some of the photographs in Abigail's portfolio, Andrew being especially interested in the city shots of bomb damage. She couldn't help noticing that his eyes lingered over a shot of a haggard man with one leg, begging outside an Oxford Street store.

'There but for the grace of God,' he muttered, shaking his head as he turned the page.

Abigail was surprised when she glanced up at the office clock and saw that it was already past midday. She stood up.

'Oh dear, I've taken up half your morning, Mr Naylor. I really must go.'

He smiled. 'No hurry. By the way, I've seen to it that your cameras and other equipment are safely stored and locked away until you can collect them, speaking of which, something has just occurred to me. I believe I might know of a property that could suit your needs.'

'Really?' Abigail's heart gave a leap. 'A shop, you mean?'

'Yes. Not exactly in the centre of town, but a very good position.'

'Does it have living accommodation, too?'

'I believe there are rooms above, though I've no idea what they are like. The premises was a hairdressing salon, and the owner, Mrs Ellington, used to advertise regularly with us. She came to see me yesterday to say that she is retiring.' Andrew smiled wryly. 'She tells me she can't keep up with some of the latest innovations, and it seems that the final straw came with the arrival of this new permanent wave that all the ladies are so intrigued by. Mrs Ellington predicts deaths from electrocution, and all kinds of horrors.'

Abigail smiled. 'I hear it's a very expensive process. Perhaps Mrs Ellington is wise to avoid it.' She leaned forward eagerly. Do you think she would be willing to rent the place to me? I couldn't afford to buy.'

'She was talking about putting an advertisement in the *Chronicle*, so I don't see why not. Look . . .' Andrew drew a notepad towards him and scribbled down the address. 'Why not go and see her now? You could discuss the details with her and probably work something out.'

Maison Adelle was a small, select hairdressing establishment in a fashionable residential district on the edge of the town. It stood in the centre of a tree-lined terrace of Georgian town houses. The sign, flamboyantly engraved in purple copperplate letters, was displayed on a small easel beneath frilled and draped net curtains in the centre of the large front window. Abigail stood for a moment, surveying the place; trying to picture it as a photographic studio. The window was certainly large enough to display half a dozen or so elegantly framed photographs. She imagined a selection of fashionable wedding pictures; perhaps some engaging baby photographs. She mused on the idea of buying a white fur rug, an elegant high-backed chair, maybe some toys; having some romantic backcloths painted. How much would it all cost? she asked herself apprehensively. Would her meagre inheritance stretch that far? But it wouldn't do to let Mrs Ellington think she was a pauper. And first she had to persuade the woman that she was the ideal tenant. Plucking up all her courage, she took a deep breath, opened the door and walked determinedly through the front door into an elegant hallway.

Mrs Ellington emerged as the doorbell rang. She was a tall, amply built woman in her late fifties. She wore a businesslike overall and her luxuriant silver hair was piled high on her head in the style now firmly rejected by modern young women. Her shrewd eyes swept critically over Abigail with her short hair and stylish clothes.

'If you've come to make an appointment, I'm afraid you're

out of luck,' she said abruptly. 'I'm closed, really – only here to clear the place out. I'm retiring, you see.'

'I know. Mr Naylor of the *Chronicle* sent me,' Abigail explained. 'I understand from him that you might be considering letting these premises,' she added hopefully.

Mrs Ellington drew herself up to her full height and sniffed. 'Indeed! I don't know what gave him that idea,' she said, her eyes raking Abigail from head to foot and back again. 'I've been in business here for the past thirty years. Hairdressing isn't what it was since the war. Girls wanting their hair chopped off in all these ugly new styles, and as if that wasn't bad enough there's all this dangerous interfering with nature now. It'll all end in tears, if not worse, if you ask me. I wouldn't want to have my customers subjected to that kind of risk.'

'Oh, you misunderstand,' Abigail said. 'I intend to open a photographic studio, not a hairdresser's.'

'Oh!' The woman's attitude softened. 'Well, now, that's different.'

Abigail moistened her lips. 'Do you own the premises?' she asked. 'I mean – were you planning to sell or let?'

'I do own it, yes, and the first floor is already let off as a flat to an elderly couple. I had thought of selling, but I wouldn't want to have to give the Carters notice. They're nice people, and they've been my tenants now for over twenty years. That really means letting the rest of the premises off for business purposes . . .' Mrs Ellington folded her arms and drew in her mouth thoughtfully. 'I was waiting, really, to see what came along. It would depend very much on the respectability of their business. I have the other residents of the street to consider, you see.' She saw Abigail's face fall, and her expression relaxed a little. 'Still, seeing as you're here you might as well have a look round. After all, the place might not be suitable for your needs, in which case we'd both be wasting our time.'

'I'd like very much to see it,' Abigail told her, brightening. 'Of course, if it's too much trouble I could always come back another time.'

'Not at all. No time like the present.'

'Thank you very much.' Abigail held out her hand. 'I'm Abigail Banks, by the way.'

Mrs Ellington nodded and shook her hand briefly. 'Ada Ellington,' she responded. 'If you'd like to come this way then, Miss Banks.'

From the moment Mrs Ellington opened the first door, Abigail's excitement began to grow. It was more perfect than she had ever dared to hope. The small front room, now used as an office would make an ideal reception area and waiting-room, and the large sunny room at the rear, the perfect studio, once the curtained cubicles had been removed. Off that room was a large walk-in store cupboard, which would make an ideal darkroom.

Mrs Ellington led the way through a back door and across a paved yard to a sturdy brick outbuilding that Abigail visualized as a workshop, for frame-making and storage.

'This can be reached by way of a passage at the side of the building,' Mrs Ellington told her. 'You might have noticed it. It means that deliveries need not come through the building, so it's quite convenient. The – er – usual office is out there, too.'

'It all looks very suitable so far,' Abigail said, trying hard not to show her rising enthusiasm in case the woman might be tempted to increase the rent.

'There's a kitchen in the basement,' Mrs Ellington told her. 'It's this way.'

She led the way back through the hall to a door at the rear of the staircase. At the bottom was a kitchen furnished with a range and a large deal table and chairs. Leading off it was a scullery, equipped with a sink. A window looked out on to a wrought-iron staircase leading up to the yard.

Abigail nodded her approval. 'I would need living accommodation,' she said. 'Are there any spare rooms upstairs?'

Mrs Ellington looked doubtful. 'Well, the first floor is already let, as I said. There are three rooms on the top floor. Though they haven't been used for some time. They are reached by the back stairs. I daresay you could fix them up as a flat at a pinch. You're welcome to look.'

They climbed the stairs to the hall again, and Mrs Ellington led the way up a spiral staircase reached by a lobby at the back. By the time they reached the top, Mrs Ellington was puffing. She looked at Abigail, pink-faced.

'Now you can see why these rooms haven't been used,' she said, mopping her face with a lace handkerchief. 'Still, you're young and slim. I don't suppose they'd present any problems to you.'

They stood in the front room and Abigail looked around her. It was dusty and cluttered with boxes and items of unwanted furniture, but in her mind's eye she visualized it as a cosy living-room with its dormer window high above the terrace.

'There's a fireplace over here.' Mrs Ellington moved aside some boxes to reveal a cast-iron fireplace inset with pretty blue and white Dutch tiles.

'I'll be sending all this stuff to the local junk dealer,' Mrs Ellington remarked, following her gaze. 'But if you fancy any of it you're welcome to take your pick before it's collected.'

Abigail had already spotted a button-backed chair and a couple of little tables, and her eyes sparkled as she said, 'Thank you. I'd be very grateful.'

Inspecting the larger of the two other rooms, Abigail could see that it would make a very nice bedroom. The third, a spare room to accommodate a guest – or, her fancy already taking flight, one day a bathroom, if her business was successful and she had saved enough money.

'So – what do you think, then?' Mrs Ellington was eyeing her speculatively.

'I like it very much,' Abigail said. 'If you were offering it to let, I'd be interested, providing the rent is within my budget – although . . .' She hesitated, looking round at the sad state of the decoration.

'You're thinking there's a lot to do to make it habitable up here,' Mrs Ellington supplied.

'Well, yes. Changes to make downstairs, too.'

'Well, you'd expect that wherever you went, wouldn't you?'

The older woman's tone was sharp. 'I could sell my business as a going concern, you know,' she said. 'I've built up a large clientele over the years.'

'Yes, but you said you didn't want another hairdresser here,' Abigail put in quickly.

Mrs Ellington's expression softened and the corners of her mouth twitched. 'I think you're going to do very well in business, Miss Banks. Got your head screwed on, haven't you?' She pursed her lips, considering for a moment.

'Tell you what I'll do,' she said. 'I'll let the premises to you on a six-month lease. And as you'd be improving the place by turning up here into a flat, you can have the first month free of charge to help you pay for the materials. Nothing structural, mind.'

'Of course not.' Abigail held her breath. 'How much, though?'

Ada Ellington gazed pensively at the ceiling for a few minutes, her eyes enigmatic, then she named a figure. Abigail's heart leapt. It was within her reach – just. And if she got some work from Andrew Naylor to tide her over till the business got on its feet, she might just manage it. Mrs Ellington was eyeing her speculatively.

'Well – does it suit, then?'

'I'd have a proper rent book and everything?' Abigail asked.

'Naturally. Rent payable on the first of every month. I'll collect it myself, then I can see how you're doing.'

Abigail held out her hand. 'I agree.' She shook the older woman's soft plump hand firmly, adding with a sudden burst of inspiration, 'And if you'd like a portrait or a family group any time, I'd be delighted to offer you a good rate.'

Mrs Ellington laughed. 'Like I said, you've got your head well screwed on, girl.' She looked thoughtful. 'Funny you should say that, though. As it happens, I've got a new baby granddaughter, so I might take you up on that offer.'

'It could go in the window,' Abigail said, warming to the idea. 'A group; yourself, your daughter and the baby girl. Three generations. I'm sure your past customers would be interested

47

to come and look at it.'

'So *I'd* be advertising *your* new business!' Mrs Ellington laughed. 'I've got an idea I'm not going to regret this morning's work,' she said, as they descended the stairs.

'And if it doesn't work out, at least you'll have a new flat to let, won't you?' Abigail saw the twinkle in the older woman's eyes and added, 'Though if I have anything to do with it, Mrs Ellington, I'll be here for a very long time, because I intend to succeed.'

'And I believe you will, Miss Banks. *That* I do.' She paused, her eyes thoughtful. 'Banks. We had a doctor of that name here once. Would you be any relation?'

Abigail smiled. 'He was my father.'

'You don't say!' Mrs Ellington shook her head. 'Well, I never. Small world, isn't it? It was Doctor George saved my daughter's life when she was little. Diphtheria. Couldn't breathe, poor little mite, but he never gave up – pulled her through, he did.' She pursed her lips. 'It was all wrong, what happened to him. Best doctor this town ever had; a really caring man. Still in practice, is he?'

'No. I'm afraid he was killed in the war,' Abigail told her.

'Oh, no!' The woman reached out and took her hand. 'My poor girl. Well, anything you ever want, you come to me. Many's the time I've wished I could pay Doctor George back for all he did for me.'

Abigail smiled. 'Thank you, Mrs Ellington.'

CHAPTER FOUR

Abigail was bursting to tell someone her news, but knowing there would be no one at home at Ashford's Yard, she went to Prospect House to share her good news with Sophie. The maid ushered her into the morning-room, where she found her friend busy at her writing-desk.

Sophie looked up in delight. 'Abby! What a nice surprise. I was just writing invitations to our dinner party. I hope a week next Friday will suit you.'

'Perfectly.' Abigail sat down. 'Oh, Sophie, I've such a lot to tell you. I would never have believed that things could happen so quickly. I've met Mr Naylor, the editor of the *Eastmere Chronicle*, and he's going to give me some freelance work. He's such a kind man. I know you'll like him. He even offered to store my cameras and equipment for me, too. And then, this morning, he told me about a shop to let.'

Sophie laid down her pen and looked up. 'A shop? How exciting. Where is it?'

'Castle Terrace. It was a hairdresser's, but the lady who owns it is retiring. It will make a wonderful studio. The first floor is let as a flat, so I won't have to rent the whole building, but this is the best bit, Sophie, there are three empty rooms at the top of the house that will make me a lovely little home!'

'Oh, Abby, what luck! This calls for a celebration. You must stay for lunch.' She hesitated as her hand reached for the bell. 'You are free, aren't you?'

Abigail laughed. 'Of course, but what about your husband?'

'Edwin never comes home for lunch,' Sophie said. 'It will be lovely to have company for once. And, as it's a special occasion, we must have a glass of sherry first.' She rang the bell.

When Sophie had ordered lunch for two and the girls were sipping their sherry, Sophie said, 'Now, I want to hear all about this shop – sorry, studio – and the rooms. What will you do about furniture?'

'Well, the whole place will need cleaning and decorating first. I shall have to buy a few things to start me off, although there were some unwanted pieces stored upstairs, and Mrs Ellington has offered me the pick of them.'

'And I shall offer you some, too,' Sophie said excitedly. 'When Edwin and I got married we refurnished some of the rooms. The old things are still stored away upstairs. After lunch, we'll go up and have a look. There may be something that would be of use to you.' She bit her lip. 'Oh dear, I hope you don't think I'm throwing all my old cast-offs at you.'

Abigail laughed. 'Not at all. All contributions gratefully received. Beggars can't be choosers. Anyway, I'm sure that nothing ever crossed the threshold of Prospect House that wasn't elegant.'

A lunch of cold meat and salad was served in the dining-room, and over it the girls chattered away, Abigail about her plans for the new studio and Sophie about the dinner party she was happily planning.

'Suppose I invite your nice Mr Naylor?' she suggested. 'It would be more comfortable for you to have someone you know there. Do you think he would come?'

'I've no idea.' Abigail looked thoughtful. 'I don't know anything about him – I don't even know whether he's married. If he is, he might not want to come without his wife.'

'I'll make enquiries,' Sophie said. 'You probably remember that the ladies of Eastmere make it their business to know the marital status of any incoming male. Nothing has changed. If anything, the competition has grown keener. There are far too many unwed daughters around since the war took off so many eligible young men.'

After lunch, the girls went up to the top floor to look at the furniture stored there, and Abigail chose enough basic items to set her up in the flat. She also found a high-backed chair with important-looking carving, which would be perfect for dignified portrait-sitters, and, rolled up in the bottom of an oak chest, a sheepskin rug.

'Oh! Just what I wanted,' she exclaimed with delight as she unrolled it. 'Can't you just see lovely little fat, naked babies having their photographs taken lying on this?' Immediately she bit her lip as Sophie's face fell. 'Oh, Sophie darling, I'm so sorry. My big mouth!'

But Sophie shook her head. 'Don't be silly. If you can use it, of course you're welcome to it. Just let me know when you want the things, and I'll arrange for someone to bring them round.' In a sudden burst of exuberance she threw her arms round Abigail. 'Oh, Abby, I can't tell you how lovely it is, having you here in Eastmere again. And I'm so glad you've found a place of your own. It worries me, thinking of you at Ashford's Yard.'

Abigail held her friend at arm's length and looked into her eyes. 'Maggie and her family are wonderful. They do their best to make me comfortable, and don't forget that there are still plenty of good people just like them living there, more's the pity,' she said. 'Decent hard-working people like that deserve better. But who knows? Maybe before long I'll change all that.'

Sophie looked at the familiar gleam in Abigail's eyes. 'I'm sure you will,' she said. 'I know that look, Abby Banks. It reminds me of the time you wanted to take in that stray cat and your father said no. You always knew how to get your own way.'

Abigail sighed. 'Father gave in because he loved me. The fight for Ashford's Yard won't be so easy. I think I'm going to make a lot of enemies before I succeed.'

Sophie looked doubtful. 'You will take care, won't you, Abby?' she said. 'You can't really afford enemies when you're in business. Father discovered that.'

'Exactly. Your father and mine gave up a lot in their fight to clear Ashford's Yard, and that is exactly why I intend to finish what they started. I can't let all their efforts be in vain, can I?' Abigail looked at Sophie's anxious face and hugged her warmly. 'Don't you worry your head about me,' she said. 'You know what I'm like when my mind's made up. I'll get there somehow, even if I do get a few bruises on the way.'

It was three o'clock before Abigail was ready to leave. She was taking her leave of Sophie in the hall when the front door opened and a man walked in. He stopped when he saw her.

'You didn't tell me you were expecting a guest, Sophie.'

'You're just in time to meet Abigail Banks. My oldest friend,' Sophie turned to Abigail. 'Abby, this is Edwin, my husband.'

Edwin Dean was a tall man with thick fair hair and piercing pale blue eyes, which flicked over Abigail with open admiration. He held out his hand. 'A pleasure to meet you, Miss Banks. Naturally, I've heard a lot about you.'

'Good things, I hope.'

'I already know that you have a very persuasive way. You've managed to succeed in something where I have failed most miserably.'

'Really? What can that be?' Abigail asked.

'You've made my wife smile again.' There was a hint of sarcasm in his tone as Edwin's eyes flicked coldly to his wife's flushed face and back to Abigail's again. 'A sight I had almost given up hoping for.'

'It's very good of you to agree to give a dinner party for me,' Abigail said, gently extricating her hand from his grip.

'Not at all,' he said. 'It will be a pleasure to have some life in the house again. Over the past months the place has felt like a mausoleum' He smiled down at her. 'An attractive feminine presence is just what we need, eh, Sophie?'

Sophie blushed. 'Certainly,' she said.

Although she had walked round the town and looked at the shops until it was growing dark, the house was still empty when Abigail arrived back at Ashford's Yard. She lit the lamps, went upstairs and took off her coat, then decided to make herself useful by starting to prepare vegetables for the evening meal.

Taking a bowl, she went out into the yard to fetch potatoes from the sack in the wash-house. Reaching in, she began to fill the bowl when suddenly a piercing pain shot through her hand. She screamed as a large brown rat jumped out of the sack and scuttled away across the floor. Horrified and repulsed, she ran back into the kitchen and slammed the door. Looking at her hand for the first time she saw that the rat had bitten deeply into the flesh between her thumb and first finger, and the wound was bleeding profusely. Pumping water at the sink, she held her hand under the flow, wincing at the throbbing pain.

'Have you hurt yourself?'

She hadn't heard anyone come in and she turned sharply to see Patrick standing in the doorway.

'It was a rat,' she told him. 'I was in the wash-house, getting some potatoes for supper. It gave me a fright.'

'You should always kick the sack first before you put your hand in,' he said, stepping up to her. 'We're used to it. The rats come up from the river. Not much you can do about it.' He reached out to take her hand, frowning at the bite. 'That looks nasty. I think Ma's got some ointment and bandages somewhere.'

Abigail drew her hand away, feeling slightly foolish. 'It's all right.' She took a clean handkerchief from her pocket and wrapped it round the wound. 'It's nothing much – I'm sure it'll stop bleeding in a minute.'

'You all right? Not feeling faint or anything?'

Abigail blushed. 'Of course not,' she told him sharply. 'I used to help my father, remember? I'm not the swooning kind.' She turned away. 'I'll get on with the meal.'

He shrugged. 'Right, then, if you don't want my help I'll take some water up and have a wash.' He took the kettle from the range and went upstairs.

Abigail peeled the potatoes as best she could with her injured hand, but the incident had shaken her. 'We're used to it,' Patrick had said. Rats in the potato sack – among the very food they ate. Not that there was any wonder, the conditions they lived in at Ashford's Yard. But that they had actually become resigned to it, even Patrick, with his resentment and his militant views. Rats carried all kinds of disease. Something must be done before there was another devastating epidemic.

When Maggie came home, she was concerned about Abigail's bitten hand, insisting on examining it.

'You shouldn't have peeled the potatoes with an open wound,' she admonished. 'You should know better than that, Abigail Banks.'

Abigail was too proud to confess that she had done so out of sheer bravado, to prove her stoicism to Patrick. Maggie applied some of her home-made salve and bandaged the wound as best she could.

Over the evening meal, Abigail shared her good news with them, and Ted and Jim offered to help her with the decorating and any heavy furniture-lifting. It was noticeable that Patrick did not join with his brothers in offering help.

Maggie looked pointedly at her eldest son. 'Sarah and me'll help you scrub the place out, and I'm sure Patrick will help, too.'

But her eldest son merely shrugged. 'Seems like she's got all the help she needs.'

Abigail dozed fitfully all that night as her hand burned and throbbed painfully. Still awake when Maggie rose to make Patrick's breakfast at six o'ciock, she got up herself and allowed Maggie to take off the bandage and look at the bite. The whole hand was now badly swollen and discoloured, and the wound itself looked red and angry. Maggie shook her head.

'Don't like the look of that,' she said. 'I said you should-n't've peeled them spuds. You've got some of the dirt in it. I think you should let Doctor Maybury see it.'

Abigail shook her head. 'Just put some more of your oint-ment on it, Maggie. I'm sure it'll soon be better.'

The older woman laid a hand on Abigail's forehead as she sat huddled close to the range, sipping a mug of tea.

'Unless I'm very much mistaken, my girl, you've got a fever

coming. If you neglect that hand it might go wrong, and you need your health, never mind the use of both hands, with what you've got coming, don't you?'

What she said made sense. 'I suppose you're right,' Abigail conceded with a sigh 'But it's such a nuisance just when I have so much to do.'

'Doctor William has an early-morning surgery for his panel patients,' Maggie went on. 'So's they can see him before work. You can register while you're there. Now, do you know where it is?'

'No, but I . . .'

'I'll take you,' Patrick put in, without looking up from his breakfast. 'It's down the south end of the quay. Near the cattle market.'

Abigail was taken aback by the offer. 'Oh, but that's out of your way. I'm sure I can . . .'

'Let him take you,' Maggie interrupted, with a meaningful look. Bending close, she said softly, 'Not often *he* offers. Take advantage while you can.'

'Of course, if you're ashamed of being seen with a man in working clothes . . .'

'Of *course* I'm not,' Abigail said. 'I just don't want to put you out.'

'Don't worry, I won't let you.' Patrick rose from the table and took his cap from the peg by the door. 'But we'll have to go now if you're coming. Can't be late. I'm in enough . . .' He bit back the rest of the sentence with a quick glance in his mother's direction. 'You coming, then?'

'Yes. I'll get my coat.'

They walked in silence to the end of Ashford's Yard and down the alley that led to the quayside.

'It's good of you to show me the way,' Abigail said, glancing at him 'Thank you, Patrick.'

He shrugged. 'It's all right.' He turned to look at her. 'Does it hurt – your hand?'

She was about to brush his question away when she looked up and saw with surprise that his eyes held genuine concern.

55

'It is quite painful,' she admitted. 'I didn't get much sleep last night.'

'I know. I heard you tossing and turning,' he said. 'That makeshift bed makes a hell of a racket.'

'I'm sorry if I disturbed you.'

'You didn't. I wasn't asleep anyway.'

'Are you worried about your job?' she asked.

He gave his characteristic shrug. 'I'm not popular at the moment. I thought I was doing the lads a favour, trying to get better wages for us. But to hear some of them you'd think I was trying to get them the sack.'

'They probably don't want to stir things up,' she suggested. 'I expect some of them have families to support.'

'That's true of some of the older men, but when your own brother is one of the people standing out against you . . .'

'Jim?' Abigail looked at him in surprise. 'But he's only a boy.'

Patrick snorted. 'Huh! Man enough to be walking out,' he said.

'He's got a young lady?'

'If you can call her that. It's Annie Pearce from number ten. They've been sweet on each other since school, daft pair.' He sighed. 'There's no helping some folk. Sometimes I think I might as well give up. It's like banging your head against a brick wall.'

'Don't give up, Patrick. I'm sure there must be others who feel as you do.'

'So there are, but not nearly enough of them.'

She turned to look at him, tentatively touching his arm. 'I know that if my father were alive today he'd be on your side, and Mr James would listen to you.'

'They're not here any more, though, are they? That's the whole point. The war was supposed to make things better for working men. Seems to me things are even worse now than before.'

'I know your heart is in the right place, Patrick.'

'You know nothing about me,' he snapped. 'You've got no idea what our life is really like, coming here to stay for a few weeks. There's no future for the likes of us. Nothing to look forward to – nothing to work for except to scratch a living, and a poor one at that. But do they appreciate what I'm trying to do? Do they hell as like! Sometimes I feel they're all against what I stand for, workers and boss alike. Even Ma keeps on at me to keep my mouth shut.' He glowered at her. 'And don't you go telling her what I've said. I can do without her on my back as well!' He stopped walking and pointed across the road. 'Surgery's over there. The house with the green door.' And with that he turned on his heel and began to walk back along the quay, his head high and his shoulders thrown back defiantly.

Abigail watched him go with a heavy heart. Why didn't he believe she was on his side? If only he wasn't so angry with everyone.

The early-morning surgery was crowded. All the chairs lined up along the wall of the hallway that served as a waiting-room were taken, and the room was filled with the sound of coughing, muted voices and shuffling boots. Abigail filled in the necessary form at the nurse's request and was then obliged to stand to wait her turn. It was almost an hour before her turn came, and she walked into the doctor's surgery, the last patient of the morning.

She was relieved to see that Doctor William Maybury was not at all like his uncle. A tall, good-looking young man in his late twenties, he had smooth dark hair and a neat moustache. He rose to meet her with a smile.

'Miss Banks. What a coincidence. I've just received an invitation to a dinner party at Prospect House – in your honour, I believe.'

'That's right. Sophie is my oldest friend. I'm here to open a photographic studio – in Castle Terrace, as a matter of fact,' she added proudly.

'Very interesting.' He glanced at the form she had filled in to register as a panel patient. 'Sophie tells me that you're the daughter of the late Doctor George Banks, who once practised here in Eastmere. I must say I'm a little surprised that you've signed on to my panel.'

'My father was a pioneer of Lloyd George's National Health Act, as you must have heard. He believed in it very strongly. I'd be letting him down to do otherwise.'

His blue eyes looked up into hers. 'Of course. I understand.'

'You may have heard that Father was killed in the war,' she said quickly.

'I have indeed, and I'm sorry. I applied to go to the front myself, but as I was still training I was deferred. By the time I qualified, the Armistice had been signed.' He swung his chair round and nodded towards her bandaged hand. 'So – you've had an accident?'

'It's a rat bite. I'm staying at Ashford's Yard temporarily, with my very old friends, the Johnson family,' she explained.

'How did it happen? May I?' He began to unwind the bandage Maggie had applied.

'I was getting potatoes from a sack and . . .' She winced as the last piece of bandage stuck painfully. 'Living conditions in that place are a disgrace to the town.'

He glanced up at her briefly, then raised her hand to look closely at the wound. 'Mmm. That looks nasty. It's already begun to be infected. Rat bites can be very toxic indeed. I'm afraid there is only one treatment for this, Miss Banks, and, being a doctor's daughter I think you probably know what that is.'

'You're going to have to cauterize it.'

'I'm afraid so. Is anyone with you?'

'No. But I'll be all right.'

'You're sure? If you'd rather come back this evening – with a friend.'

'No. I'd rather get it over with.'

She watched as he fetched equipment and dressings from a cabinet, noting with relief that he had one of the new electric cauterizing-irons. It took only moments to be ready, and she held out her hand, taking a deep breath and bracing herself for the inevitable pain.

As the rat's teeth had penetrated the flesh between thumb

and forefinger, it was necessary to cauterize both the entry and exit wounds. The pain and the sickening smell made her head swim, but she gritted her teeth until the ordeal was over.

'All over. Well done, Miss Banks.' He applied a sterile dressing and a clean bandage. 'Try to keep the hand elevated as much as possible,' he said. 'And I'd like to see you again in a couple of days, just to make sure it's healing satisfactorily.' As she rose to put on her coat, he added, 'I'm off on my rounds now. I'll be passing Ashford's Yard. Please allow me to take you home.' His blue eyes twinkled. 'Can't have my newest patient fainting in the street, can I?'

'I'm not the fainting kind, but if you're sure it isn't out of your way – thank you very much.'

As Abigail seated herself in the passenger seat of Doctor Maybury's Model T Ford, she remarked that it must be one of the very few in Eastmere. William Maybury smiled.

'I daresay cars are an everyday sight in London. You probably remember my uncle using a horse and carriage as his transport.'

'I do indeed,' Abigail said, picturing the large stern-faced man with his mutton-chop whiskers, riding haughtily through the town behind a pair of fine horses. 'It was rather different for my father, though. He did *his* rounds on a bicycle.' She glanced at him. 'Apart from your car and your panel patients, Doctor Maybury, things have not moved on much in Eastmere. I hope conditions are about to improve, now that the war is over.'

He shook his head. 'Unfortunately, Miss Banks, there are still a great many people who are against change,' he said.

'Wealthy people, you mean?'

'Not altogether. For instance, it might surprise you to know that there are people among my poorer patients who still resort to opium just as they did in your father's time here.'

Abigail remembered the opium pills readily available, and how her father had done his best to deter his poor patients from the noxious habit. 'Surely that just shows how wretched many people still are?' Abigail frowned. 'But surely there was a Royal Commission to prevent it?'

'It isn't as widely available as it was. Now it is mainly taken in the form of laudanum,' he told her. 'And often obtained on the pretext that it is for animal treatment. In spite of the Commission, it was never actually outlawed. It's cheaper than alcohol, and many educated people still think of it as a harmless drug. It's a losing battle. I'm afraid people who sit on commissions don't see its outcome as I often do.'

'But if the lives of poor people were better, they'd have no need for it,' Abigail said. 'If living and working conditions improved . . .'

He shook his head. 'Mmm. I wonder.' They had reached the end of the alley that led to Ashford's Yard, and he stopped the car and turned to her with a wry smile. 'If wishes were horses, Miss Banks, beggars would ride.'

Her eyes widened and she turned to him, an angry retort on her lips. She bit it back. She had no wish to make an enemy of him. He had treated her with nothing but courtesy. If she was to get him on her side, she must use diplomacy. Besides, she liked him. She swallowed hard and smiled.

'Thank you so much for the lift, Doctor Maybury. Good morning.'

He tipped his hat, his eyes twinkling as he reached across to open the door for her. 'Not at all. Look after that hand, and come back to the surgery to let me check it.'

Maggie was waiting anxiously when she got in. She was concerned to hear about the cauterization, saying that she should have gone with Abigail to support her.

'I know Sarah wouldn't have minded getting herself off to work for once. Does it pain you?' She looked earnestly into Abigail's face as she helped her off with her coat. 'I'll make you a nice cup of tea before I go off to Prospect House. I'm sure I don't know what Miss Sophie will think. I feel to blame, that I do.'

'Of course you're not to blame,' Abigail assured her. 'I should have been more careful.'

'Well, now, just you take it easy today. I'll pop home this

afternoon to see how you are. There's some soup on the stove if you feel like it later.' As she began to put on her coat, she asked, 'Was Patrick all right with you? I know he can be a bit sharp at times, but he's a kind lad under all that anger.'

'He was very thoughtful,' Abigail said.

Maggie sighed. 'I just wish he'd drop all this union stuff. It'll lose him his job before he's done. What bothers me is that he keeps trying to involve Jim, too. Poor lad is torn between loyalty to his brother and wanting to keep his job.'

'Patrick told me that Jim has a young lady.'

Maggie smiled. 'Annie, that's right. They've been going together since they were babes, bless 'em.' She pulled on her brown felt hat. 'Now, will you be all right?'

'I'll be fine, Maggie. Don't worry about me.'

Abigail couldn't bear to be lazy. She was bored and restless all that day with nothing to do but nurse her injured hand. She kept thinking of all the things she could be doing to prepare for her move to Castle Terrace. Later in the morning the sun came out, so she put on her coat and took a walk into town. Peering in through the window at Mr Hudson's chemist's shop she saw that there were no customers, so she went in to see Sarah. The girl was pleased to see her.

'How is your hand?' she asked. 'Ma said you were bad all night. Did Doctor Maybury make it better for you?'

'He had to cauterize it.'

'Oh, no!' Sarah shrank in horror. 'It must have hurt you something awful!'

'He has an electric cauterizing-iron,' Abigail told her. 'It's quicker and cleaner than the old method.'

Sarah shuddered. 'All the same . . . Will it leave a scar?'

'Probably. But it will fade with time.'

'You'll still be able to go to Mrs Dean's party though, won't you?'

'Of course I will.' Abigail laughed. 'I might even have the bandage off by then.'

Sarah leaned forward, her cheeks pink. 'Ma's going to ask

Mrs Dean if I can come and help on the night,' Sarah said. 'To wait tables. I've done it before,' she added. 'Ma showed me how to go on – what's proper and everything. What are you going to wear?'

Abigail smiled. 'That's not something I need to think about. I'll wear my one and only evening dress.'

Sarah's eyes widened. 'I've always wanted an evening dress. Did you wear it in London?'

'Yes. When Mr Cusak and I went to take photographs at society functions, it was necessary to mingle with the guests. I've worn it lots of times, so it's far from new. In fact, I may have to make some alterations to bring it up to date.'

'Will you let me help you?'

'Of course.'

'And your hair?'

'It's short, so there isn't much I can do with it. I've got a little *diamanté* clip that my father bought me. I might wear that.'

Sarah sighed. 'I'm sure you're going to look lovely. I can't wait to see you.'

CHAPTER FIVE

'Oh, Abby, it's *lovely*! You are clever.' Sarah was admiring Abigail as she stood before the full-length mirror that Maggie had unearthed from the back of a cupboard so that she could see the full effect of her handiwork. 'I thought it was nice before, but you've done wonders with it,' she went on. 'I bet you'll be the best-dressed lady there.'

'I doubt that, but I think it will probably do,' Abigail said. 'It's three years old, but at least it's more fashionable now.'

'I've had most of my clothes more like *twenty*-three years,' Maggie put in, as she came into the room. 'But I must say you've made a good job of that. You've got a real way with your needle – and you with a poorly hand too. If you weren't a photographer, I swear you could make your living at dress-making.'

Abigail looked at her dim reflection in the ancient mirror. The dress was made of watered silk in a vibrant shade of red. It had once been ankle-length, with a deep flounce of material at the shoulders, dropping to the elbows. After studying current fashions in a copy of *Vogue* that Sophie had lent her, she had shortened the dress to mid-calf length and added a black silk fringe to the hem. Using some of the material from the unpicked flounce, she had made thin shoulder straps and left the bodice plain. Earrings and a long string of jet and crystal beads that her aunt had given her gave the finishing touch.

'You'll be the belle of the ball and no mistake,' Maggie said with satisfaction.

'But what will you wear over it – to go in?' Sarah asked.

Abigail pulled out a black silk shawl that had been her aunt's. It was edged with a fringe that echoed the one she had stitched to the hem of her dress.

'Do you think this will do?' she asked.

'No two ways about it,' Maggie said. 'I'm glad I've seen you now, 'cause tomorrow I'll have to be at Prospect House most of the day, getting everything ready. And Sarah is coming there straight from work, so we won't be here to see you off.'

'Wasn't it nice of Doctor Maybury to offer to be your escort?' Sarah said. 'I think he's ever so handsome.'

Abigail had mixed feelings about it. When she had gone to the surgery two days before to have her hand examined, William Maybury had suggested that as they were both going to the dinner party alone, it would be sensible for them to team up.

'I can pick you up in the car and drive you there,' he said. 'After all, you can hardly walk to Prospect House, can you?'

'I don't see why not,' Abigail said. 'It's not very far, and I walk everywhere else.'

'But after dark – and in all your finery? Of course, if you'd rather not . . .'

'No! It's very kind of you,' Abigail said quickly. 'I didn't mean to sound ungracious. I accept your offer.'

'Right. That's settled then. I'll come for you at about half past seven.'

Abigail called in to see Sophie later that morning, and told her about the doctor's suggestion. Sophie smiled her approval.

'William is such a nice man. I'm sure you and he will get along famously. Now – you're quite sure your hand is better?'

Abigail held out her injured hand, now free of bandages. 'Much better. Doctor Maybury was very pleased with it. You can still see the puncture marks, but I'm sure they'll soon fade. The cauterization killed off the infection.'

'Still, you should be careful of it. The sooner you can move out of that awful Ashford's Yard, the better.'

Abigail was silent. She longed to remind Sophie that it was

her own husband who was responsible for the conditions his workers were obliged to live in. If Edwin were *her* husband, Abigail would do all in her power to make him do something about it, but for some reason Sophie seemed to be slightly fearful of him. She knew instinctively that her friend would be upset if she expressed her views too strongly, so she held her tongue.

'When are you going to move in to your new premises?' Sophie asked.

'Quite soon, I hope. Ted and Jim, Maggie and Sarah are going to start helping me next weekend. I'm so eager to begin, Sophie. I can't tell you how exciting it all is.'

Sophie looked wistful. 'I do envy you, Abby.'

'*Envy* me? When you have all this?'

Sophie shook her head. 'You have a *life*, Abby. You have an aim – something to strive for. Sometimes I feel so useless, with nothing to do but run the house and sit here day after day, watching the world go by.'

Abigail hugged her friend. 'Useless – you? When you're giving this party just for me, to help me get my business off to a good start? Don't let me hear you speak like that again. Besides, I'm sure your husband doesn't see you as useless.'

'Edwin?' Sophie opened her mouth to say something else, then closed it again. 'I'm sure you're right,' she said with a shrug. 'I'm just being silly.' Her face suddenly cleared. 'Oh, by the way, I forgot to tell you. I discovered that Andrew Naylor is a widower. His poor wife died and left a little daughter. She's three years old now. Isn't it awful? Poor man.'

'I had no idea,' Abigail said. 'Who is bringing up they little girl, then?'

'He is. His sister lives with them and looks after the child. She's a war widow.'

Abigail sighed. 'The war took away so many people's loved ones. It's sad.'

'But he's coming to the party,' Sophie said. 'I've invited his sister, too, and he's accepted for both of them. He tells me someone will sit with the child; his secretary, a Miss Audley.'

Abigail smiled. 'That's wonderful. And I'm quite sure no child would dare misbehave with Miss Audley to keep her in line!'

When Abigail came downstairs on the evening of the dinner party, Maggie's three sons were sitting round the table in the living-room. Ted, who faced her, looked up and beamed with delight.

'You look very nice, Abby,' he said.

Jim blushed and nodded agreement. Ted reached across the table and nudged his older brother.

'Look at Abby, Pat. Don't she look nice?'

Patrick turned and stared at Abigail, his eyes dark with the enigmatic look that was becoming so familiar to her.

'All right, I suppose,' he muttered. 'If you like that sort of thing. I bet your posh friends don't know you're living in Ashford's Yard, though. You'll be keeping that dark!'

'Why should I?' Abigail said. 'It's not the address that impresses, it's the people who live there.'

'Fine words don't—'

'*Butter no parsnips*,' Ted interjected, and he and Jim collapsed into giggles. 'You sound just like Ma, our Pat!'

'Oh, grow up, the pair of you!' Flushing darkly, Patrick got up from the table and took down his cap, ramming it over his hair. 'I'm going out,' he growled. But as he reached for the door handle, there was a knock from the other side. Patrick opened it to see William Maybury standing there, looking handsome and imposing in evening dress, a white silk scarf around his neck.

'Good evening. Is Miss Banks ready?'

Patrick pushed rudely past him. 'She's ready,' he grunted. 'Help yourself!'

'That young man has a massive inferiority complex,' William remarked, as they got into the car.

'Is it any wonder,' Abigail asked, 'being born and growing up in a place like Ashford's Yard, and working at the timber yard for a pittance?'

'I hear he's getting quite a name as an agitator.'

66

'I think he sees it as his duty. These people have no chance of a good education, and no prospects of a better life. Patrick has a good brain. He has every right to be angry.'

'I daresay that is true, but Rome wasn't built in a day. Sometimes, people like Patrick Johnson do more harm than good. Only two months ago, a general strike in Glasgow ended in a riot, and many people were badly injured. And all for nothing.' He glanced at her. 'I believe your father and Theo James were campaigning to demolish Ashford's Yard before the war,' he said. 'Clearly that memory has left its mark on you.'

'A lot of things left their mark,' she told him. 'For instance, I remember the typhoid epidemic that took off so many of the Yard's residents; including Patrick's father and his baby brother. Father managed to get piped water laid on after that, but more should have been done long ago. Decent people like the Johnsons deserve a living wage and a decent place to live. Surely that's not too much to ask for?'

'We have had a world war since then,' William reminded her. 'And now Lloyd George's government has a slum clearance programme in place. It will all happen eventually. As I said, Rome wasn't built in a day.'

'But there is so much that could be done in the mean time,' Abigail argued. 'Proper drains and sewerage for instance. The local council could do so much if they really wanted to.'

William turned to her. 'Abigail . . . I may call you Abigail, I hope?'

'Of course.'

'A word of well-meant advice. Stay off your political soapbox this evening. Sophie Dean is giving this party to help you in your future business. I would hate you to ruin your own chances before you've begun.'

Abigail felt the hot colour flood her face. 'I'm sorry,' she said. 'I was speaking to you in confidence, and of course I won't get on what you call my *political soapbox* this evening. I wouldn't embarrass Sophie for the world.'

He was drawing up outside Prospect House now, and he nodded with satisfaction. 'I'm delighted to hear it, because I fear that you would embarrass more than one of this evening's guests if you expressed some of the thoughts you've just put into words.'

'I can think of worse discomforts than embarrassment,' she said. 'But I hope I know how to behave in company, Doctor Maybury. You can rest assured that I can be as flippant and frivolous as the next woman when I have to.'

'I'm delighted to hear it!' He smiled at her. 'And by the way, the name is William.'

'William – yes. But that doesn't stop me from thinking,' she added. 'Nor does it change my resolve to do all in my power to change things for the better, one way or another.'

The twinkle in his eyes could have been admiration or scepticism. She could not quite decide which as he inclined his head towards her and said quietly, 'I'd be sadly disappointed if it did, Abigail.'

Sophie came out into the hall to meet them when they arrived. She looked fragile and pretty in a long dress of palest pink and her mother's diamond earrings. She greeted William warmly and kissed Abigail.

'Almost everyone is here,' she whispered. 'There is sherry in the drawing-room Do come in and meet everyone.'

Besides herself and William Maybury, also present were Andrew Naylor and his sister Anne, a tall, pleasant-looking woman in a black evening dress. Abigail was introduced to several couples from the town's oldest families. Sophie presented her friend to the other guests in glowing terms, making sure to tell them that she was soon to become the town's most accomplished photographer. As the clock struck nine, Sophie's housemaid came in to tell them that dinner was served, and William offered Abigail his arm.

The dining-room looked breathtakingly elegant. The long table was laid with a pristine white damask cloth, and candlelight from twin candelabras gleamed on Sophie's mother's silverware and crystal, which had been wrapped in tissue paper and stored away ever since Sophie's wedding. Sophie herself had chosen the flowers and arranged them, and their spring freshness perfumed the air, mingling with the aroma of delicious food.

Edwin sat at the lead of the table. He looked distinguished in his evening dress, his fair hair brushed smoothly back from his forehead and a diamond signet ring sparkling on his left hand. Sophie took her place at the other end of the table, and the guests looked for their place-names. To her relief, Abigail found herself seated between William and Andrew Naylor's sister, Anne March. Some of the other guests looked slightly redoubtable, and she was glad not to have to sit next to them, but she was determined not to allow herself to be intimidated.

Anne smiled at Abigail warmly.

'I've heard so much about you through Andrew,' she said. 'I've been looking forward to meeting you and hearing about the exciting work you did in London.'

Abigail relaxed. Talking about the interesting functions she had attended in London with Jeremy soon made her forget her initial nervousness, and before long she realized that everyone at the table had stopped talking to listen to what she was saying.

'Did you meet any of the Royal Family?' an elegantly attired woman sitting opposite asked.

'Only once. We were engaged to attend the coming-out ball for the Duchess of Mey's youngest daughter last year. It was at The Savoy Hotel, and a lot of interesting people were there, including the Prince of Wales.'

The eyes round the table widened with interest. 'Really? How fascinating.'

'Did you photograph him?'

'Did you speak to him?'

'Was he as handsome as his pictures?'

'We took the photographs at a reception for Douglas Fairbanks and Mary Pickford in January, just before I left,' Abigail went on. 'When they came on a visit from America. That was at The Waldorf. Charlie Chaplin was one of the guests,' she added. The remark was greeted by gasps, and at once everyone wanted to ask questions. The ice was well and truly broken.

The food that Maggie had prepared was delectable, and Sarah looked very pretty in her neat uniform as she served it. After the ladies had retired to the drawing-room for coffee, Abigail found herself the centre of attention. The ladies all wanted to know about the London fashions; who was being presented at Court, the latest hairstyles, and gossip about the aristocracy. Abigail obliged with as many answers as she could, reminding them that her work was confidential and anything she might have seen or overheard was not for repeating, a fact that many of them clearly appreciated.

Towards the end of the evening Mrs Welland, a handsome middle-aged matron, moved closer to Abigail and said, 'Our eldest daughter will be twenty-one in June. I'm sure my husband and I would be delighted if you would take photographs at her party.'

'My studio is not open yet,' Abigail told her, 'so I have yet to have cards printed, but I would be delighted to photograph your daughter's coming-out party and if you would like to give me your address, I will get in touch with you.'

The time flew, and it seemed no time at all before the clock was striking midnight. One by one the guests took their leave, but before they departed several had indicated that they would spread the word and that Abigail would certainly have their patronage in the future.

At last the Deans stood at the door to bid Abigail and William goodnight. Abigail kissed Sophie and thanked her for a successful party.

'Mrs Welland has already asked me to attend their daughter's coming-out party,' she whispered excitedly.

Sophie laughed. 'Then you're made! Where the Wellands go, everyone else follows. Well done, Abby.'

'I couldn't have done it without you,' Abigail said. 'And I had an idea the other day. Sophie, you said you have no wedding photograph. If you still have your dress, I could take one for you – as a special thank you.'

Sophie's eyes lit up with delight. 'Oh, Abby! That would be—'

But Edwin cut in quickly, 'There's really no need for that.'

'It would be a pleasure, though. I'm sure Sophie must have made a beautiful bride. It's so sad that there is no record of it. And I have so much to thank you both for.'

'Not at all. Besides, it would hardly be a wedding photograph after all this time, would it?'

'Oh, but Edwin . . .' Sophie was silenced by a look from her husband. The expression on his face made it clear that he wished the matter closed.

'It's a long time since this house was as cheerful as it has been tonight,' he said, turning a sugar-sweet smile on Abigail. 'You are already breathing new life into the place.' He took her hand and raised it to his lips. 'Oh dear, you've hurt your hand,' he said, as he noticed the tiny purple marks near the base of her thumb.

'Yes.' Abigail cleared her throat as she prepared a reproach about the living conditions in which Edwin's workers were housed, but before she could speak William quickly intervened.

'Moving into new premises has its hazards, doesn't it, Abigail? Nailed boxes to unpack – impatient fingers.' The pressure of his hand on Abigail's arm made his warning all too clear. 'Thank you both for a very pleasant evening. Goodnight.' He gently drew Abigail down the steps towards his car.

'Yes, thank you again,' she said, her heart sinking at the lost opportunity.

In the car neither of them mentioned Abigail's near-gaffe. She was thoughtful as they drove along the deserted streets, then suddenly she remembered something and gave an exclamation.

'Oh!'

'What is it?' William looked at her.

'I've just thought. The Wellands live out of town, don't they? And I have no means of transport.'

'That could certainly be a problem,' William conceded. 'You

could always ask them to send a car for you.'

'Oh, no. That would look unprofessional. I'd rather be independent,' Abigail said quickly.

He laughed. 'Why doesn't that surprise me?' For a moment he was silent, then he said hesitantly, 'There's a bicycle in the shed at the back of the house where I have my practice. As far as I know it doesn't belong to anyone. It's yours, if you want it.'

'Can I come and see it?'

'Of course you can,' he said, slightly taken aback by her enthusiasm, 'But it might need some attention – and with all your equipment . . .'

'It's a start, and I'll find a way of making use of it. Thank you, William, that would be marvellous!'

He drove on in silence. The young woman sitting beside him was clearly not to be deterred by anything. He wondered if that augured well for the future – or if he should expect trouble.

CHAPTER SIX

'It's just amazing, what you've done in such a short time.'

Abigail and Sophie were standing in front of Abigail's window display at the Castle Terrace Studio. In the front of the window was a gilt-scrolled sign bearing the words, *Abigail Banks, Photographer*, in bold black lettering. The window was decorated with a swathe of velvet in royal blue, and on a small black easel was the group photograph of Mrs Ellington, her daughter and baby grandchild.

'My first customers,' Abigail said. 'Although they weren't quite customers. Taking their group was part of the deal I made with Mrs Ellington.'

'They look very proud, whatever it was,' Sophie said. 'You really are very clever, Abby. The way the light catches Mrs Ellington's velvet dress is lovely.'

'Has Edwin had any more thoughts about letting me take a wedding photograph of you?' Abigail asked. 'I'd love to display that in the window, too.'

Sophie shook her head. 'I only wish he had. Edwin hates being the centre of attention,' she said. 'I've tried to persuade him, but he's adamant.'

It was Sunday afternoon, and Abigail had invited her friend to Castle Terrace for tea and to look round her new establishment for the first time. She proudly took her on a tour of the studio and reception area, and even across the yard to see the building where she hoped eventually to employ someone to do framing for her.

Sophie spotted the ancient bicycle that William had given Abby, propped against the wall.

'Don't tell me you actually ride that!' She was laughing.

'Of course I do.'

The smile vanished from Sophie's face. 'Really? Where on earth did you get it?'

'William gave it to me, and I was very grateful. How else would I get to people who are too far away? I'm not going to turn away good business.'

'But your equipment?'

'Ted is making me a little trailer,' Abigail told her. 'It hooks on to the back, see, just here. I've even got a waterproof cover for it, in case it rains.'

Sophie looked incredulous. 'Are you sure it's quite – safe?'

Abigail laughed. 'What you really mean is, is it quite lady-like?'

The other girl blushed. 'You must admit that it's a far cry from dressing up and going to society functions with Mr Cusak.'

'Well, you're right there,' Abigail conceded. 'But one can't have everything. I'm my own boss here, Sophie. I love Eastmere and the people who live here – at least, some of them.'

Sophie looked at her. 'You must have heard that Edwin has decided to stand for the Town Council.'

Abigail had heard, though she secretly felt that Edwin would be more concerned with furthering his own interests than those of the local people.

'I did hear,' she said. 'And I want to come and talk to Edwin about Ashford's Yard soon. I'm sure he'd prefer his workers to have decent housing, wouldn't he?'

'Well, yes, of course,' Sophie said, without conviction.

'There is so much he could do,' Abigail went on. 'It would be much easier to get the Council to agree to lay on services with someone like Edwin on my side. Will you ask him for me?'

'Me?' Sophie's cheeks paled. 'Oh no! I don't think that

would be a good idea. He'd think I'd put you up to it.'

'No, he wouldn't. Everyone knows that Edwin owns the timber yard.'

'But not that he owns the land adjoining. It isn't common knowledge.'

'Then maybe it's time it was.'

Sophie looked uncomfortable. 'I'd really rather you didn't speak to him, Abby. I know he wouldn't agree anyway.'

Seeing her friend's obvious distress, Abigail dropped the subject, but she was determined to get Edwin Dean to listen to her somehow, with or without Sophie's help.

'Come upstairs and see my flat,' she invited. 'Tea's all ready. I've only to put the kettle on.'

The bleak storeroom on the second floor was now transformed into a little sitting-room. Abigail had worked hard with the help of Maggie and Sarah. They had scrubbed and dusted, later making curtains and covers on Maggie's ancient sewing machine while Ted and Jim moved in to paint and decorate. The pieces of furniture and the carpet that Sophie had given her looked just right, and Abigail had added the finishing touch with a vase of lilacs on the window-sill, filling the room with their heady perfume. Sophie looked round in admiration.

'Oh! It's lovely, Abby. So comfy and welcoming.'

'Thanks to your generosity. I was so grateful for the pieces you gave me,' Abigail reminded her. 'I couldn't have done any of it without the help of my good friends.'

'Speaking of friends, Anne March called on me the other day,' Sophie said, 'to thank me for the dinner party, and to invite Edwin and me for supper next week. She said she was inviting you, too.'

'That's right. I think she's inviting William also.'

Sophie looked coy. 'I believe William is very taken with you, Abby, and I have to say that you make a very handsome couple.'

Abigail laughed. 'Don't start match-making, Sophie. I'm sure nothing is further from William's mind, and it certainly hadn't occurred to me.'

'He should be married,' Sophie said. 'It's only right for a family doctor. The patients prefer it, and you would make a perfect wife for him.'

'At the moment I've no intention of getting myself tied down,' Abigail said, pouring the tea. 'I'm far too busy.'

'But what if you fall in love?'

'That's a state of mind I intend to avoid,' Abigail said firmly.

When Sophie had gone, Abigail put on her coat and walked across town to make her weekly visit to the Johnsons at Ashford's Yard. As she walked, she thought about Sophie's remarks concerning herself and William Maybury. William was a pleasant companion, clearly a good doctor and, she had to admit, attractive too, but that kind of attachment was the last thing on her mind at present. In fact, it could only hinder her future plans.

The early June evening was mild and mellow with the first promise of summer, but as she made her way down the narrow alley that led to the yard, the odour of raw sewage and the rankness of the river at low tide made her wrinkle her nose. There were no streetlights in the alley or the yard, and the closeness of the buildings made it so dark that she had almost bumped into the couple standing at the end of the alley before she saw them The girl was clearly distressed, and as she passed Abigail heard her say,

'I *can't* tell him. He'll kill me, Jim. What are we going to do?'

Abigail stepped aside, muttering an apology, but as the boy turned his face towards her she recognized young Jim Johnson. He said nothing and she hurried on, hoping he hadn't recognized her.

At number seventeen, she knocked on the door and walked in. Maggie sat by the fire with her knitting, Sarah opposite with a pile of darning. They both smiled.

'Abby! How nice, come and sit down. I'll make a brew,' Maggie said, making room on the sofa and plumping up a cushion. 'Now, we want to hear all your news. Whose likenesses have you been taking this week?'

Abigail told them about the two portraits and several baby pictures she had already taken at the studio, and the two assignments she had done for the *Chronicle*; one of the new flower beds being planted up in the municipal park, the other of women harvesting daffodils at Gardiner's Farm, picturesque in their traditional cloth bonnets.

'Mr Naylor was very pleased with them,' she told them. 'And his sister has invited me to supper next week. I'm looking forward to meeting his little girl.'

'Poor motherless baby,' Maggie said, as she poured the tea. 'Far too many of them, thanks to the war.'

When they had finished their tea, Sarah asked Abigail if she would come upstairs with her to see the new blouse she had bought. When they were safely inside the bedroom with the door closed, Sarah turned to her conspiratorially.

'I wanted to get you away from Ma for a minute.'

'Why? Is something wrong?'

'Yes. It's awful. I don't know what she's going to do when she finds out,' Sarah said, with a shake of her head. 'It's Annie – Jim's girl. She's expecting.'

'Oh, Sarah!' Abigail remembered the weeping girl out in the alleyway.

'Poor Jim. I know what he did was wrong, but he doesn't deserve to be so worried, not at his age. He hardly earns enough to pay Ma for his keep. I don't know what they're going to do.'

'What about Annie's family?'

'There's just her dad. He's nearly always drunk and he's got a terrible temper. He used to knock his poor wife about. I pity Annie when he gets to know, and he'll be after our Jim all right – nothing surer.'

'I think you should tell your mother,' Abigail said.

'That's what I said, but it's down to Jim to do that,' Sarah pointed out. 'It's not really my business. I've tried to talk to him, but he won't listen. He's talking about taking Annie and running away together, but how could they do that? What would they live on? Annie's dad will turn her out, and that

77

means the Union workhouse is her only hope. I'm just so feared that she might go and do something silly.'

Abigail didn't have to ask what. She remembered the incident that had resulted in her father's unjust expulsion from the town, and the women who lived off other women's misery with their barbaric methods of terminating pregnancy. 'Silly' was hardly the word to describe it.

'You'll *have* to talk to your mother,' she said. 'If Jim won't, then it will have to be you. You can't risk something awful happening to poor Annie. She and Jim need help.'

'I know.' Sarah twisted her hands together. 'I'll give him one more chance, then I'll have to say something. Thanks for letting me talk to you, Abby. I had to tell somebody.'

A thought occurred to Abigail. 'Does Patrick know?'

'He might. The boys keep things to themselves. It was Annie who told me. I'd never have heard it from Jim.'

Patrick came home just as Abigail was leaving. He nodded curtly to her as she stood to put on her coat.

'You'll see Abigail home, Patrick, won't you?' Maggie prompted. 'It's almost dark, and I don't like to think of her walking home alone.'

'I'll be quite all right,' Abigail protested. 'Patrick has only just got in.'

'He won't mind, will you, Pat?' It was Sarah who put in this last, with a meaningful look at her brother.

Patrick shrugged. 'Not as long as you're ready now. I don't want to hang about.'

As they walked in silence along the alleyway, Abigail wondered whether to broach the subject of Jim and Annie's problem, but decided to keep to more familiar subjects.

'How are things at the timber yard?' she asked. 'Are you still meeting opposition?'

'A few of the diehards are still against risking any trouble,' he said. 'But I'll win them round in the end, you see if I don't. It's obvious we'll get nothing unless I can get them to agree to a strike.'

'A strike?' She looked at him 'That's drastic, isn't it?'

'Like I said, it's the only way to make men like Edwin Dean listen. It's not only wages, it's safety, too. There are men injured every week, and if they can't work it's the sack. It's not fair.'

'What about Jim?' Abigail asked. 'You said he was reluctant to back you.'

'He's got others who need his support at the moment,' he said, without looking at her.

'You mean his girl – Annie?'

Patrick stopped walking and turned to face her. 'You know about Annie? Who told you – our Sarah?'

'Yes.'

'She'd no business, bringing in outsiders. This is something we have to work out ourselves, as a family.'

'But it seems you're not talking to each other. Sarah was desperately worried. She needed someone to talk to. You should be trying to work something out, Patrick.'

'What the hell has it got to do with you anyway?' His face was like thunder.

'Nothing, but I was asked for my opinion.' She glanced at him. 'It seems that not every member of your family thinks of me as an outsider. Sarah knows I won't betray her confidence.'

'No. All right – sorry. Oh!' He shook his head in exasperation. 'I can't understand how he could be so *stupid*!' His voice was tight with anger. 'He knows she's got a brute of a father who thinks nothing of taking his belt to her. Who's going to take care of the girl and her kid? That's what I want to know. Haven't we got enough mouths to feed? Why didn't he think of the trouble and upset it would cause?'

'When you're in love, practicalities fly out of the window,' Abigail said softly.

He looked at her with raised eyebrows. 'I thought well-brought-up young ladies weren't supposed to have thoughts like that,'

'You forget, I'm a doctor's daughter,' Abigail reminded him. 'I was brought up to face the realities of life. Young people have strong feelings and emotions that sometimes overwhelm them. It's a basic fact of life. Everyone makes mistakes.' She shot him a wry glance. 'Even you, I daresay. You're in love with your ideals, and you don't always consider the consequences of them, do you?'

'I do. It's just that I get so – so *frustrated* sometimes.' For a moment he walked in silence, then he said gruffly, 'Folks like us can't afford mistakes. We can't even afford luxuries like love either, half the time. According to those who control us, we're sub-human, with no right to feelings of any kind – except things like cold and hunger. We're welcome to those.'

'Oh, come on, Patrick. That's a bit melodramatic, isn't it?'

He rounded on her. 'Do you have any idea how it feels to be the eldest son in a family like mine?' he demanded. 'When my dad died, I felt it was up to me to support my family. I felt I should be the breadwinner. So how do you think it makes me feel seeing Ma still having to go out to work – especially cooking for Edwin Dean?'

'Maggie loves working at Prospect House,' Abigail said. 'She's looked after Sophie all her life. She loves her, and she'd never desert her. It's more than just a job to her.'

'All the same, without the money she earns we'd be a lot worse off,' he said gruffly. 'She's getting old. She should be taking things easy now. And it should be up to me to see that she does.'

'No one expects you to work miracles, Patrick. You shouldn't blame yourself.' They'd reached the terrace now and Abigail reached into her bag for her keys. 'Will you come in for a hot drink? We could talk.'

He hesitated. 'No. Better be getting back.'

'Actually, there's something I wanted to discuss with you.'

'Can't you tell me here?'

'I'd rather tell you over a cup of cocoa. It's getting chilly out here.' She smiled. 'Besides, it's not something I'd care to talk about in the street. Do come in, Patrick.'

'Oh, all right then. But only for a minute.'

In the kitchen behind the studio, Abigail made cocoa while

Patrick sat at the table looking slightly ill at ease.

'I'll come straight to the point, Patrick,' Abigail said, as she handed him a mug of cocoa. 'I've thought of a way to do something about Ashford's Yard. I think Mr Naylor would let me take photographs and write an article about it for the *Chronicle*.'

He shrugged. 'So why are you telling me?'

'I'd have thought it was obvious. I need to ask whether you feel it would be invading your privacy, having your home and the way you live featured in the paper,' she said. 'Not only you but the other people who live here. I know how proud you all are, and I wouldn't want to do anything to offend anyone.'

'Do you think it would do any good?'

'I've already written the article,' she told him. 'I describe it as a disgrace to the town, a town that likes to think of itself as forward-looking.' She opened her bag and took out a sheet of paper. 'You can read it and see what you think.' She passed it across the table to him. 'Who knows, it could even help you in your quest for better wages and working conditions.'

As he read the article, his face brightened. 'This isn't bad. Do you really think you could get it published?'

'I still have to get Mr Naylor to agree,' she said. 'That is just a rough draft, and he would have to approve it, but I wouldn't even show it to him without sounding you out first.'

For the first time since she had known him as an adult, she saw respect in his eyes. Suddenly he smiled, and his face was transformed. The brooding green eyes brightened and the tightness round his mouth softened. The effect was dramatic, and Abigail felt her heart lift in immediate response.

'Patrick! Don't say I've done something you approve of!'

He coloured, and cleared his throat. 'Well, I think it's a good idea, of course. But why should you stick your neck out for the likes of us?'

'Because you're my friends. And because it was what my father tried to do. It's for him, too. That's partly why I came back here.'

'Look – Abby, speaking plainly, your father's dead. You can't please him or avenge what happened to him any more. And you could harm this new business of yours.'

'You're a fine one to talk.'

'I'm not taking the same kind of risks as you. You've put the money your father left you into this business. You could lose everything if you get on the wrong side of folks with influence.'

'I'd ask for the article to go under a different name.'

'People already know you take photographs for the paper. They're not daft. It wouldn't take them long to put two and two together.'

'I'm willing to risk that. I've even tried to talk to Edwin Dean.'

'You've *what*?' He looked shocked. 'I don't think you know who you're dealing with there.'

'He's the husband of my oldest friend.'

'He's a nasty piece of work! I just thank God he's not our landlord at Ashford's Yard. If he was, I'd be risking more than my job. He'd not think twice about putting us all out on the street.'

Abigail's blood curdled at the thought of her friend being married to such a man. 'Who *is* your landlord, Patrick? Do you know?'

He shook his head. 'Nobody does. The rent gets collected every Friday by a ferrety little man called Jack Gittins. I don't think even *he* knows who employs him.'

'I'll find out,' she said. 'I'll get to know somehow. There has to be a way.'

'Well, just be careful,' Patrick warned. 'It must be someone who wants it kept quiet. You could find yourself in trouble.' He stood up and pulled his cap out of his pocket. 'I'd better be off. Ma will be wondering where I've got to.'

'Yes, of course.' She paused, wondering whether to voice what was in her mind. 'Patrick – have you ever thought about picking up your education again?'

'What do you mean?' His brow gathered into a frown. 'Are you saying I'm thick or something?'

'No! Quite the opposite. You're bright and intelligent, and you obviously want a better life and conditions for you and your fellow workers.'

He shrugged. 'I left school at thirteen and went straight to work at the timber yard – there was no option.'

'But there are evening classes you could go to,' she told him.

'Night school? The lads would think I'd gone soft.'

'It's not like you to care what people think. You're taking on a huge task, Patrick' she told him. 'I don't think you realize just how huge. There'll be educated people for you to deal with – people who could talk you down in five minutes with long words and phrases you don't understand. You need more than just anger to succeed, Patrick, a lot more. You need knowledge, education.'

He shook his head. 'I don't see how . . .'

'Patrick, listen, there's something called the Workers' Educational Association. It was started a few years before the war by a man who had to leave school early, like you. He felt that people with good minds should be offered a chance to better themselves.'

He looked doubtful. 'Well, that's all very well, but surely it's too late for me?'

'Not if you have an open mind – if you really want to succeed in this dream of yours. There are classes on just about everything, Patrick – right here in the town. They hold them at the Institute Hall. Teachers volunteer their time to teach people just like you. It would help you in so many ways. And you'd do well, I know you would. Why not give it a try?'

'I don't know . . .'

'Will you let me find out about them for you?'

'No!' He coloured. 'Just hold your horses. I can find out for myself – if I'm interested.' The old independent defiance was back. 'Anyway, how do you know it wouldn't just be a waste of time?'

'Because I've been to their classes myself and I know.'

He stared at her. 'You have?'

'The only education I had was at Prospect House with

Sophie's governess. When I knew I wanted to be a photographer, I needed to know more about chemistry and physics. Girls aren't supposed to need subjects like that. Father and I were quite poor, so there was no money for college. Then I found out about the WEA.'

Patrick looked impressed, but still unconvinced. 'I don't have that much free time, and there's so much I want to do with it.'

'I'll leave it to you, then, Patrick. Just promise me you'll think about it.'

'All right, but I'm making no guarantees, mind.' For a long moment he stood looking at her, then he pulled on his cap. 'Well – I suppose I'd better be off now.'

'Yes. Goodnight, Patrick.' Abigail walked with him to the door.

As he stepped out into the street, he turned to her. 'You're the first person who's ever believed in me.'

She opened her mouth to reply, but before she could say anything he had gone, walking quickly away into the darkness.

Anne March had assured her guests that the evening was to be casual and informal. 'Just a relaxed supper,' she'd said.

When William called to pick Abigail up, he found her dressed in her favourite blue dress, her hair freshly washed and brushed into a shining bob that swung around her face.

He smiled. 'You look very nice.'

'Thank you.'

In the car, he turned to her. 'I've been thinking about Julia Welland's twenty-first birthday party the week after next. How are you proposing to get there?'

She smiled. 'How do you think? On my trusty bicycle and trailer.'

He stared at her. 'You can't be serious.'

'Why not?'

'Do you realize how far it is? It takes me almost half an hour to *drive* out to Willow Fen.'

'Then I shall have to set out early.' She frowned thoughtfully.

'It may even mean shutting the studio earlier on that day.'

'*Abigail*! You'd be completely exhausted after cycling all that way.'

'I think I'm a bit tougher than that.'

'Suppose it's raining?'

'I've got a waterproof cover for the trailer.'

'And what about yourself? You'll want to wear something dressy for an occasion like that.'

'Then I'll wear my mackintosh over it.'

He laughed and shook his head. 'I've never met anyone like you! Listen, will you let me come and pick you and all your equipment up?'

'Why should you do that?'

'You really are the most infuriating girl!' He took a deep breath and said slowly, 'Look. I'm invited to the party anyway, and the car will be empty apart from me. You need to get all your equipment there, so it makes sense for me to give you a lift – doesn't it?'

She laughed. 'All right, I accept. Thank you very much. But there are bound to be times when I'll have to cycle to appointments; I'll have to get used to it sometime.'

'I agree, which is why the best thing you can do is buy yourself a motor car and learn to drive.'

'Which is exactly what I intend to do, just as soon as I've bought all the other essential things I need. Which could be quite a long way off.'

He laughed and shook his head. 'I give up!'

Andrew Naylor and his sister, Anne, lived in the first-floor flat of a Victorian villa overlooking the park. Anne greeted them at the door and took them up to the sitting-room, where Andrew was waiting with his small daughter, who had been allowed to stay up late to meet the visitors. She was a pretty little girl of about four, with huge dark eyes and straight brown hair, cut in a fringe. She wore a red dressing-gown and clutched a rag doll. She peered shyly at Abigail and William.

Andrew nudged her towards them. 'Mary, this is Miss Banks

and Doctor Maybury. You remember Doctor Maybury. He came and made you better when you had the measles.'

Mary extended a small hand and said solemnly, 'How do you do?'

'How do you do, Mary?' William replied. 'I hope you're well now.'

The child nodded. 'Yes, thank you.'

Abigail shook the small hand and sat down, accepting the sherry that Andrew offered them. A few moments later, the doorbell downstairs rang again and Anne went to answer it. Voices could be heard on the stairs, and a moment later Sophie and Edwin appeared in the doorway. Andrew stood to greet them.

'Two more guests, Mary,' he told his daughter. 'This is Mr and Mrs Dean.'

Abigail saw at once the instant rapport between Sophie and the child. Sophie's eyes were bright with tears as she took the plump little hand, and a moment later she had put her arms around the little girl and kissed her forehead.

Anne stepped forward, smiling. 'High time all good little girls were in bed. Say goodnight, Mary.'

'Can Mrs Dean come and read me a story, please?' Mary's eyes were still fixed on Sophie.

Anne looked embarrassed. 'Not tonight, Mary. Mrs Dean is a guest, and supper is almost ready.'

'Oh, may I?' Sophie said impulsively. 'I would so love to.' She looked at Andrew and his sister. 'If you don't mind, of course.'

Andrew laughed. 'If *you* don't mind, of course it's all right. But don't let her talk you into reading more than one. She can be very persuasive.'

'I can imagine.' Sophie smiled down at Mary, who put her hand into Sophie's as they went off together with Anne.

Andrew poured a sherry for Edwin, and refilled William and Abigail's glasses. Edwin leaned back in his chair and took a sip from his glass. 'You're a widower, I understand,' he said.

Abigail was shocked at his directness, but Andrew seemed

unembarrassed by the remark. 'Unfortunately, yes. My wife caught influenza soon after I came back from France two years ago.'

'Invalided out of the army?' Edwin gestured towards Andrew's leg.

'That's right. No use to the army with only one leg. Mind you, it was a price almost worth paying to get away from the carnage in France. Many others weren't so lucky.' He took a sip from his glass. 'Did you see action yourself?'

It was Edwin's turn to remain unabashed. 'No. I was involved in the clothing trade at the time, in London. We made uniforms.'

'A reserved occupation then.'

'Quite.'

Anne appeared in the doorway. 'Supper is ready, if you'd all like to come through to the dining-room.' She looked at Edwin. 'Your wife will be with us directly. I'm sorry to say Mary is taking advantage of her quite dreadfully.'

'She's frightfully broody, I'm afraid,' Edwin said, draining his glass and putting it down on the table beside him. 'We lost a child, you know. It was quite a while ago now, but she doesn't seem to have recovered from it.'

Anne looked shocked. 'Really? I'm so sorry. I had no idea.'

'We don't talk about it,' Edwin said. 'At least, I don't. Sophie would, but I try to steer her away from the subject. Not healthy, is it – to keep brooding on what's over and done with?'

If Abigail had not already decided that she didn't like Edwin that remark would have confirmed her opinion.

Sophie joined them as they seated themselves at the table. She looked flushed.

'What a delightful little daughter you have, Andrew,' she said. 'She's so bright and intelligent for her age. You're so lucky.'

Andrew smiled. 'I know. She was born while I was away at the war, so I missed her babyhood. She didn't know who I was when I first came home, and after her mother died – well, it was very difficult to begin with.' He smiled across the table at his sister. 'I don't know what I would have done without Anne.'

'Does she go to school yet?' Sophie wondered.

'Not until next year,' Anne told her. 'She could have started at Easter, but she was quite poorly with measles last winter so we decided to keep her at home a little longer. I'm afraid she gets dreadfully bored, poor child. As you say, she's bright. It's difficult to keep her amused sometimes. I take her to the park most days.'

'Isn't there a garden here?' Sophie asked.

Andrew shook his head. 'There is, but it belongs to the people who own the house. They have the ground-floor flat. It was one of the reasons we took the place. Gardening is out with my leg, I'm afraid.'

'Then you must bring Mary to play in ours,' Sophie said excitedly. 'I'm sure she'd love it, and I'd love to have her.'

Edwin cleared his throat. 'Really, Sophie, you mustn't try to monopolize other people's children.'

Sophie blushed. 'I meant for Anne to come, too, of course. We could all have tea together. I'd like it very much.'

Anne smiled. 'That would be lovely. I'm sure Mary would be delighted.'

'Right. That's settled then. Shall we say next Wednesday?'

For the first time Abigail saw defiance in Sophie's eyes, and she silently applauded her for it.

The food was delicious, and the rest of the evening was spent pleasantly, but as they were leaving Abigail took Andrew aside. 'I've got something I'd like you to look at,' she said quietly. Opening her bag, she took out the article she had written about Ashford's Yard. 'I'd like to take some photographs to illustrate it, too – if you agree.'

He unfolded the paper and glanced briefly at it, then at her. 'We'll talk about it later,' he said. He lowered his voice. 'I hope you know what you're doing.'

'I think so,' she said.

'It's going to be pretty controversial.'

'That's the whole point.'

'There'd be a lot at stake, both for you and for the paper.' For a few moments he held her eyes. 'All right. Let me read it carefully, then we'll talk.'

On the drive home Abigail was silent, busy with her own thoughts. William glanced at her from time to time.

'Is everything all right, Abby?' he asked at last.

'Yes, thank you, William.'

'What was the paper you gave to Naylor as we were leaving?'

'Just an idea – something I thought might interest him.'

'Not another of your political hot chestnuts, I hope?'

She shrugged noncommittally. 'It depends on who you are and how you look at it.'

As he pulled up outside the studio, he turned to her.

'Abby – you're a beautiful and independent young woman, and so far you're doing very well. You won't do anything to put all that in jeopardy, will you?'

She turned to look at him, her brown eyes bright and clear. 'William, if I didn't know you better I'd say that sounded almost like a threat!'

CHAPTER SEVEN

The evening of 28 June was warm and mellow. William called for Abigail at eight o'clock and helped her to load her equipment into the back of the car: the large camera in its case, plus a large black cloth to cover it; the glass plates in their holders and a black velvet bag in which to hold the exposed negatives; finally, the folding tripod.

'I don't know how you thought you were going to get all this lot on your bicycle all the way out to Willow Fen,' he said, as he seated himself back behind the wheel.

Abigail smiled. 'You'd be surprised what I can do when I've made up my mind.'

He raised a quizzical eyebrow at her. 'No, I wouldn't, and frankly, Abby, the thought of it sometimes frightens the life out of me.'

As he had predicted, it took almost half an hour to make the journey. Abigail enjoyed the ride, feeling that the lack of features in the fen landscape was more than compensated by the beauty of the evening sky. After a warm summer day the panorama was breathtaking as the sun slowly set in a blaze of rose and turquoise, violet and crimson.

At last William turned the car into a driveway lined with chestnut trees, still frothy with pink and white blossom, and Abigail gave a gasp of delight as the house came into view. William smiled at her.

'Willow Grange. Beautiful, isn't it?'

Three storeys high and of early Georgian architecture, the

house was built of rose-coloured brick and surrounded by smooth lawns. The drive ended in a circular carriage sweep, and other cars were already parked, their owners mingling on the lawn, where maids in black dresses circulated with trays of drinks.

'I'll help you with your equipment,' William offered.

She shook her head. 'No, you're a guest. You must present yourself to your hostess, but I'd be grateful if you could ask her if someone can show me where to set up.'

Abigail began to unload her photographic equipment from the car, and presently a maid arrived to help her carry it into the house. The large square hallway had been cleared, its floor polished for dancing, and musicians were tuning up their instruments above on the galleried landing.

Abigail was setting up her camera on its tripod when Mrs Welland appeared, accompanied by a pretty fair-haired girl in a glamorous pink dress, copiously embroidered with beads and crystals.

'Miss Banks. Good evening. This is my daughter, Julia. We thought this might be a good moment for you to take a portrait of her. I hope you will find this a suitable location.'

Abigail was slightly taken aback. She would have preferred to take Miss Welland's portrait at the studio, but if this was what the sitter's mother wanted, she could hardly refuse. She looked around for a suitable background and spotted a console table against the wall, backed by a gilt-framed mirror. On the table was an exquisite flower arrangement.

'If Miss Welland could sit over there,' she suggested. 'Half turned, I think, so that we could achieve an interesting reflection. She has a beautiful profile.'

Mrs Welland and her daughter seemed to like the idea, and Abigail arranged the girl on a carved chair and moved her camera into position. Luckily, the light was good and she would not need a flash. She disappeared under the cloth to view the effect, and was satisfied by the inverted image.

Emerging, she said, 'That looks very nice. Now, if you could hold that for me . . .' She pressed the bulb. 'Very good. Maybe

91

we'll have one more, facing the other way. I'd like to try something else.' She removed the exposed plate and stowed it in its
light-proof bag, then, after replacing the plate with a new one,
she attached a filter to the camera lens and adjusted the focus
slightly before taking the second shot.

Abigail was kept busy for the early part of the evening,
photographing the other members of the Welland family, the
new arrivals and guests of importance who were pointed out to
her. During supper, a sumptuous buffet laid out in the dining-
room, she moved her camera and snapped groups of revellers
chatting and enjoying themselves. It was some time before she
realized that Sophie and Edwin were not among the guests,
and, asking William, she learned that Edwin had had a last-
minute engagement and so had sent apologies for himself and
Sophie. Abigail could only guess at her friend's disappoint-
ment.

Later, when the dancing was well underway, Mrs Welland
suggested that Abigail might like to partake of supper herself,
and she found herself being ushered below stairs to the kitchen
by a maid and presented with a plate of food left over from the
buffet table. The only other person in the kitchen was a stout
woman with a red face, who looked at her compassionately.

'Evenin'. I'm Mrs Carne – Cook, most call me.'

'How do you do? I'm Abigail Banks.'

'So I've 'eard.' Cook stoked the range vigorously and came
to join Abigail at the table. 'I reckon it's a bit thick.'

'Sorry – what is?'

'You're good enough to take photos of 'em, but not good
enough to eat with 'em upstairs!'

'I don't mind. It's good to have a break and something to
eat. This evening has been quite hard work.'

'Oh, it would be,' Cook said with a nod. 'They'd take care
o' that all right. The Wellands believe in getting their money's
worth.' She peered at Abigail 'Is it right that you're Doctor
Banks's daughter? Him what used to be the panel doctor?'

'It is.'

'A finer man never lived,' Cook said baldly. 'Worked his

socks off for the poor of Eastmere, and little good it did 'im! I wonder you wanted to come back 'ere.'

'We were happy for much of the time,' Abigail responded. 'I have some good friends here, and I like the fen country.'

Cook shook her head. 'Well, I reckon you deserves a medal after what they done to your dad!' She rose and went to a cupboard. Taking out a bottle she poured two generous glasses of dark red liquid. 'Get that down you, girl,' she said, pushing one glass towards Abigail. 'Nice drop o' port. Do you the world o' good.' She took a deep drink and smacked her lips. 'Aah! One o' the perks o' this job.'

'They provide you with port?' Abigail said.

'Oh, yes.' Cook tapped the side of her nose knowingly. 'Not that they knows it, mind.' Abigail laughed and sipped the thick, sweet wine. 'That's the ticket, girl,' Cook said approvingly. 'Down the 'atch, and to 'ell with them upstairs.' She hiccupped slightly, suggesting that this was not the first drink she had taken this evening. 'Now, then – what do you think of our Miss Julia?' she asked.

'She's very pretty,' Abigail said.

'Handsome is as handsome does, I always say.' Cook leaned towards Abigail confidentially, her elbows resting on the table. 'This party's by way of a sprat to catch a mackerel, if you ask me,' she said. 'Reckon they thinks it's high time they got 'er off their 'ands. They got two other girls and a lad, y'know. She's the eldest.'

'Yes, I've photographed them all this evening.'

'They got their eyes on young Doctor Maybury, or I'm a Dutchman,' Cook added. 'There's money there, y'know. They reckon 'is family owns half the property in Eastmere. He's not your average sawbones, if you'll pardon the expression, you bein' a doctor's daughter.'

'Not at all. And I know Doctor Maybury quite well.'

The woman's face fell. 'Oh. I 'ope I'm not speakin' out o' turn.'

'Of course not.' Abigail finished her food and stood up. 'I'd better go now,' she said. 'They might be wanting more photographs, and it wouldn't do to take advantage. Thank you for the port. It was nice meeting you.'

'Just as you wish, Miss Banks, though I'd take longer if it was me. Good luck with the photos.'

It was after midnight when William helped her pack her equipment into the car. She had promised Mrs Welland that the proofs of the photographs would be ready by the following Wednesday. Normally she asked her clients to wait a week, but Mrs Welland had made it clear that she expected special treatment, and half promised to recommend Abigail to all her friends if the photographs turned out well.

As William turned the car out of the gates of Willow Grange he said, 'I hope you're going to charge an appropriate fee for all the work you've put in this evening.'

'All I hope is that the photographs turn out well, and that Mrs Welland and her daughter are pleased with them,' Abigail said. 'Normally I only do portraits in the studio, where I can adjust the lighting and use my own props.'

'Is that why you used the mirror?' he asked.

'Partly. It was by way of being an experiment. I can't wait to get it developed and see if what I've done has paid off. If it hasn't, I shall offer to take another portrait in the studio, free of charge.'

William smiled. 'I'm sure there'll be no need for that.'

Abigail looked at him speculatively. 'Have you known Julia Welland long?'

'Quite a long time, yes.' He looked round at her. 'Why do you ask?'

'I just wondered. She's very pretty.'

He smiled. 'She is rather, isn't she?'

'I expect she has a lot of admirers.'

'I daresay. I wouldn't know for sure, but a girl like Julia is bound to have.'

Abigail said no more. Secretly she wondered if he was oblivious to the Wellands' plans for him, or if he just considered it none of her business.

At the studio, William helped her inside with her equipment. She offered to make him a hot drink, but he declined with a smile.

'It's getting on for one in the morning, and this is a highly respectable neighbourhood. Can't have your reputation torn to shreds, can we?' He put his hands on her shoulders and drew her to him, kissing her lightly on the forehead. 'See you again soon, Abby. Maybe we could have a spin down to the coast one Sunday, now that the summer's here. Take a picnic. Would you like that?'

She smiled. 'Very much.'

But as he drove away, she wondered what the Wellands would think of their designated son-in-law taking a common photographer out for the day.

Abigail couldn't wait to get into her darkroom with the negatives of the photographs she had taken at the Wellands' party, but she had to wait till the following evening, when her day's work was finished. Andrew Naylor had sent word that he had an assignment for her. It was at the local printing works, the owner of which was also the owner of the *Chronicle*. A new and up-to-date press had just arrived, and it was to be featured in this week's paper.

It was late when she got back to the studio. She made herself a quick meal, and then put on her overall and carried all the negatives waiting to be developed through to the darkroom, which she had converted from the old pantry under the stairs.

She began with the Wetlands' party photographs. Waiting for the developing fluid to take effect had never seemed to take longer, but at last the image merged into view. At the right moment she retrieved it and immersed it in the fixing solution. So far so good, but she was eager to see how the other portrait, her experimental one, had turned out. It was better than she had dared to hope. The soft filter gave Julia's sweet face a dreamy quality, and the background of flowers framed her reflection in the mirror in the most attractive way. Of course, it would be up to the girl and her mother to choose the one they liked best, but Abigail had already decided that, with their permission, it would be the soft-focus one that she would display in her window.

The photographs of the new printing press had come out well, too, and as she hung up the proofs to dry she decided that as she had no appointments for the following morning, the *Chronicle* office would be her first call.

Andrew was pleased to see her, and delighted with the photographs. On her own initiative Abigail had taken some shots of the building as well, and suggested to Andrew that the arrival of the new printing press might be a good time to publish a short history of Halliwell's Press.

'I believe the press is coming up to its centenary,' she said. 'And it's been in the same family since the beginning, which is surely something to celebrate.'

Andrew smiled. 'Sometimes I wish I had you on my regular staff,' he said. 'Which brings me to the little matter of this article you've written about Ashford's Yard.'

Abigail's interest was instantly aroused. She hadn't liked to broach the subject herself, but she had been wondering what Andrew thought of the article. He indicated the chair opposite.

'Sit down a moment.' She did as he said, holding her breath. 'Abigail,' he began, 'the article as it stands is very good. Straight to the point and effective. If I owned the paper, I'd publish and be damned, as they say. The trouble is, I don't. As you know the *Chronicle*'s owner is Mr Halliwell, who also prints it, and I dread to imagine what his view would be.'

Abigail frowned. 'Well – couldn't you ask him?'

'It's not as simple as that. I know that like all local business-men, Edgar Halliwell relies on local people for business – advertising and so on. I'm not quite sure how many sets of feathers an article of this sort would ruffle, but I'd say a good many. Whoever owns the houses in the yard, for instance, not to mention Edwin Dean, who owns the land. Most of his workforce live in the Yard, and you indicate in your article that employers are as much to blame as landlords.'

'So – are you saying you can't publish it?' Abigail asked,

trying not to sound too disappointed.

Andrew pushed his chair back. 'Not exactly. Do you think you could tone it down, or approach it from another angle?'

'My whole plan was to shock,' she said. 'I wanted to make an impact.'

'Of course you did, and, off the record, I'm in complete agreement. Something should be done about that place. It's a disgrace, But maybe there's a more subtle way of doing it.'

'Would subtlety work, though?'

'I think it would, if it were done in the right way. You've just mentioned that Halliwell's Press is approaching its centenary. You've a talent for ferreting things out. Why don't you do some research into Ashford's Yard? Maybe there's a clue there.'

'Yes, perhaps I will. Thank you, Andrew.'

'By the way,' he said, 'I'd like you to cover the Council by-election next week. Did you know that Edwin Dean is standing?'

'Yes. That's interesting.'

'I'll let you know where and when.' As she stood up and prepared to leave, he said, 'You know, it's high time you had a telephone. I have to send the boy round with messages for you. It isn't very convenient.'

'I'm beginning to show a profit, but not enough to pay for a telephone just yet.'

'Well, I think the paper could run to that for you,' he said. 'After all, you are on the payroll, and it would be to our advantage.'

'Oh, Andrew, thank you.'

'I'll arrange it. And, by the way, what happens to the studio while you're away from it – here, for instance?'

'I have to close it.'

'That's what I thought. You could do with an assistant, you know; someone to mind the place and make appointments when you're not there. You must be losing business.'

'I probably am, but it can't be helped. I always leave a note on the door to say when I'll be back.'

'Not very professional, though, is it?' he said, with a wry

smile. 'I think a young girl is what you need. Give it some thought, Abby.'

Abigail did give it some thought. She thought about it all that day, but her heart sank when she thought of what it might cost. It was true that business looked promising, but there were so many demands on her bank account that so far she was barely breaking even.

After the studio had closed, she worked in the darkroom until her rumbling tummy reminded her that it was supper-time. She had just washed her hands and was taking off her overall, when she heard someone tapping on the shop door. It was past closing-time, and she had locked up long ago. Going through to the front and opening the door, she was surprised to see Sarah Johnson standing outside.

'Hello, Sarah! This is a surprise.

'Can I come in and talk to you, Abby?'

'Of course, come upstairs to the flat,' Abigail invited. 'I'll make some tea, You look as though you could do with a cup.'

Sarah followed her upstairs and stood looking round the cosy little living-room wistfully while Abigail made the tea. She looked out of the window across the town to where she could just make out the curve of Ashford's Yard winding along the river's edge like a snake. She stroked the soft material of the curtains.

'You've made it lovely here,' she said. 'I can't imagine what it must be like to have all this space to yourself. We're so crowded at home.'

'I know.' Abigail began to pour. 'I appreciated your mother putting me up, and I did my best to make my stay as temporary as possible.'

Sarah turned quickly. 'Oh, I didn't mean that. It was wonderful having you to stay, honestly it was. But now Annie's moving in with us, and that *won't* be temporary.'

'She's moving in?'

Sarah nodded. 'She couldn't keep it to herself any longer that she was expecting. She plucked up the courage and told her dad.'

'What happened?'

Sarah shuddered. 'He went mad – beat her something shocking. When Ma saw the state she was in, she was so angry she went right round there and had it out with him. She told him it was a wonder Annie hadn't lost the baby. He didn't care, though – said it would have been best all round if she had. He told Ma that we'd better take her in if we were so fond of her, 'cause he was chucking her out.'

'What a horrible man! I'm so sorry, Sarah. I suppose she and Jim will be getting married.'

'Oh, yes, her dad insisted. Jim always wanted to do the right thing anyway. But they won't be able to afford a place of their own, and how we're all going to fit into the house I don't know, especially after the baby's born.'

'I'm so sorry to hear all this, Sarah.'

The girl sighed and took a sip of her tea. 'That's not all, though, Abby. There's worse – Mr Hudson's given me the sack.'

'Oh, Sarah! But why?'

'Not because of anything I've done. His daughter's turned fourteen now, and she's leaving school. He always promised her a job in the shop, and he says he can't afford two shop assistants, so I've got to go.'

'That's awful, Sarah. I'm so sorry.'

'It only happened yesterday, and I haven't told Ma yet,' Sarah went on, her voice trembling. 'I'm dreading it. She'll be so worried. We need all the money we can get now, and once Annie has to leave off work we'll have to support her and the baby, as well. And you know what Patrick's like. Ma's worried to death that he'll end up getting the sack before long, too.'

'I wish there was something I could do.'

Sarah looked at her. 'You don't know of any jobs going, do you? I'd do anything – even scrub floors.'

'Oh, Sarah.' Abigail's heart went out to the Johnson family. They'd been so kind to her. If only there were some way she could pay them back. She put down her cup, shaking her head, then suddenly she remembered something Andrew Naylor had said that morning, and she thought of all the times lately when she'd had to close the studio to go out to assignments. He was right, of course; she should be able to keep open and not lose business.

'There might be something I could do, Sarah, but I don't know if it would be suitable for you . . .'

'What is it? I'll do *anything*.'

'I could offer you my spare room and your keep, plus a small amount of pocket money in return for minding the studio and making appointments for me while I'm out. I know it's not much, but . . .'

Sarah's eyes lit up. 'You mean I'd *live* here with you? Have a whole room all to myself?' She clapped her hands. 'Oh, that would be marvellous!'

But Abigail was shaking her head. 'It isn't a real job, though. There wouldn't be much future in it . . .' Suddenly an idea presented itself. Sarah was bright and keen to make something of herself. 'Unless . . .'

'*Yes*?' Sarah was watching her face intently. 'Unless what?'

'How would you like to learn photography, Sarah?' Abigail asked. 'You could be my apprentice.'

'*Oh*!' Sarah's eyes were like saucers. 'Learn to be a photographer, like you? Oh, I'd . . .' Her face fell. 'But apprentices have to pay a premium, don't they? Ma couldn't afford to pay you.'

'She wouldn't have to. You'd be earning your keep. It would mean taking some evening classes, too, and studying,' Abigail warned. 'It would be hard work. But you would have a trade at the end of it. What do you say? Would you like time to think about it – talk to your mother and the boys?'

'*No*. I want to take it – please.' Sarah's eyes were alight with eagerness. 'When can I move in?'

Abigail laughed. 'I think I'd better come and talk to your mother first. I don't want her to think I'm taking over your life. Tell her I'll come tomorrow evening, after the studio closes.'

*

100

When Abigail arrived at Ashford's Yard the following evening she could sense at once the atmosphere of despondency. Annie sat in the corner by the range, a pile of mending in her lap. She was a thin, pale girl of about seventeen with lank fair hair. When she saw Abigail she picked up her darning and scuttled upstairs like a frightened rabbit. Abigail looked apologetically at Maggie.

'I didn't mean to scare her away.'

Maggie shook her head. 'Poor lass. She's afraid of her own shadow, and no wonder, the life she's had with that pig of a man. Not fit to call himself a father.'

'When is the baby due?'

'Around October, as far as I can tell,' Maggie said. 'She doesn't rightly know herself, so we'll have to wait and see. You can see what she's like – skinny and run down. There isn't twopenn'orth of her. She needs plenty of good food and building up, if she's to get through the birth. How we're going to manage, I don't know.' She reached out a hand to Abigail. 'But that's not your problem, bless you. What am I thinking of keeping you standing there? Sit you down while I make a brew.'

Abigail sat down. 'Maggie, has Sarah told you that she came to see me yesterday?'

'That she has, and about that mealy-mouthed Hudson giving her the sack. I can't tell you how grateful I am for what you've offered her.' She sighed. 'And it's kind of you. But I can't help feeling like I'd be throwing my own girl out to make more room.'

'You mustn't feel like that. Sarah's keen to work for me, and she can come home and see you as often as she likes.'

'She's a good girl. She'll not let you down,' Maggie said. 'She'll cook and clean for you, as well as work in the shop – sorry, studio.'

'I don't mean her to be a servant, Maggie,' Abigail said. 'We'll do the chores between us. I won't be able to pay her much, just her room and keep and a little pocket money, really, but if she would like to learn photography I'll take her on as

101

my apprentice. If you're in agreement, that is.'

'Well, of course, if that's what she wants. And, I must say, she does seem keen.

'Right. That's settled, then. She can move in whenever she likes.'

At that moment Sarah appeared in the doorway, her cheeks scarlet with excitement. Abigail smiled at her.

'Did you hear that, Sarah?'

'Yes. Oh, thank you, Abby. And thank you, too, Ma. I have to work a week's notice with Mr Hudson, so would this time next week be too soon to move in?'

'Not at all,' Abigail replied laughing. 'I'll get the spare room ready for you.'

Abigail drank the tea that Maggie had made, then took her leave. Dusk was falling as she left. It was dark as she entered the alleyway at the end of the yard, and she had almost walked past the man coming in the opposite direction before she recognized who he was.

'Oh, Patrick!'

'Good evening.' He pulled off his cap.

'I've been to see your mother,' she explained. 'We've arranged for Sarah to come and work for me. She's going to be my apprentice.'

'I see.'

'Yes.' She stepped closer to look into his face. 'You *are* in agreement with your sister working for me? You weren't there, so I couldn't ask you.'

'What right have I to say who she works for? Beggars can't be choosers, can they?' He shook his head. 'Sorry, that sounds ungrateful. It's just that it's a shame Sarah has to move out to make way because of the mess our Jim's got himself into.'

'Don't say that, Patrick. Sarah wants to come, and I'm happy to have her. Jim and that poor girl need your support.'

'It's easy to see it like that when you don't have to live with it.' He looked at her. 'Look, I'll walk home with you. It's getting late.'

'You don't need to do that. I'm quite . . .' she began. But

already he had turned in the direction she was walking.

'I know I don't *have* to,' he said gruffly, 'but I've said I will, haven't I?'

They walked in silence for a moment, then she asked, 'Have you been to a meeting?'

He turned to look at her. 'If you must know, I've been to night school.'

Abigail was so surprised she was almost lost for words. 'Really?' she said at last. 'That's wonderful.'

'I thought about what you said, and it made sense,' he said. 'I made enquiries and went to see the man who runs the classes. I've signed up for English, history and political studies.'

'I'm glad. Are you enjoying the classes?'

'More than I thought I would,' he told her, his voice warming with enthusiasm. 'I thought it'd be like being a kid at school again, but it's not. You're encouraged to join in and discuss things.'

'I've got some books of my father's you might like to borrow – if you want to.'

'Thanks. Maybe I will.' He paused. 'Look, no one knows about the classes, so I'd be glad if you'd keep it to yourself for the time being.'

'Of course. Anything you say.'

'So, our Sarah is going to live at your place?'

'That's right. It will make more room, now that Annie's moved in with you.'

He nodded. 'As you know, Ted's working at Eastmere Hall now, under Mr Brown, the head gardener. The Browns have offered him a room at theirs so without him and Sarah I'll be the only one in the way. When Annie and Jim get wed, I'll have to sleep downstairs on the sofa.' He sighed. 'If I thought Ma could manage without my money I'd move out, too – find some digs somewhere. It's not going to be easy to study with no space of my own and a baby yelling its head off day and night.'

'Perhaps it will be a good baby,' Abigail said hopefully. They had reached the studio now, and Abigail opened her bag to search for her key. 'Do you want to come in for a drink,

Patrick?' she invited. 'I could look out those books for you.'

He shook his head. 'Better not. It's getting late.'

'You know you'll always be welcome to come and study here, don't you, Patrick? It's quiet in the evenings, and you could work downstairs in the studio. No one would disturb you there.'

'Thanks. It's good of you. I'll remember.' He looked at his feet. 'Is it true you're going out with Doctor Maybury?' She laughed, and he coloured. 'Said something funny, have I?'

'No, it's just the idea. I'm not going out with Doctor Maybury, or anyone else for that matter,' she told him. 'We've become friends, and he's helped me out with his motor car once or twice, that's all.'

'I shouldn't have asked. None of my business anyway. 'Night then.'

'Don't forget that you're welcome to use the studio for studying,' she called. But he appeared not to hear as he walked quickly away along the terrace without a backward look.

Mrs Welland and her daughter Julia came to the studio the following day to inspect the proofs of the photographs Abigail had taken at the party. To Abigail's relief they were both delighted with the results, and made a generous order for enlargements.

'Do you do framing?' Mrs Welland asked.

Abigail had to tell her regretfully that, as yet, she did not. 'I hope to find someone to frame for me before long,' she said. 'I have an outbuilding in the yard that would make an ideal workshop.'

Mrs Welland paid for the photographs, and as Abigail gave her change for the five pound note she handed over, Mrs Welland said casually, 'I believe that William – Doctor Maybury – has been helping you with transport.'

'He very kindly gave me an old bicycle that was in his shed,' Abigail told her. 'But on the night I came to your house, he helped me out with his motor car.' She sighed. 'There are so many things I need to build up my business here. Someone to make frames is one, and a reliable form of transport is another.'

'Naturally. And a modern young woman like you must surely want to be independent,' Mrs Welland said. She smiled reassuringly at her daughter as she said it, and when they had gone Abigail remembered what Mrs Carne, the cook, had told her on the night of the party. If it was true that the Wellands had their eye on William as a prospective son-in-law, they surely didn't see *her* as a threat, did they?

To her surprise, William came into the studio the very next day. On hearing the shop doorbell, Abigail came out of her studio to find him standing at the counter.

'Good morning, Miss Elusive,' he said. 'This is the third time I've been round to see you only to find the door locked and a note pinned to it.'

'I'm getting the telephone installed shortly,' she told him proudly. 'And a new apprentice. I shall soon be completely professional.' She smiled at him 'What can I do for you, William? A nice studiously posed portrait perhaps, or a photograph of your motor car?'

'Neither, and I'll thank you not to make fun of me. I'm here to hold you to that Sunday picnic down at the coast,' he told her. 'The weather is perfect, so are you free this coming weekend?'

Abigail hesitated, remembering Mrs Welland's veiled warning.

'What's wrong – changed your mind?' William asked.

'No, it's a lovely idea. But I'm going to be busy this coming weekend. My new apprentice is arriving on Sunday and I shall be preparing a room for her. Could we make it the one after that?'

'If we must, then I shall wait,' he said, with a slightly mocking smile. 'Is that settled then?'

'Yes.'

'If I call for you at ten o'clock, would it be too early for you?'

'Not at all. I'll be ready.'

'Wonderful. I'll look forward to it. And don't worry about food. I'll take care of all that.'

When he had gone, she wondered if she should have accepted. But William was not engaged to Julia Welland. In fact, he seemed blissfully unaware of the plans the Welland family had in store for him. And a Sunday picnic by the sea did sound inviting.

Mrs Ellington came in person on the first of every month to collect her rent, and the following Wednesday was her day. At first, Abigail had wondered if she was checking up on her tenants, but the woman was always friendly and pleasant in spite of her forthright manner.

'I must say you've made it very nice,' she said, as she looked round the studio at the draped curtain and the carved chair Abigail used for portrait-sitters.

'There is still so much I want to do,' Abigail told her. 'For instance, I've been asked if I do framing. The workshop is there in the yard, but I don't know anyone who would work for as little as I'd be able to pay.'

'Mmm.' Mrs Ellington looked thoughtful. 'How do you get on with the Tarrants?'

She was referring to the elderly couple who occupied the first-floor flat, and Abigail wondered why she was changing the subject so abruptly.

'I hardly see them,' she replied. 'But they always seem very pleasant when we do meet. Why do you ask?'

'Joe Tarrant used to be a carpenter,' Mrs Ellington said. 'I suspect they find it quite hard to manage on the little they've got, and it occurred to me that he might welcome a nice little job.' She looked at Abigail. 'They're proud people. You wouldn't say that it was my idea, would you?'

Abigail was busy over the days that followed. She covered the by-election as Andrew had asked, and was surprised when Edwin Dean was elected to a seat on the Town Council. All her free time was occupied in trying to prepare the spare room for Sarah's arrival. There was already an iron-framed single bed in the room but nothing else. She tried the bed, and found the flock-filled mattress impossibly hard and lumpy. Taking a walk into town, she looked around the local second-hand shops, but could find nothing that wasn't either worn out or ugly. At last, with only one day to go, she decided to go along to Prospect House and see if Sophie had any more unwanted pieces in her attic.

She found her friend in a good mood and eager to help.

'Let's go up and see what there is,' Sophie said. 'I'm sure there are one or two pieces you could use, and there's certainly a single feather bed up there to replace the lumpy flock one.'

Together, they rummaged in the attic, and as well as the feather mattress Abigail was delighted to find a small dressing-table and a bedside cabinet. They were about to leave when she suddenly spotted a carpet rolled up in one corner.

'Oh, may I take that, too?' she asked. 'I don't think Sarah has ever had a carpet in her bedroom before. She'd be so thrilled.'

'Of course you can take it,' Sophie said. 'Take anything you want.'

Downstairs, over tea, Abigail studied her friend's pink cheeks and bright eyes. 'You're looking so much better, Sophie. I expect you're excited that Edwin won the seat.'

'Hardly,' Sophie said. 'I suppose I'll see even less of him now.'

'But you seem much happier. Has something else happened?'

'Yes, it has.' It was almost as though Sophie had to bite back the smile that lit her face. 'For the past two weeks I've had little Mary Naylor here to play in the afternoons. Oh, Abby, she's such a darling little girl. I love having her. It's so sad to think of her losing her mother so young.'

Abigail's heart sank. Was Sophie becoming too attached to the child?

'She is a sweet little girl, isn't she?' she agreed. 'Andrew obviously adores her, and it's so lucky that she has a doting auntie to bring her up.'

'Yes . . .' Sophie was thoughtful for a moment. 'I've been thinking lately, Abby. Edwin and I could give an orphaned child so much; a very good home and upbringing, not to mention so much love.'

'But Mary isn't an orphan,' Abigail pointed out. 'Andrew would never give her up. I think he feels that Mary is all he has left of the wife he loved.'

'I know.' Sophie's eyes filled with tears. 'Oh, Abby, I do so long for a child of my own. I know it's never to be, but sometimes the pain of longing is such agony that it's almost unbearable.'

Abigail took her friend's hand and squeezed it. 'I know. My poor Sophie, I do feel for you, but don't give yourself more pain by growing too fond of someone else's child.'

'You think I should stop her coming here?' Sophie looked into her eyes with such sadness that Abigail's heart ached for her.

'Let her come if it gives you both pleasure,' Abigail said. 'As long as you know it's only temporary. After all, she'll be going to school very soon now.'

'I've tried to speak to Edwin about adopting a baby.'

'And what does he say?'

'Edwin says I should forget about ever being a mother. He doesn't understand how I feel, Abby. Sometimes I think he never wanted children anyway.'

'Then why don't you just enjoy having little Mary here to play now and again?' Abigail suggested. 'Perhaps you could invite Anne and Andrew to come too sometimes. They're such nice people.'

'I'll try,' Sophie said. But the light had gone out of her eyes and Abigail felt guilty, as though she had spoilt her friend's pleasure.

Sophie had the pieces of furniture sent round to Castle Terrace that evening, and Abigail occupied herself on Sunday morning happily preparing Sarah's room. When she had finished, it looked very cosy. She was on her way down to the studio again when she met the Tarrants coming in from church. It seemed a good time to sound them out about Mrs Ellington's suggestion. She smiled.

'I've been meaning to ask you up to my flat for tea as we're neighbours,' she said. 'There's something I want to ask you about. If you're not busy this afternoon would you like to come up at about four?'

Mrs Tarrant looked pleased. 'I'm sure we'd like that very much, wouldn't we, Joe?'

Joe Tarrant nodded. 'That we would, Miss Banks. Thank you very much.'

When the Tarrants arrived that afternoon, dead on the dot of four o'clock, Abigail had tea and cake ready in the living-room. Mrs Tarrant had on her best brown dress with the bead trimming, and Joe looked slightly uncomfortable in his best suit, complete with starched collar and tie. They exchanged pleasantries. Both Tarrants had known Abigail's father, and they talked a little about him.

As she refilled their teacups, Abigail said, 'I wonder if you know anyone who would do some framing for me, Mr Tarrant? I hear that you were a carpenter before your retirement. Perhaps you know of someone who would be free to take on some part-time work.'

The couple looked at each other. Mrs Tarrant nodded encouragement, and Joe turned to his hostess, clearing his throat. 'Well, Miss Banks, I daresay I could do a job like that for you. As long as the hours weren't too long.'

'Could you really?' Abigail tried hard to sound surprised. 'I would appreciate that very much. It would probably only amount to a couple of days a week,' she added, 'to begin with, of course. We'd have to see how things went. The outhouse in the back yard would make an excellent workshop, I think. Perhaps you'd like to inspect it with me?'

'I will. And I've still got my own tools,' Joe added.

'Then shall we say tomorrow morning?' Abigail asked. 'At about nine o'clock?'

Soon after the Tarrants had gone downstairs to their own

flat, Sarah arrived, carrying all her possessions in a shabby carpet bag. When Abigail opened the door of the spare room, the girl stood on the threshold and gasped.

'*Oh*! Is this really to be mine?'

'Yes, to do as you like in,' Abigail told her. 'You might like to paint the walls a different colour later on, or make yourself new curtains. You must please yourself.'

'Oh, no, I shan't change anything. It's beautiful as it is.' Sarah sat down on the bed, her face alight with pleasure. 'Oh. It's so *soft*! Thank you, Abby.' She stopped, biting her lip. 'Oh – I'd better call you Miss Banks now that you're my boss, hadn't I?'

Abigail laughed. 'Well, perhaps while we're working. And I shall call you Miss Johnson. It sounds more professional.'

'I'll remember. I'll do my best for you, Abby, I promise.'

'I know you will, Sarah.'

CHAPTER EIGHT

Abigail sat on the cliff top, her large straw sun-hat on the grass beside her as she watched the sun dancing like scattered diamonds on the sea below. She and William had finished their meal, the remains of which lay spread out before them on the white cloth William had produced from his hamper. He held up the half-empty bottle of wine.

'Help me finish it?'

She shook her head. 'I couldn't. It was a lovely lunch, William. Thank you.'

He poured the remainder of the wine into his own glass. 'Don't thank me. Mrs Yates, my housekeeper, packed it all. All I added was the wine.'

She smiled and lay back on the rug, her arms behind her head. 'I'm not used to eating chicken salad and strawberries and cream in the middle of the day. I feel very spoilt.'

'You deserve it.' He began to pack away the used plates and glasses and the remains of the food. 'I wonder if you know how much I admire you, Abigail.'

'I can't think why.' She opened one eye to look at him. 'I've done nothing special.'

'Oh, yes, you have.'

She sat up and turned to look out over the sea, lifting her face to the fresh, salty breeze as it lifted her hair away from her face.

'It was so nice of you to ask me to come today,' she said. 'It's a real treat to get away from the town for once.'

'You're changing the subject,' he said, his eyes twinkling. 'There's something I've been meaning to mention to you, Abigail.'

'Yes?' She turned to look at him.

'I think you should find yourself another doctor.'

'Are you throwing me out?' She laughed. 'Don't worry, I'm not planning any more rat bites, and apart from that I'm pretty healthy.'

'I'm serious, Abigail,' he said. 'If you and I are to continue seeing each other like this, and you are still my patient, tongues will start wagging.'

'But we're friends. Surely even a doctor is allowed friends?'

'Not of the female variety, when they're patients, too. The medical profession holds strong views on that kind of thing.'

'What *kind of thing*?' Her cheeks coloured. 'Are people really so narrow-minded?'

He reached out a hand to touch hers. 'Abigail, you're missing the point I'm trying to make. Surely you realize that I feel – *hope* – it's possible that we might become more than mere friends.'

'Oh.' She sighed, a little dismayed. 'I like you very much, William,' she said carefully, 'but for the moment I'm busy building my business. I really haven't time for being "more than friends", as you put it; not with anyone, doctor or otherwise.'

'Time is one thing, but what about feelings?' he asked. 'Sometimes these things just happen without our planning them.'

'Not to me.'

His eyebrows rose. 'Are you really so cool-headed and in control?'

'I have to be.'

'I see.' As he let go of her hand she saw that he was hurt, and she reached out to take his hand again, pressing it lightly.

'Please don't be offended, William,' she said softly. 'I really value our friendship, but there are things you don't understand about me. Father and I had a hard time of it after we left

Eastmere. Working as a panel doctor in the East End of London was a hard grind, and we were almost as poor as Father's patients. When you live like that, you have to learn to control not only your feelings, but even your basic needs. We saw how much misery lack of control could cause. I learned a lot from my father, but the most important thing he taught me was how to cling on to dignity and independence. Since I've been alone, that has stood me in good stead. Now I have a chance to build a life.'

'You had a new life in London – a good job with that society photographer.'

'All that was just a preparation for coming back to Eastmere and putting right the wrong that was done to my father. I need to do it on my own.'

'But what about *you*, Abigail? I know you loved your father very much, but he's gone now, and surely above all things he would have wanted you to be happy?'

'I *am* happy. I'm doing better than I could ever have hoped.'

'But you're a lovely young woman. If you fall in love – what then?' His eyes looked intently into hers. 'It could happen, whatever you think now.'

'*If* I fall in love – though I don't intend to – nothing will change,' she told him. 'And if the man I love can't accept that, then I shall give him up.'

'Oh dear! We are getting serious, aren't we?' He leaned across and kissed her softly on the cheek. 'All right, Abigail. I think you've signalled loud and clear what your intentions are.'

'But I'd still like you to be my friend.'

'Naturally.'

'*And* my doctor.'

'Not a chance! I'll be passing your notes over to Doctor Fenning first thing tomorrow morning. Oh, and by the way,' he said, as he fastened the strap of the hamper. 'He's in his late fifties, with a wife and seven children, so I think I'm quite safe in giving you up to him.'

On the drive back to Eastmere they were quiet, each busy with their own thoughts, until Abigail suddenly asked him,

'William, do you know who owns the houses in Ashford's Yard?'

He glanced at her. 'Still on that hobby-horse, are you?'

'Yes, and I shall be until I get something done about it. *Do* you know, William?'

'I only know who used to own them.' Aware that she was looking intently at him, he added, 'My uncle.'

Her mouth dropped open as she stared at him. 'Doctor Gilbert Maybury?'

She was silent, absorbing the information and piecing together past events. Clearly the elderly doctor had had a double reason for wanting to get rid of her father. Not only did he believe that Doctor Banks was stealing his patients, but he was also afraid he was about to uncover his unprincipled business practices.

'I see. That explains so much.' She looked at him 'You said he *used* to own them. So, are you saying he sold them?'

'When he retired, he decided to give the properties up.'

'So – who bought them?'

He frowned. 'You can't expect me to tell you that, Abigail.'

'But I *do*! I need to know.'

'What would you do with the information, if you had it? What good would it do you?'

'You can let me worry about that.'

'I don't like this, Abigail. It feels like sitting on a powder-keg.'

'Tell me, and I promise not to light the fuse.'

'You mean that?'

'Not under *you*, anyway.'

'You're not going to like it.'

'Tell me anyway.'

He took a deep breath. 'I can see that you're not going to let go until I tell you. Ashford's Yard was bought by the man who owned the land. He'd been wanting to get his hands on the houses for a long time.'

She stared at him as the information sank in. 'Theodore James – Sophie's father?'

'Just before he died, yes.'

'He must have meant to pull them down and build better houses for his workforce. It was his dream.' She turned to look at him as an even more significant truth dawned. 'And now Edwin Dean owns them!'

'I said you wouldn't like it.'

They were back in Eastmere now, and as William drew up outside the studio she gathered her things together.

'Thank you so much for a lovely day, William. Thank you for the information, too. I promise not to tell anyone who told me.'

'You're not going to do anything silly or impulsive, are you, Abigail?'

'I never do anything without thinking carefully about it first.'

'I believe you,' he said, with a wry smile. 'When will I see you again, Abigail?'

'You know you're always welcome to come here,' she said. 'I enjoy your company so much, William – and your friendship. We won't let anything spoil that, will we?'

He smiled. 'Of course not. And Abigail . . .'

'Yes?'

'Just be careful.'

'I will.' She picked up her bag and straw sun-hat. 'Goodbye, William. And thanks again for a lovely day. See you soon.'

In the kitchen at the back of the studio, she was surprised to find Sarah and Patrick drinking tea together. Sarah sprang up guiltily.

'Oh, I hope it's all right, Abby. Patrick came to borrow some books from you. I said it was all right for him to have a cup of tea while he waited.'

'Of course it is. Hello, Patrick.' Abigail threw down her hat and bag. 'It was wonderful by the sea, but I'm so thirsty. Is there any more tea in the pot?'

'I'll make you some fresh.' Sarah jumped up and took the pot through to the scullery.

Abigail sat down at the table opposite Patrick and noticed

for the first time that he was wearing his Sunday best suit. Smoothly shaved, his unruly copper hair brushed neatly back, he looked quite handsome, but there was a glint of hostility in his green eyes as he asked,

'Been seeing how the other half lives?'

She frowned. 'I'm sorry, I don't know what you mean.'

'I suppose you've got to keep in with the snob crowd, though,' he added. 'Good for business, although I wouldn't have thought you'd get much business from the medical profession.'

'Doctor Maybury invited me to take a drive down to the coast for a picnic lunch – if you *must* know,' Abigail said, her own eyes flashing. 'For your further information, we had chicken salad, with strawberries and cream to follow. Oh, and wine, too. Is there anything else I should tell you? Have I forgotten anything?'

He coloured and looked away. 'None of my business what you do with your free time.'

'Exactly!'

Sarah came back with the teapot and looked from one flushed face to the other. 'Is everything all right?'

'Absolutely. I'm dying for that tea,' Abigail said, fetching a cup and saucer from the dresser.

In the silence that followed, Sarah cleared her throat. 'Well, I've got a pile of stockings upstairs to mend, so I'll leave you to it.' She shot her brother a look full of meaning. 'I expect Abby's tired, Pat.'

He didn't reply or even return her gaze as she went out of the room. Abigail held up the teapot.

'Do you want another cup?'

'Thanks – then I'll get out of your way.'

'There's no hurry. When I've had my tea, I'll look out those books for you.'

'Right.' He took a sip of his tea, then said, 'Abby – look, I didn't mean – I'm sorry if you thought . . .'

'How are the classes going?' she interrupted.

'Very well. I'm enjoying them.'

'I'm rewriting that article for the *Chronicle*.

'Oh I wondered about that.'

'Mr Naylor thought it needed toning down,' she told him. 'I've been doing some research, too, and I think I've got a new angle on it. I'd like to come round to Ashford's Yard and take some photographs in the week. Now that the evenings are lighter, it'll be ideal. Is that all right with you?'

'Yes – any time.'

'You'll make sure your mother knows I'm coming?'

'Yes. But you know you're always welcome anyway – as far as she's concerned.'

'Only as far as *she* is concerned?' She looked up and met his eyes.

He chose to ignore the question. 'Ma's half off her head with worry,' he said.

'Because of Jim and Annie?'

'She heard last Friday that the landlord is putting the rent up.'

Abigail stared at him. '*More* rent? For those hovels? That's a disgrace!'

'I know, but what can we do about it? It's still cheaper than anything else we could find.'

Abigail was silent, her fingers drumming on the table. Edwin Dean was paying his men with one hand and taking it away with the other. She thought that kind of extortion went out with the truck shops. Should she try to speak to him, or just publish her article and shame him? And was it her duty to tell Andrew that she now knew who the landlord was? It was a dilemma. She realized that Patrick was looking at her. 'I'll get you those books,' she said. 'Come up to the flat, and you can pick what you want.'

He chose three books on politics and history from Doctor Banks's collection.

'You can borrow any of the others when you've read those,' Abigail told him.

Patrick was leafing through one of the books. 'People like us have always been oppressed,' he said. 'But the time is coming

117

when we'll have our say.'

'And *all* of us women will get the vote soon now,' she said. 'It was so disappointing last year when they decided that only married women over thirty should have it. What difference does it make? Do they think our brains aren't fully developed until some man puts a ring on our finger?'

Patrick laughed, his eyes sparkling. 'You should have been a suffragette,' he told her. 'You'd have made them sit up and listen.'

It was the first compliment he'd ever paid her, and she was surprised to find herself blushing. 'Thank you, Patrick. It's not fashionable for women to make themselves heard. Most men hate women who speak up for themselves.'

'Not me. I think you're . . .' Embarrassed, he cleared his throat and picked up the books. 'Well, I'd better be off now. Thanks for these.'

'Don't forget, you can borrow the others whenever you want,' Abigail said, as she followed him down the stairs.

At the door, he turned to her. 'Thanks for taking Sarah on,' he said. 'It means a lot to her. She's worth more than just a shop-counter job. She's bright.'

'I know. I'm very fond of her, and I'm sure she'll learn quickly and do well. She's only been working for me for a week but she's picking things up really fast.'

She let him out and watched him walk away along the street, shoulders back and his head held high. There was a definite change in him since he'd been going to evening classes. He still had a chip on his shoulder, but some of his anger had gone, to be replaced by a newly developing confidence. She felt a little stab of pleasure that she had helped to make this happen.

All that evening Abigail worked on the article for the *Chronicle*. She had decided not to name Edwin Dean as landlord of Ashford's Yard. She decided that subtlety was the best policy. She hoped that Edwin alone would realize that she was getting at him, though once others read the article, it would be only a matter of time before they put two and two together and uncovered him for the scoundrel he was.

She worked until long past her usual bedtime, writing and rewriting until she was satisfied, then she made a fair copy and put it into an envelope to take round to Andrew's office in the morning.

'Mmm, quite hard-hitting stuff.' Andrew removed his pipe from his mouth and looked up at her. Abigail had been holding her breath for his reaction.

'It's still too much?'

'No. This kind of thing needs to be strong. And, after all, we're going to back it up with photographic evidence, aren't we?'

'Yes. I'll go and take the photographs this evening, if you agree. I do have permission.'

'Good.' Andrew puffed on his pipe, looking at her speculatively. 'I think you've taken my advice and done some research I get the distinct impression from this that you know who the landlord is.'

'Yes, I do.'

'Well, you're right not to name him. Do you mind me asking who it is?'

She bit her lip. 'I – think I'd better not say – at least for the present. If I told you, you'd automatically know who told me.'

'Well, journalists are not obliged to name their sources, so it's up to you.' He frowned at her. 'If I publish this, Abigail, I'm going to have to trust you that you've got your facts correct.'

'I'm quite sure about it, I promise.'

He nodded. 'Right. Go ahead and take the photographs, and I'll publish as soon as I can.'

Abigail felt elated as she left the *Chronicle* office. At last she was getting somewhere in her quest to avenge her father.

Sarah accompanied her to Ashford's Yard that evening to take photographs. It had been a hot day, and the evening was still warm and airless. As soon as they entered the alleyway, the stench of raw sewage and rotting rubbish filled their nostrils. Sarah looked at her, her nose wrinkled.

'You see what it's like here in summer? It can't be good for anyone's health, can it?'

'It certainly can't,' Abigail said, as she knocked on the door of the Johnsons' house. It was opened by Maggie, who looked worried.

'Come in and close the door,' she said. 'The smell and the flies have been terrible this week. Annie's in bed, poorly. Doctor's been to see her today, and he says she's to give up work till after the baby's born, and she's to have complete rest and all the good food we can get her to eat.' She sighed. 'It's all right for the likes of him. Little does he know what he's asking. Now the rent's gone up, it's even harder to stretch the money, and now that Annie can't work . . . Not that she can help it, poor lass.'

'I'm so sorry, Maggie.'

'I hope she'll be well enough for the wedding,' Maggie said. 'It's arranged for next Friday. The vicar's agreed to marry them at eight o'clock in the morning, so that we can keep it as quiet as possible.'

'Would you like me to come and take photographs?' Abigail asked.

Maggie shook her head. 'No. There'll be no wedding dress or special clothes. It's nothing to celebrate – just a case of " 'aving to".'

'I've come this evening to take photographs of the yard,' Abigail explained, 'to go with the article the *Chronicle* is to publish. Did Patrick tell you I'd be coming?'

'He did mention it.' Maggie nodded distractedly. 'He's out, no doubt at another of those meetings again. Seem to be more and more of 'em these days. Out nearly every night, he is.'

Abigail made no comment. Maggie was clearly unaware that he was taking evening classes. 'I'll leave you and Sarah to have a chat,' she said, 'while I take my photographs. I'll try not to be too long.'

Outside in the yard, she photographed the gully where the slops were deposited, the communal privy, and the neglected exteriors of the mean little houses with their rotting window-frames and crumbling brickwork. Then she took pictures of inside the Johnsons' home, with the aid of her flash equipment; the damp patches on the walls and the disintegrating plasterwork. At last she was satisfied and, with the exposed negatives safely stowed away, she went to see if Sarah was ready to return. Maggie had made tea, and invited her to sit down and take a cup.

'Did Doctor Maybury say what was wrong with Annie?' she asked.

'The lass is undernourished,' Maggie told her. 'The baby is making her anaemic. He's given her an iron tonic, and he says she needs fresh greens and red meat, 'specially liver, to eat. Our Ted says he'll bring some fresh greens from the garden where he works, and I suppose I'll have to find the money for the rest. I know Miss Sophie would help if I asked, but you know me, I'd rather die than ask for charity.' She looked at Abigail, her face furrowed with anxiety. 'This article that's going in the *Chronicle* – it's not going to cause trouble, is it?'

'It's intended to make things better for you, Maggie.'

'I know, lass. It's just that, the way things are at the moment, I couldn't face anything else going wrong.'

Abigail developed the negatives that night and took them round to the *Chronicle* office first thing the following morning. Andrew was pleased with them. He told her that there were news items scheduled for several weeks to come and he always had to keep space for breaking news, but he promised that the article would go in as soon as there was space for it. Abigail hoped it would not be too long.

Joe Tarrant turned out to be a treasure. His work was reliable and meticulous, and after the trial period they had agreed on, Abigail was happy to offer him permanent work. The customers who left their finished photographs to be framed by him were more than delighted with the results.

Sarah, too, was proving her worth She was a willing and enthusiastic apprentice, eager to learn everything about the photography business. She managed the front shop with ease,

121

taking quickly to the appointments system Abigail had organized and making herself agreeable to the customers, with
whom she quickly became popular. Her only real concern was
the newly installed telephone. At first she jumped every time it
rang, terrified that she would be electrocuted the moment she
picked it up, but she soon became used to it and managed to
answer it without panicking, even progressing to making calls
herself.

Abigail took her along whenever she had evening assignments, so that Sarah could learn about the process of
camerawork, and once the studio had closed in the evenings
she would take her into the darkroom to teach her how to
develop and print. Sarah also learned how to touch up the
negatives, taking out blemishes and wrinkles with the aid of the
scalpels and soft pencils Abigail used. She was shown how to
retake the photograph afterwards and tint the finished picture
with watercolours and fine brushes – everything to improve
the sitter's appearance. She watched carefully as Abigail eradi-
cated backgrounds on children's portraits, using the intricate
'aerograph', which had to be pumped by foot, replacing them
later with carefully applied artwork. All of it fascinated her,
and she began to enjoy the work more each day. She did her
best to make herself useful around the flat as well as downstairs, and insisted on taking her turn with the cleaning, and
preparing a meal for Abigail when she finished work. They
would eat together after the studio closed and discuss the day's
work, but the girl tried never to intrude on Abigail's privacy.

Part of the arrangement was that Sarah should have Sunday
afternoons and one evening off each week to go out for her
own amusement. She was to be in by nine o'clock. She usually
visited her mother on Sundays, but she used her precious free
evening to visit friends or go to the cinema. Sometimes, if there
was a dance on at the Drill Hall, Abigail allowed her to be in
later.

Since her success with the photographs at Julia Welland's
party, bookings had poured in and the appointment book
gradually filled up. Abigail began to feel happy and satisfied

with her progress. She now had a proficient framer, and a keen and willing apprentice. She was becoming an established and successful businesswoman.

Although she was busy, Abigail made sure that she made time to visit Sophie as often as she could. She was concerned that her friend was becoming too attached to Andrew's small daughter. She had heard from Andrew that the child visited Prospect House twice a week now, to play in the garden, that if Anne was busy Andrew sometimes dropped in himself to collect his small daughter. Clearly, he and Sophie were developing a friendship, and on the afternoon when Abigail dropped in for a flying visit, Sophie was full of her new friend.

'We have so much in common,' she said, her eyes bright as she poured the tea. 'We've both lost someone dear to us. We like so many of the same things, music and the theatre. Plays and concerts are few and far between in Eastmere, but when he came to collect Mary yesterday, Andrew said that he has tickets for a concert in Cambridge. He asked if Edwin and I would like to go with him and Anne.'

'What does Edwin say?'

Sophie looked doubtful. 'He says he'll look in his diary and see if he's free that evening. Now that he's on the Town Council, he has so many meetings to attend.'

'I hope you can go,' Abigail told her. 'I know you'd enjoy it.'

Sophie nodded. 'Andrew is such good company. He always stays for a cup of tea and a chat when he comes to pick Mary up. It's lovely to have someone to talk to. Anne always seems to be in a hurry when she comes to pick up Mary.'

'I expect she has to get home to make Andrew's dinner,' Abigail pointed out, reflecting that Sophie knew very little of domestic life or how busy other women's lives were.

Sophie looked wistful. 'I know. It must be wonderful to be busy all day; to have things to attend to and someone to please. When Edwin and I were first married, I used to like to cook for him sometimes, as I did for Father, but he's been out so much lately. He's hardly ever in for dinner these evenings. I often just have a tray in my room.' She looked at Abigail despairingly. 'I get so *lonely*, Abby. Sometimes it's as though I have no husband. I don't know what I would do without darling Mary's visits, and the little talks with Andrew.' She passed Abigail a plate of biscuits. 'I've almost made up my mind to go to the concert whether Edwin can come or not.'

Abigail was surprised at her friend's sudden rebellion. 'Well, perhaps you should,' she said. 'After all, Anne will be going, too, so you'll have female company.'

What she really meant was that Anne would provide a chaperon, and Sophie would not be compromised by being seen out with a man who was not her husband.

'That's what I thought,' Sophie said, nibbling at a chocolate biscuit.

Abigail looked at the clock. She had to get back to the studio, but she still hadn't accomplished what she had come for.

'Sophie, I want to ask you a favour,' she said. 'I don't know whether Maggie has told you that she is to become a grand-mother.'

'No! Oh, how lovely. I must be sure to congratulate her.'

'It's hardly a matter for congratulation to Maggie,' Abigail said. 'Her son, Jim, and his girl have had to be married – quickly.'

'Oh, I see.' Sophie's face fell. 'When is the baby due?'

'Around October time. Not long to go now.'

'Poor Maggie. Is she upset?'

'She likes the girl well enough. Annie has moved in with her. They're very overcrowded at Ashford's Yard, and she's finding it hard to manage financially. Now Annie is ill and can't work. She needs plenty of good food and complete rest.'

'I do wish Maggie had told me,' Sophie said. 'Shall I go and visit them? I could take the poor girl some flowers from the garden. The roses are still blooming – the second flush, you know.'

'I think perhaps they might find that embarrassing,' Abigail said. 'Maggie isn't proud of her home. To be honest, at this time of year Ashford's Yard is nothing more than a stinking hole.' She looked at her friend. 'But there is something you can do.'

'What? Tell me, Abby. Those poor things.'

'It's very simple, really. Just give Maggie permission to take the leftovers home.'

'Is that all? I can do better than that,' Sophie said. 'I'll send her a hamper. I'll order one from London – from Fortnum's. Port and pâté de foie gras; asparagus and some of those little cakes that . . .'

'Whoa!' Abigail was laughing. 'Rich food like that would probably make her worse. Just simple fare. As I said, anything left over from your meals will be fine. Maggie would be so grateful and you know she'd never take advantage. She wouldn't even ask you herself, so don't mention that I asked you on her behalf.'

'I'll speak to her first thing tomorrow,' Sophie said. 'And I'll make her think it's my idea.'

Abigail's article about Ashford's Yard was published in the *Eastmere Chronicle* the following week, along with the photographs she had taken. Andrew had given it a centre-page spread, and when she saw it in print she was delighted. Andrew had allowed all of her photographs to be printed, and they made harrowing viewing, and the article, which Andrew had edited only to the minimum, was even more shocking. The byline he had given it was simply 'By our town correspondent'.

Recently, Halliwell's Press reached its centenary and cele-brated by bringing its equipment up to date. By a strange coincidence, Halliwell's shares its anniversary with another, less salubrious feature of this town – Ashford's Yard, a shameful blot on the town, which should long ago have been replaced by dwellings fit for a civilized commu-nity.

This slum is a disgrace to the character of a town that considers itself go-ahead and innovative. The houses are in a scandalous state of disrepair, with medieval drainage and sanitation, which cannot fail to impair the health of its residents.

In winter, there is hardly any protection from the elements. The roofs leak and the walls are damp. In summer, the stench from the river at low tide is almost suffocating. The inadequate drains and the open effluent gully running between the houses are a threat to the health of all the residents, especially the children.

Six years ago there was an outbreak of typhoid fever at Ashford's Yard, but incredibly no steps have ever been taken to improve the conditions for its unfortunate residents. Apart from running water laid on soon after the outbreak had abated, not even the most basic of improvements has been made, and if the present situation is allowed to continue there is little doubt that another epidemic will ensue that could rapidly spread to other parts of the town.

Unbelievably, in spite of the conditions that prevail, the landlord of Ashford's Yard has recently increased the rents. His identity seems to be a closely guarded secret, which is hardly surprising, but whoever he is, he should attend to his duty by these people without delay. He owes it not only to the reputation of Eastmere and the residents of Ashford's Yard, but to humanity at large, to wipe this shameful scar from Eastmere's smiling face once and for all, and give these deserving people a fair deal.

Abigail cut the centre pages from the paper and proudly pinned them up in the small room she used as an office. She had the strongest feeling that her father was smiling approvingly down at her. Perhaps now, at last, something would be done.

All that day the people who came into the studio were full of the article, but their opinions varied. Some were pleased that Ashford's Yard had at last been brought to the attention of the townspeople and shamed for the disgrace it was; others were only afraid of the epidemic mentioned in the article. Then again there were the ignorant ones, who believed that people actually *liked* to live in slums.

'What would be the point of putting people like them in decent places?' one woman said scathingly. 'They're born filthy and wouldn't know what to do with a nice house. In a week the new place would be as bad as Ashford's.'

Abigail had to bite her tongue to keep back the angry retort. Even though she longed to speak out, she was determined that no one should guess that she was the author of the article. The diverse opinions expressed were enough to prove that she would not improve her business or her popularity by admitting to it and, much to her regret, she could not afford to say openly what she felt, however much she wanted to.

She had finished for the day, and had sent Sarah upstairs to make a start on their evening meal, when the studio door burst open and Edwin Dean strode in.

'I wish to speak privately with you,' he said.

'I'm sorry, but I've finished business for the day,' Abigail replied.

'What I have to say has nothing to do with your business, and it is extremely important, so close the door so that we can speak privately.'

Angry at his dictatorial attitude, Abigail tried to assess the situation calmly. She and Sophie's husband had met only a handful of times, so what could he possibly have to say to her?

She closed the shop door, turned over the CLOSED sign, and pulled down the blind.

'Yes? What is it?'

'I insist that in future you stay away from my wife.'

Abigail's eyebrows rose. 'Sophie and I have been friends since we were children.'

Children grow up,' he said. 'And become very different people. You are a bad influence on Sophie.'

'A bad influence?' She laughed. 'How on earth can you say that?'

'You are filling her head with all sorts of harmful ideas.'

'What ideas?'

'This ludicrous adoption idea for one,' he said. 'And encouraging her to go out unaccompanied.'

Abigail frowned. 'I haven't the least idea what you are talking about.'

'It was you who introduced her to this Andrew Naylor person.'

'Yes. Andrew and his sister are very respectable people. You met them at a dinner party in your own home.'

'I did indeed, and their respectability is a matter of opinion! Are you aware that last Friday she went to a concert in Cambridge with him – alone? My wife and the editor of this scurrilous local rag?'

'No, I was not aware of it. I have absolutely no influence over what Sophie does or who she sees.' Abigail was smiling inwardly. *This scurrilous local rag.* Now they were getting to the heart of the matter. Could his conscience be pricking him at the exposure of the dire conditions in Ashford's Yard?

'The wife of a prominent businessman – out with a single man,' he went on. 'What do you think people will make of that?'

'Sophie told me that you had *both* been invited to the concert,' Abigail said. 'The last time I spoke to her, she said that you were going together – if you had no other commitments.'

'Well, I *did* have another commitment. But in this new rebellious mood, inspired by *you*, Sophie decided to go without me.'

'Perhaps you should have cancelled your other engagement,' she said boldly. 'Perhaps if you made more time for your wife . . .'

His face darkened. 'That is none of your business, but apart from that, you are missing the point!' he shouted. 'Which is that she would never even have *thought* of doing something so foolhardy before *you* returned to Eastmere!'

'I'm sure that going to the concert did Sophie the world of good,' Abigail said. 'She has been very depressed since your baby daughter died. And anyway, Mr Naylor's sister Anne was with them.'

'*No, she was not!*' Edwin thundered. 'The woman had a headache on the night in question and decided to stay at home.'

'That could not be helped, surely? You are speaking as though the whole thing was planned.'

'I did not come here to bandy words with you, Miss Banks!' He took a step towards her. 'I could tell that you were trouble the moment I set eyes on you. With your London ways and your suffragette liberalism. I forbid you to have anything more to do with my wife. Do you hear me?'

Abigail stood her ground. 'I could hardly fail to hear you, unless I were stone deaf,' she said quietly. 'You have no right to come here telling me what I should and should not do.'

'I have every right to protect my wife from women like you! It is easy to see now why that quack father of yours was kicked out of Eastmere,' he sneered. 'The man had dangerous radical ideas. You're his daughter, all right! You come here and you think you can stick your interfering nose into . . .'

'I shouldn't say any more, if I were you,' Abigail interrupted. 'You're very angry, and any moment now you're going to let slip something you'll regret – like the fact that you are the landlord of Ashford's Yard, for instance.'

Edwin Dean blanched, then hot colour began to suffuse his face. 'So! I was right, it *was* you who wrote that slanderous rubbish in the *Chronicle*! Well, Miss Banks, at least you were sensible enough not to make an accusation like that in print! I advise you to get your facts right in future,' he said, his voice ominously quiet. 'As it happens, I am *not* the owner of Ashford's Yard.'

'*Not?*' She stared at him, taken aback. 'I don't believe you. If you don't own it, then who does?'

'My wife. Yes, your dear friend Sophie. Her father left the yard to her, so it is at her door that your complaints and accusations come to rest. Now perhaps you can see why I'm asking you to stay away from her. I won't have her upset like this.'

Abigail stood and watched, speechless, as he left the shop, slamming the door so hard that the bell rang on for several seconds.

To a shaken Abigail, it sounded ominously like a death-knell.

CHAPTER NINE

Defying Edwin's demand that she stay away from Sophie, Abigail went along to Prospect House the very next morning, hoping against hope that Edwin would not be at home and that Sophie would agree to see her.

The maid asked her to wait in the hall, reappearing a few minutes later to usher her into the morning-room, where her friend sat looking out of the window. The moment the door closed behind the girl, Abigail spoke.

'Sophie, I daresay you know that Edwin came to see me yesterday. He insisted that I stay away from you. Is it true that you don't want to see me again?'

'Of course it isn't,' Sophie said. 'He was angry. We had a quarrel. It's his way of punishing me.'

'He said something else,' Abigail said. 'Something I can scarcely believe. I have to ask you: is it true that you are the owner of Ashford's Yard?'

Sophie turned slowly to face her, and Abigail started with shock as she saw the livid bruise that ran down the left side of her face.

'*Sophie*! Your face, what have you done?'

The other girl waved a hand dismissively. 'It's nothing. I slipped and fell. As to your question, yes, it is true. I do own the yard.'

Shocked and appalled, Abigail sank on to a chair. 'I don't understand. Why didn't you tell me this before?'

'Do you suppose I'm proud of the fact?' Sophie drew in a

shuddering breath. 'It was partly the reason I stopped writing to you. I've always known how much it meant to you to carry out our fathers' plans.'

Abigail shook her head. 'You're not making any sense, Sophie. If you own Ashford's Yard then surely you're free to do as you wish with it?'

'No. I'll try to explain. Father already owned the land, as you know. The houses were built on part of it, leased for the purpose. It was all done so long ago that Father couldn't discover who drew up the original contract. The lease ran out eventually, shortly before he died, and he bought the houses. You can imagine how pleased he was. At last he could pull them down and rebuild, just as he and your father had always intended. Edwin was furious when we discovered that Father had left the yard to me. He refused to allow me any money to fulfil Father's wishes, and furthermore he said that as I owned Prospect House as well, I must use the rents to pay for its upkeep.' She bit her lip, looking at Abigail appealingly. 'I had no choice, Abby. I felt so bad, not being able to carry out Father's wishes. Then with the price of everything going up so much after the war, the expenses of running the house began to get out of control. Edwin again refused to help, so I had no choice but to increase the rents.' She swallowed hard. 'What would people like Maggie think of me, if they knew I was her landlord?'

'But how did you manage to keep your ownership quiet?' Abigail asked.

'The rent collecting is in the hands of a solicitor, just as it always was. They employ a man who collects them, and the money is paid into my bank account. I have nothing to do with it.' Her eyes filled with tears. 'I'm so ashamed. I've been closing my mind to the poverty of those poor people.'

'But why didn't you tell me all this when I first came back to Eastmere?'

'Until I saw you again and heard you talking about carrying your father's plan through, I just refused to let myself think about it.' Sophie dabbed the tears from her cheeks. 'As you know, Maggie never complains, and I – I just didn't *want* to face up to it.' She looked up at Abigail. 'Do you think it's easy, living with that? I hate myself, especially when you tell me about the Johnson family's struggle, and that poor girl's illness. Now I suppose I've lost you, too. You'll never forgive me for this, will you, Abby?'

Abigail swallowed her impatience. Sophie had been cosseted all her life. She had never been faced with a problem of this magnitude. It must be very hard for her. She went to her friend and took her hands, pressing them. 'Please, Sophie, don't upset yourself. It's an impossible situation for you. I see that. Don't worry. Somehow, we'll think of something.'

'You haven't heard all of it yet. There's worse to come,' Sophie said. 'Edwin has been approached by a property developer, who wants to buy up that parcel of land and redevelop it. Now that it's all under one ownership, that is a possibility.'

'But surely that's good.'

'No! The developer doesn't want it for housing. The plan is to build a large warehouse to rent out. The riverside location would be ideal, and after the shaming article in the *Chronicle* the Town Council are all for it. Ashford's Yard has become an embarrassment to them. But you see what it will mean. The present tenants of Ashford's Yard will be evicted.'

'But *you* own the yard,' Abigail pointed out. 'Edwin can't sell it without your agreement, your signature.'

'I have no choice but to agree, Abby!' Sophie cried. 'I can't go on as I am. I have hardly any money of my own, and I'm already in debt. I even thought of trying to sell some of my jewellery, but Edwin put it all into the bank when I was ill. I've asked for it back, but he refuses. The only other option would be for me to sell Prospect House!'

'Surely Edwin wouldn't want that.' Abigail considered for a moment. 'Selling Ashford's might be for the best,' she said. 'With the money from the sale, you could find more land somewhere not too far out of town and build new houses. You'd still get an income from the rents, and people like the Johnsons would have somewhere decent to live.'

'You still don't understand, do you? Edwin would never let me keep all the money. He will handle the sale and he'll make me an allowance from the proceeds; just enough to run the house on.'

'But that's outrageous! It's *your* money,' Abigail said indignantly. 'It's *your* inheritance.'

'Edwin has his own way of making me do as he says.' Sophie hung her head. 'A very effective way, I'm afraid.'

Abigail gasped. 'He *hits* you, doesn't he?' she said. 'He did that to your face!'

Sophie's anguished eyes met hers. 'It was after I went to the concert with Andrew, and if he finds you here . . .' She didn't have to finish the sentence. Abigail rose and went to her friend, gathering her in her arms.

'My poor Sophie, things are worse than I thought,' she said. 'I wish you'd told me all this before I wrote the article for the *Chronicle*. I see now that it's done more harm than good to Maggie and her neighbours, and to you. I've brought you all nothing but trouble, haven't I? Perhaps Edwin was right when he said I should never have come back to Eastmere.'

'Don't say that,' Sophie said. 'If you hadn't come back, I'd probably be in an asylum by now. I could feel my mind slipping away fast before you came. Now, through you, I have dear friends like Anne and little Mary and – and Andrew. I can't tell you how much I enjoyed going to the concert with him last week. It was such a treat.'

Abigail said nothing, but deep inside she feared for her friend. It seemed to her that her growing friendship with Andrew Naylor was destined to bring her even more trouble.

'I'll stay away for a while,' she told Sophie. 'Just until things calm down.'

'What shall I do about Ashford's Yard?' Sophie asked.

'Try to hold out for a while,' Abigail advised. 'Edwin can't do anything without your signature. Meantime, I'll try to think of something.' A thought struck her. 'Does Andrew know any of this?'

Sophie shook her head. 'I was too ashamed to tell him. I

don't want to lose him as a friend, but if he knew I ran my household on the rents from Ashford's Yard, he'd surely despise me.'

'If he knew the circumstances, he'd understand,' Abigail told her. 'Would you mind if I discussed it with him? Together, we might think of a plan.'

Sophie sighed. 'If you think it best,' she said. 'I'd given up hope of finding a solution. It's such a relief to tell you.' She looked up. 'But, Abby, you won't tell anyone else, will you?'

'Of course I won't. Your secret's safe with me.'

Although she didn't visit Sophie again for fear of what Edwin might do, she thought about her constantly. She confided in Andrew about Sophie's ownership and the bind that Edwin held her in. Although he appeared calm, she saw his mouth tighten with anger.

'The more I hear about that man, the less I like him,' he said. 'I knew that planning permission was being sought for the building of a warehouse on a riverside site, but I'd no idea it was Ashford's Yard. Sophie will have a breathing space at least until planning permission comes through.' He smiled at Abigail. 'Don't look so worried. I think I know of a way this can be resolved. Just leave it to me.'

Patrick was a regular Sunday evening visitor, bringing back the books he had borrowed and exchanging them for others until he had almost exhausted Doctor Banks's collection. Abigail watched him grow and change, week by week. His anger had gradually been replaced by a calmer attitude towards the injustices he resented so much. His hot-headed aggression had abated, and he seemed prepared to accept that the changes he wanted to see would not be achieved by precipitating the men at the timber yard into an ill-timed strike.

They had long Sunday evening discussions over tea and biscuits in the studio kitchen. He had been impressed by Abigail's article in the *Chronicle*.

'I can see now why you urged me to sign on for the classes,' he admitted. 'I could never have put things as well as you did. You really hit the nail on the head, without going on and on like I might have done. I only hope some good comes of it, though I doubt it, knowing some of the old fogies on the Council. All they're interested in is whose turn it is to be Mayor.'

Abigail laughed. 'Never mind, I'm booked to take the next mayoral portrait, so I can't complain.'

But although she joked about it, she was even more frustrated about the plight of the residents of Ashford's Yard. It was only a matter of time before the planning committee met and passed the plan to redevelop the site. Then the whole matter would rest in Sophie's hands, and for how long would she be able to hold out against Edwin's bullying tactics?

Andrew kept Abigail busy all that summer with assignments for the *Chronicle*. In August she visited the largest farm in the neighbourhood, to photograph the crops being harvested and, a month later, she was at the village hall to record the harvest supper and to photograph the decorations in the church. She was busy with her own work, too, the demand being mainly for portraits and family groups, and when she could not be there she was confident that Sarah would manage efficiently on her own. The girl was quickly making herself an indispensable part of the business.

Abigail had seen William regularly since the seaside picnic they had shared in June. He often looked in at the studio when he was passing, to invite her out for a drive with him on Sunday afternoons, but when she tried to talk to him about her crusade for better housing, they always ended up arguing.

'Why can't you support me?' she had asked him one late September afternoon, when they were on the way home from a pleasant drive. 'You're a doctor. Surely you know all too well how unhealthy places like Ashford's Yard are? You have only to look at poor little Annie Johnson.'

Annie and Jim had been married for almost two months, and the baby's birth was imminent, but in spite of Maggie's care and the food that Sophie had allowed her to take home, the girl's health had continued to deteriorate.

'She's so frail. How she'll have the strength to survive the birth, I don't know,' Abigail said, looking at William accusingly. 'I wouldn't be surprised if the poor girl had tuberculosis. Father and I saw it so often when we were here. What do you think?'

He sighed. 'Abigail, you know very well that I can't discuss my patients with you.'

'I know you can't, and I'm sorry.' She bit her lip. 'It's just that I worry about them.'

'I had hoped we could have a pleasant couple of hours together without the usual argument.' He looked at her. 'Don't you think it's time you stopped agitating over this? It's only a matter of time before people realize who is trying to stir things up. You'll make yourself extremely unpopular and begin to lose business. Is that what you want?'

'Of course it isn't. I do want something done, though. Are you really prepared to wait for another epidemic like the one six years ago to strike?'

'People are more hygiene-conscious nowadays,' he said. 'Poverty isn't the problem it used to be. There's Public Assistance for the poor. Many of the trade unions have pension schemes, and wages are higher than before the war, too.'

'And so is unemployment! A lot of employers sack workers who join trade unions – Edwin Dean, for instance. You must know how abysmal the safety record is at the timber yard,' she challenged. 'How many injuries do you treat from there in a year? And how many men become permanently disabled and lose their jobs because of it? You must know how many Ashford's Yard babies die within their first year, as compared with other parts of the town?'

They had reached Castle Terrace and he sighed again as he drew up outside the studio.

'Abby – you're in the wrong profession. You should be a politician.'

'I don't *want* to be a politician,' she told him. 'I just want to live in a world where conditions are fair and equal – like we were promised they would be after the war.'

'Oh, Abby – *Abby*. Life's not as simple as that, my dear girl. Changes take time.'

'And in the meantime must some people put up with filth and squalor when others live in luxury and comfort? There are men from Ashford's Yard who fought for their country, and what have they come home to? I tell you, William, there'll be an uprising before long. Some of them are almost at breaking point.'

William switched off the engine and turned to her. 'Abigail . . .'

She held up her hands. 'I know. All right, I'll shut up about it.'

'But you won't, will you? That's the point.' He turned in his seat to look at her. 'If I ask you something, will you answer me truthfully?'

'Don't I always?'

'Did you write that article for the *Chronicle*?' As she opened her mouth to reply, he added: 'I know the photographs were yours, and I'm guessing that the article was, too. Am I right?'

'All right then, yes. But I'm not prepared to let it be publicly known – for obvious reasons.'

'I thought as much. So you're not prepared to come out and stand up for your beliefs?'

'That's not fair. You know I can't afford to.'

'Then perhaps you should keep quiet about them alto-gether.' He took both her hands in his. 'Think about it, Abby. You'll lose friends as well as business, and I assure you, you won't gain anything. The article was a nine-days wonder. People talked about it, but nothing was done, was it?'

'At least I tried. So many people just stand aside and do noth-ing.'

He smiled and shook his head. 'You're so stubborn. The odd thing is that it's what I love about you.' He drew her close and kissed her. 'Marry me, Abby,' he said softly. 'Marry me, and forget about scraping a living for yourself.'

'Be free to come out into the open, you mean?' she asked,

her eyes searching his. 'If I did, would you join forces with me and help me fight to clear Ashford's Yard? Would you support me in that way, too? Someone like you – a respected doctor – would have so much more weight to throw behind it.'

'Abby – you know that might not be possible.'

'Why not?'

'Do you really have to ask? What happened to your father could easily happen again.'

'I see. Then the answer would have to be no.'

'If you loved me, you'd be prepared to make sacrifices.'

'But it wouldn't be *my* sacrifice, would it?'

'Let it go, Abby! What good did it do your father, when he tried? What good have you done with your article, writing and campaigning? Nothing but raise false hopes for nothing.'

'I couldn't give up now. I couldn't let those people down.'

'And what about letting *me* down?' He pulled her close and looked into her eyes. 'You never say what you feel for me, Abby. I have to know.'

She swallowed hard. 'I'm terribly fond of you, William. Just not – not fond enough, I suppose.'

'Not enough is not at all in my book.'

'I'm sorry.'

'Perhaps we should stop seeing each other,' he said.

'Don't say that.'

'But I *am* saying it, Abby,' he insisted. 'It's becoming impossible, being with you and knowing that it's going nowhere. Better we say goodbye.'

'Is that what you want?'

'Of course it isn't what I *want*!' His eyes burned with hurt. 'But you obviously don't feel enough for me. I've been hoping that if I waited, perhaps it might happen, but you've just dashed my last hope. Your intentions lie elsewhere, don't they, Abby?'

She had the distinct impression that he was referring to more than just her efforts on behalf of the residents of Ashford's Yard.

'I value my independence, William,' she said. 'I'm proud of

what I've achieved.'

He nodded. 'And rightly so. I admire you so much, and I wish you all the luck you deserve for the future, my darling, but I know it doesn't include me. I only wish it did.'

She stood on the pavement and watched with a heavy heart as he drove away. It was hard to let him go. William was handsome and clever and funny, and she valued his friendship so much, even loved him in her way, but she knew it could never be in the way he wanted to be loved – to the exclusion of everything else in her life.

Upstairs in the flat, Abigail took off her outdoor things and stood looking out of the window. She could see Prospect House from here, and she wondered what Sophie was doing. She missed her friend very much. Andrew had confided in her that he had advised Sophie to sell Ashford's Yard herself through her solicitor. She had a perfect right to do that, as it was her property. The solicitor would hold the money for her in a separate account to which only she would have access. Abigail only hoped that her friend would have the courage to do this. It was the one frail hope that the tenants of Ashford's Yard would get the new homes they deserved.

Both the studio and the flat were empty. Sarah was out. Abigail hoped she was visiting her mother. Maggie needed all the support she could get at the moment, though privately Abigail couldn't blame the girl for wanting to spend her precious free time somewhere more cheerful. Annie spent most of the time confined to bed, exhausted with the burden of her pregnancy and debilitated by the cough that grew steadily worse as the weeks passed. William had told Maggie that there was a good chance that she would recover once the baby was born, but the girl's pale face and sunken eyes alarmed her mother-in-law, who shared Abigail's fears about her.

Sarah had not visited her family for several weeks. She'd been asking permission to stay out later on her evenings off lately, too. Abigail sympathized with the girl. She was young, and the atmosphere at Ashford's Yard was heavy with gloom. Going home was hardly the pleasure it once was, with her mother constantly worried and preoccupied with Annie. Abigail had asked Sarah once or twice where she went on Sundays, but received only a vague reply. She didn't want to pry, believing that the girl should have some freedom and deserved her trust, but all the same, she did feel responsible for her. Sarah had mentioned a new friend and visits to the cinema, which she loved, and for the moment Abigail had decided not to press for details.

On impulse, she decided to put on her coat again and walk across town to Ashford's Yard to see Maggie. She was welcomed in as usual, and Maggie busied herself making tea.

'Miss Sophie misses you a lot,' she said, in answer to Abigail's enquiry. 'Little Mary Naylor don't go round to play in the garden any more, not since she started school, but Mr Naylor sometimes brings her round of an afternoon. Seems his sister has her Ladies' Guild meetings on a Wednesday afternoon, so Mr Naylor picks his little girl up from school and takes her to have tea with Miss Sophie. My poor little love just lives for those days,' she went on, shaking her head. 'That husband of hers should be horse-whipped, if you ask me. She's still grieving for the baby, and she's so lonely now that you don't go round.' Maggie looked at her. 'Why don't you go to see her no more?'

Abigail shook her head. 'Her husband has forbidden me to. He says I'm a bad influence.'

' 'Cause you speak your mind, no doubt.' Maggie nodded. 'He likes to keep her under his thumb. Poor girl might as well not have a husband, as far as company goes. He's never there, what with his Council meetings and weekend trips up to London. At least, that's where he *says* he goes,' she added darkly. 'Wouldn't trust him as far as I could throw him, meself.'

'Well, I don't want to make trouble for her, but tell her that she can always come to the studio. After all, it *is* a public place. He can hardly forbid her to go into town.' She sipped her tea and looked around. 'You're on your own this evening?'

Maggie nodded. 'Ted always comes for his Sunday dinner with us, bless him. He's the only one of my family who seems to have time for his ma these days. Patrick's out. Never says where, but then, you know him. Lately, he's taken to going out all spruced up in his Sunday best.' She smiled. 'Some lass, if you ask me. I hope it is – might explain why he stopped tryin' to make trouble at work.'

Abigail said nothing. Clearly, Patrick still hadn't told his family about the WEA classes. On the other hand, had he met a girl – at the classes perhaps? She was surprised at the sudden feeling of dismay that sprang up inside her. He'd never mentioned that he'd found a girl.

'Jim's taken Annie for a walk to try to get some colour back in the girl's cheeks,' Maggie went on. 'Poor lad. He's hardly a man yet, but to look at him you'd think he had the troubles of the world on his shoulders.'

'And Sarah?'

Maggie shrugged. 'Hardly ever see her these days,' she said. 'Can't blame the lass, though, can I? This house is hardly the kind of place a young girl'd want to come to on her day off.'

'She's a good girl and works hard,' Abigail said. 'But it's not like her to neglect you. I'll have a word with her.' She looked at Maggie. 'And Annie – how is she?'

'Still coughing. Started with a cold, and just won't clear up. Doctor Maybury says she'll be better once the baby's born, but I don't know. That cough – sounds to me like consumption.'

'Oh, I do hope not, Maggie.'

'So do I, love, but if I've learned one thing it's to face up to what's coming. I've seen too many go that way not to know the signs, and there's nothing but skin and bone to the poor lass. God knows I've tried to build her up, and Miss Sophie's been so good, letting me bring food home for her, but it don't seem to make a ha'porth of difference. She's got nothing to fight with.'

Abigail was disturbed by what Maggie had told her, and her mind was full of it as she walked home later. If only there was more she could do. The result of her article had dealt her confidence a severe blow. All it had done was make matters ten times worse and deprive her of the company of her best friend.

Still deep in thought as she turned the corner into Castle Terrace, she stood at the door, looking in her bag for her keys.

' 'Evening, Abby. I've brought the books back.'

She looked up, startled. 'Patrick! I'm sorry, I didn't see you. Are you coming in to change them? I think there are still a few you haven't read.'

'Thanks. I'd like to, if it's not putting you out.'

As they went upstairs to the flat, she wondered where he had been. There were no classes on a Sunday. Could Maggie have been right when she suspected Patrick's interest in a girl?

Patrick chose the books he wanted as Abigail looked on.

Suddenly, he said, 'I've met someone, Abby. Someone really interesting. That's where I've been tonight.'

Her heart missed a beat. So – Maggie had been right.

'Really? Who?' she asked, her face still turned away as she searched the shelf for books that might interest him.

'Mr Jeffries. He's a teacher at the Methodist School and one of the WEA tutors. He's a member of the Labour Party, and he realized I was interested so he invited me round to his house. I went there this evening – met his wife. She invited me to stay for supper. They've been telling me all about the party's history, its aims and everything. It's really exciting, the way it's growing. There are now sixty-three Labour seats in Parliament. We're now the official opposition party.'

Abigail raised an eyebrow at him 'We?'

He smiled. 'I've joined. I'm now an official member of the Labour Party.'

'Congratulations!'

'Mr Jeffries says it's only a matter of time before we win an election and form a government. Lloyd George has done a lot for working people, but a Labour government – just think!' His eyes sparkled. 'There'd be fair wages for all, and places like Ashford's Yard would be a thing of the past. Sidney Webb has already suggested nationalizing the coal industry. Think what that could mean to the miners! No more greedy private mine owners exploiting them.'

Abigail nodded, remembering William's warning that

changes take time. She was about to repeat it, but the elated expression on Patrick's face stopped her.

'It sounds exciting, Patrick. I'm so pleased for you.' Suddenly she laughed and he coloured.

'What? Have I said something funny?'

'No, forgive me for laughing, Patrick. It's just that your mother's convinced that you're courting.'

He stared at her. 'How could she think that?'

'Sunday suit – the new spruced-up look. And you haven't told her about the classes, or what you do with your free time, have you? What is she supposed to think?'

'I'd have thought she had enough to worry about at the moment.' He blushed. 'Don't want to go about looking like a tramp, do I?'

'You look very smart,' she told him. 'The evening classes have given you a new interest and confidence in yourself. I'm not surprised she thought you had a girl!'

'No time for that – at least, not at the moment.' He hesitated, then, 'Abby, can I tell you something? Just between ourselves.'

'Of course. I promise it will go no further.'

'Bill Marshall, the head foreman of the timber yard, is retiring and I'm going to apply for his job. Mr Jeffries has encouraged me. He thinks I'm well qualified for it and could do a lot of good. I've been at the yard since I left school, and I know the business inside out. I know the men, too, and now that I've got a bit of learning under my belt, maybe I'll be able to talk to Mr Dean about the safety measures and the wages.'

Abigail's heart sank. Had she been wrong to instil such false hopes in him? Edwin Dean was hardly likely to change, however eloquent and reasonable Patrick's arguments might be, but she hadn't the heart to discourage him.

'That's wonderful, Patrick,' she said. 'I do wish you luck. You deserve to get it.'

The look of hope and optimism on his face made her feel a sudden rush of tenderness and, on impulse, she reached up and touched his cheek. For a moment their eyes met and held, then his hand came up to cover hers. His fingers were warm on hers, and in the moment of stillness between them she could feel a tiny pulse beating in his palm. Then the sudden slam of a door and footsteps on the stairs heralded Sarah's return, and broke the spell.

Each took a step backwards, hands falling to their sides.

CHAPTER TEN

Annie and Jim Johnson's baby daughter was born on the fifth of October at five minutes past midnight. Maggie came round to break the news to Abigail and Sarah soon after nine o'clock. As it was a Sunday, the studio was closed and they were having their breakfast upstairs in the flat.

'It's all over,' she said, puffing for breath in the kitchen doorway. 'Annie had a five-pound girl just after midnight. She's a tiny little scrap, but I think she'll do. Got a good pair o' lungs on her, I'll say that!'

'Come and sit down.' Abigail pulled out a chair for her at the table. 'Sarah, get your mother a cup. I'm sure she could do with some tea. How is Annie?' she asked, as the girl got up to get a cup from the dresser.

Maggie shook her head. 'Worn out, poor lass. She didn't have it easy. In pain since yesterday dinner-time. Jenny Knowles, the midwife from number six, came and delivered her. There was a time when I thought we'd have to get Doctor Maybury out, but you know it's not our way to bother the doctor for something natural like a lyin'-in.'

'Perhaps he could have made things easier for Annie,' Abigail suggested.

'What could he have done that we couldn't?' Maggie said. 'No one wants them forceps used if they can help it, do they? Mother Nature knows best in the long run. A towel knotted round the bedrail to pull on, that's the best. Anyway,' she

146

sighed, 'it's all done and dusted, thank God, and they're both alive.'

'Is Jim all right?' Sarah asked.

Abigail noticed that the girl couldn't quite look her mother in the eye, and she guessed she felt guilty about the recent infrequency of her visits.

'Bearing up, poor lad. He's relieved, of course,' Maggie said, eyeing her daughter. 'Maybe you'll come home more often my girl, now that there's a new baby to cuddle. My only daughter, and you weren't there when I needed you most!'

Sarah took the hint. Colouring, she said, 'I'm sorry. You should have sent for me, if you wanted me.'

Maggie sniffed. 'Reckon I would, if I'd thought it'd do any good. The way you've been lately, I'm beginnin' to wonder if you think we're not good enough for you!'

'It's nothing like that! I don't get that much time off, and when I do there's things I want to do.' She cast a tearful look at her mother. 'I'm sorry, Ma. I know I should've come more. I'll be round today, if that's all right.'

'Good,' Maggie said, draining the last of her tea. 'You can help with the washing. There's a great pile of it waiting for the copper to heat up. I lit the fire before I came out, and by half ten the water'll be ready. Least, it will if Jim can tear himself away from that baby for long enough to keep the fire going.' She stood up and drew her coat around her. 'I'll have to get off to Prospect House now to see to their Sunday dinner, so I'll go. I'll see you later, then, Sarah.'

When Maggie had gone Abigail looked at Sarah who was beginning to clear the table.

'You can get off now, if you like,' she said. 'There's obviously a lot to do at home, and I'm sure you're dying to see the baby.' She looked at Sarah. 'And by the way, Sarah, if you need more free time you could always try asking me. I don't want to be blamed for your neglecting your family.'

Sarah reddened and shook her head. 'I didn't mean it to sound like that. I couldn't explain to Ma.' She hesitated, biting her lip. 'You see, the thing is, I've met someone.'

'A boy?'

'A man, and I don't think Ma would approve.'

'Oh. Why is that?'

'Well,' Sarah sat down at the table again, 'he's older than me, quite a bit older, and very well off. Ma would say he's not our class.'

'That shouldn't matter, if you like each other. Where did you meet him?' Abigail asked.

'I was coming home from visiting Ma one wet Sunday evening, and he stopped in his car and asked if he could drive me home.'

'Was that wise?' Abigail asked.

'Oh, he wasn't a stranger. I already knew him, a bit.' Sarah blushed and looked at her hands.

'So, does he have a name?'

'I'd rather not say, if you don't mind.'

'Why not?'

'He might not want me telling people. Not yet, anyway.'

Abigail was uneasy. 'I'd be careful if I were you, Sarah,' she said. 'A wealthy older man and, as you say, from a different class. Are you sure he isn't playing with your affections?'

'Oh, no! He'd never do anything like that. He's kind and thoughtful. He's given me some lovely presents, only I can't wear them, 'cause people'd wonder where I got them.'

'Well, be on your guard.' Abigail reached across the table to touch Sarah's hand. 'Sarah, he isn't married, is he?'

The girl coloured to the roots of her auburn hair. 'I can't say any more. I shouldn't really have told you. I promised.'

'Sarah, if this friendship needs to be kept secret, then there's something wrong about it. I think you already know that. Or is that half the excitement?'

Sarah jumped up from the table and began to run water into the sink, her red face averted. 'I'm not saying any more. Anyway, it's my business what I do with my free time.'

Abigail got up and went to the girl. 'Sarah, I don't mean to interfere, but you're very young, and as your employer I feel responsible for you.'

Sarah spun round, her eyes blazing. 'You're going to tell *them*, aren't you? Ma and Patrick. I wish I'd never told you now. I trusted you. I thought you were my friend.'

'Of course I am, and I won't say anything if you don't want me to,' Abigail said. 'But my advice to you is find out more about this man. What does he really want from you, and where is your friendship with him going?'

Sarah bit her lip. 'We love each other,' she said. 'I never knew you could feel like this. I want to be with him all the time. I'd do anything for him. So, if he says we have to wait, I will, 'cause I trust him.' She raised imploring eyes to Abigail's. 'Promise me you won't say anything, Abby. If he knew I'd told you it'd be the end of us.'

'I promise,' Abigail said, but inside she felt a deep unease. 'I'll come with you to help with the washing. Maggie could do with all the help she can get. I'll bring the beef we were going to have for our lunch. We can make a meal, too.'

'You're just making sure I *do* go home and don't just sneak off to meet *him*, aren't you?' Sarah accused.

'No, I'm just trying to help out,' Abigail said firmly. 'You'll have to make up your mind whether you can trust me, Sarah. If you can't, then perhaps you shouldn't be living here with me at all.'

Chastened, the girl hung her head, he lip trembling. 'I'm sorry.'

At Ashford's Yard, washing was piled high in the wash-house; soiled sheets and clothing from the birth were soaking in the tin bath, but the water in the copper was heated almost to boiling point, and Abigail helped Sarah to dissolve the soap and load the rinsed washing into the hot water. Leaving it to boil, Abigail climbed the stairs and tapped gently on the bedroom door. It was opened by Jim, who had been sitting with his wife and new baby daughter. She was moved to see how tired and haggard he looked; far too gaunt for a seventeen-year-old.

'Come in,' he whispered. 'Annie's still asleep, but the baby's awake.'

149

The tiny baby was lying in a bed hastily made up in a drawer taken from the tallboy. Abigail thought she had never seen such a pretty child. Large blue eyes looked up at her, and one tiny fist waved.

'Oh, Jim, she's beautiful. What are you going to call her?'

'Annie wants to call her Rose,' Jim told her.

'It suits her. She's just like a little flower.' Reaching into her pocket, Abigail took out a sixpence and put it into the baby's hand. The tiny fingers instinctively closed round it. She laughed. 'There, she'll never be a spendthrift. Isn't that what they say?'

He smiled. 'Thank you.' He glanced anxiously towards his wife, her sleeping face heartbreakingly fragile and almost as white as the pillow. 'It won't be easy for Annie. She's been so poorly. If – if she doesn't get better . . . I mean, if she can't take care of the baby, it'll be hard on Ma.'

'I'm sure she'll improve, now that the baby is here,' Abigail said. 'Don't worry.' But looking at the sleeping girl, she feared for the future of the tragic little family.

By the time Maggie returned the two girls had the washing rinsed, mangled and hanging up in the yard. Sunday it might be, but on occasions such as this there was no day of rest.

'You shouldn't have done all this,' Maggie protested as she took off her coat. 'Washing like that ain't no job for a young lady.'

Abigail laughed. 'Nonsense! Sit down, Maggie. I brought my Sunday joint and Sarah has cooked dinner for us all. I'm sure you're ready for it, and afterwards you should lie down and try to get some rest. You were up all night, remember.'

'I'll not forget it in a hurry.' Maggie nodded towards the stairs. 'How is she?'

'Still asleep,' Abigail told her. 'Where are the other boys, by the way? We've cooked enough for them, too.'

'Patrick'll be here soon. I turfed him out to sleep at a neighbour's when Annie got bad last night. No place for fellers; they only get in the way. Ted'll be here soon too. He'll be that pleased about the baby. Loves the little 'uns, does Ted.'

Patrick and Ted returned, and Annie wakened in time for

dinner, looking slightly better. Sarah had made a large Yorkshire pudding to help eke out the meat, and they all tucked into large portions covered liberally with gravy. Jim took his upstairs to eat with Annie, and the rest of them sat round the table in the living-room.

'This is just like old times,' Maggie said. 'When you first come home, Abby.'

The word 'home' gave Abigail a warm glow, and as she looked round the table she realized that the Johnsons were the nearest she had to a family of her own. She only hoped that she wouldn't be obliged to let them down. The proposed sale of Ashford's Yard to the un-named property developer was never far from her mind.

After the meal was over and the washing-up done, Abigail announced that she was leaving. 'You and Sarah will enjoy some time to yourselves,' she told Maggie. 'And I have things to do at the studio.'

Patrick left with her. He told her he was on his way to see Malcolm Jeffries and his wife, Evelyn. He showed her the book he was carrying.

'Malcolm lent me this, *The History of Trade Unionism* by Sidney Webb. Did you know that he and his wife, Beatrice, founded the Fabian Society?'

'I did know, yes,' Abigail told him.

'There's so much to learn,' Patrick said fervently. 'Sometimes I feel that the more I learn, the less I know.'

'I do recognize the feeling.' She glanced at him. 'Sometimes it's the same with people. You think you know and understand them, and then suddenly everything changes.'

'You feel that, too?' His eyes were solemn as he took her hand and held it warmly. 'I owe so much to you,' he said.

'No! You owe me nothing.'

'If it hadn't been for you, I'd never have thought of joining the classes, never have met the Jeffries or known what I know now. You opened up a whole new world for me.'

'You would have done it in the end, Patrick, with or without me.'

151

'*No!* I would never have felt I was good enough, or that someone like me had anything to offer.'

'You have a lot to offer, Patrick. So much.'

They had arrived at the place where their paths diverged on the town side of the bridge that spanned the river. The street was deserted as they stood to face each other.

,Thanks to you, I'm beginning to feel that I might have,' he said. 'But I still have to find out. I've got so far to go, Abby, and I think you know that I must go alone.'

'I know.' To her horror, her throat tightened and she felt tears fill her eyes. 'I know, Patrick, but my hopes and – and my heart will be with you, whatever you do. You won't forget that, will you?'

He lifted her hand and held it against his face. Turning his face into the palm, he pressed his lips against it, then released it, turned and walked away, leaving her looking after him, her heart heavy with longing.

She watched until he turned a corner and disappeared from view. As she turned to continue walking, she caught sight of a car emerging from the mews opposite. She recognized the driver. It was Edwin Dean. On a sudden impulse she made up her mind. If Edwin had taken his motor car, he was going some distance and would be away for some time. She would take the opportunity to go and see Sophie. She was anxious to hear the latest news of the sale of Ashford's Yard.

Sophie was delighted to see her, and hear the news about Annie and Jim's baby.

'I envy them,' she said wistfully. 'They may be poor, but they have something I can never have.'

Abigail noticed with concern that Sophie had lost weight since they had last met. Her hands constantly twisted in her lap, and her eyes darted nervously at the slightest sound.

'Are you well, Sophie?' she asked.

'Things between Edwin and me are difficult at the moment,' Sophie said. 'If he were to find you here . . .'

'It's all right, I've just seen him driving away in his motor car,' Abigail told her. 'He surely won't be back for a while?'

'No, perhaps not.'

'You seem upset. What is it?'

Sophie took a deep breath. 'Like you, Andrew insisted that I must stand up for my rights over the Ashford's Yard sale,' she said. 'I am trying, Abby, but it isn't easy. Edwin goes on and on about it. He gets so angry, and keeps saying that through my stupidity and stubbornness I'm going to lose us a great deal of money. He keeps telling me that, as a woman, I'm incapable of handling the sale on my own.' She looked at Abigail. 'There's only one thing saving the situation at the moment, and that is that the planning permission didn't go through. Apparently someone objected at the first meeting. Edwin says that the Council will solve that problem, though, and the plans will go through next time.' Her knuckles showed white as she clenched her hands together. 'I don't know what to do next, Abby. I'm almost on the point of giving in. I can't go on living like this. If it wasn't for the support I've had from you and Andrew, I don't think I'd have held out as long as this.'

'You still see Andrew, then?'

For the first time, Sophie's mouth softened into a smile. 'I meet him in the park when he takes Mary to the swings after school,' she said. 'We sit and talk while Mary plays. It's all I have to look forward to. Oh, Abby, if only I'd met him years ago. Before . . .' She broke off, and Abigail said softly:

'Before you met Edwin?' She reached across to touch her friend's hand. 'Do you love him, Sophie?'

The other girl looked up, the answer in her tear-filled eyes. 'He's so kind; so thoughtful. He hasn't said anything. I know he wouldn't, because he's too honourable, but I believe he loves me too, Abby. But Edwin holds me in a grip of iron, and I know nothing can ever come of it.'

'You mustn't give in over the yard,' Abigail said. 'The property is yours to sell, and you have wonderful plans for it. You are certainly not stupid, and anyway, you have a solicitor to handle everything for you, and plenty of support from Andrew and me.'

'But Edwin is still my husband. I have to live with him. If he knew that Andrew and you had been suggesting that I go against him,' she bit her lip, 'I don't know what he would do. I honestly believe he's capable of anything.'

'Well, I for one am not afraid of him!' Abigail said. 'But you're right. Unfortunately, he is still your husband. You're just going to have to prove to him that you're a person in your own right and not just a chattel. We're not living in the Dark Ages. Those days are over.'

Sophie nodded. 'I know. I'll try.'

'Promise me?'

'I promise.'

'I'd better go.' Abigail stood up. 'I don't want to cause you any more trouble.' She reached out to hug her friend, but as her arms tightened around her Sophie gave a cry of pain. Abigail searched her eyes. '*Sophie*! You're hurt! Has he been beating you?'

'No, I fell.'

'That's what you said last time.' She took her friend gently by the shoulders. 'Now he's doing it carefully – where it doesn't show. He's a brute, Sophie. This can't go on. Whatever would your father say if he knew?'

Sophie shook her head. 'Poor Father. He thought he was leaving me in the hands of a man who would love and care for me as he did.'

'I can see how hard it must be to be strong under these circumstances. Does Andrew know?'

'No! And please don't tell him,' Sophie begged. 'I feel ashamed; humiliated, as though it's somehow my fault.'

'Of *course* it isn't your fault! Why don't you confide in Dr Maybury? You should ask him to look at your injuries, anyway. You might need a witness.'

'No!' Sophie was shaking her head dismissively. 'Please, Abby, just leave it. I'll keep trying for as long as I can, I promise, but I'm terribly afraid that Edwin won't give up until he's worn me down.'

Abigail walked back to the studio thoughtfully. It disturbed her to see what her friend was going through; that she was suffering so much through something that she, Abigail, had encouraged her to do. Clearly, Sophie would give in before much longer. No woman could live like that. Endlessly harangued, and under the constant threat of violence.

She felt partly to blame. Had she been selfish in trying to fulfil her father's wish? Was it *her* fault that poor Sophie was suffering like this? It was a frustrating thought that a man like Edwin Dean could snatch away all that was within a hair's breadth of achievement.

Abigail did not visit Prospect House during the weeks that followed, afraid that it would create an even wider rift between Sophie and her husband. She worried constantly about the situation, and, although she had promised to say nothing to Andrew about the violence Sophie was suffering, she did speak to him again about the deadlock over the sale of Ashford's Yard.

'I discovered that it was Doctor Maybury who objected to the redevelopment plans,' he told her. 'On the grounds of hardship to the tenants. I also found out that the prospective buyer is a property developer from Norwich, and it seems that Dean has convinced him that it is only a matter of time before the plans will be passed. He's clearly confident that he can wear Sophie down in the end.'

'And I'm afraid that he might,' Abigail said. 'It can't be easy for someone as gentle as Sophie, living with a ruthless man like Edwin Dean.'

'I have a horrible feeling that he's using more than verbal forms of wearing her down.' Andrew said, his face grim. Abigail shrugged and said nothing.

'There must be some way of getting to him,' Andrew went on, his fingers drumming on the desk.

'Conditions at the timber yard are terrible,' Abigail told him. 'Patrick Johnson says that there are no safety measures in place – no guards on those huge circular saws. The men don't complain, because to do so would mean instant dismissal. If only there were some way of bringing it to the public's notice.'

Andrew looked thoughtful. 'Maybe there is a way. I've been planning to do a feature on local industry for the paper. There's Halliwell's Press and Hadley's canning factory, as well as the cattle-feed mills. The timber yard would need to be part of that, too, and I'm sure that Dean is greedy enough to welcome free publicity.' He smiled at her. 'I'm sure you'd like an excuse to get in there with your camera.'

'But he'd be on his guard,' she said. 'That's no good. We'd have to drop in unexpectedly to get the true picture.'

Andrew smiled. 'Leave it with me,' he said. 'I'm sure I can think of something.'

As Abigail was on her way out of the office, Sybil Audley stood up from behind her desk and cleared her throat nervously.

'Miss Banks, may I speak to you a moment?'

'Of course.' Abigail was surprised. She had always felt that the strait-laced Miss Audley rather disapproved of her. 'What can I do for you?'

Sybil glanced round as though making sure they were not overheard, although Andrew's door was firmly shut.

'I'd rather not speak here,' she said. 'I'll be taking my lunch-break in ten minutes' time. I sometimes go to the Cosy Teashop in Bridge Street. Could we meet there?'

Abigail knew that she had no appointments until half past two, so she was free for an hour and a half.

'Of course,' she said, intrigued. 'I'll meet you there in ten minutes, shall I?'

Abigail sat at a table in the window of the Cosy Teashop, where Sybil would see her. It was five past one when she arrived, slightly out of breath and looking uneasy. They ordered tea and sandwiches, and Abigail prompted Sybil to begin:

'You have a problem, Miss Audley? Something I can help you with?'

Sybil crumbled her sandwich, staring down at her plate as though wondering where to begin.

'I have a younger sister, Miss Banks,' she said at last. 'Celia is twelve years younger than me, and she's all the family I have. Our parents died when she was still at school, so it was left to me to bring her up. She did well. She was bright at school, and so I paid for her to go on to a secretarial college. Eventually she became a qualified secretary and obtained a post in London.'

Abigail was beginning to wonder where this was leading, but she knew by Sybil's halting tones that she was finding it difficult. Miss Audley was an intensely private person, and would not find it easy to speak about anything remotely personal. Abigail saw that two spots of bright colour had appeared in her cheeks, confirming her opinion.

'Take your time, Miss Audley,' she said. 'What happened next?'

Sybil swallowed hard. 'Celia met a man called Francis Blake and fell in love. She wrote to say that they were to be married after only three months. I had reservations about the marriage. It all seemed so rushed, but at the wedding Celia seemed so happy that I was reassured. Francis was charming and good-looking, and I felt sure that my sister would be settled for the rest of her life. Then, just six months later, disaster struck.' She paused to fumble for a handkerchief in her bag.

'Her husband was taken ill – he died?' Abigail asked gently.

'Oh, no!' Sybil looked up, her face flushed. 'In some ways it was worse. He suddenly left,' she said. 'There was no warning. No note or anything. Poor Celia got up one morning and found him gone. All his clothes were missing and so, unfortunately, were the few valuables she possessed.'

'I'm so sorry.'

'Worse was to follow,' Sybil said. 'Very soon she discovered that he had cleared their bank account of money, and that he hadn't paid the rent on their flat since they moved in. There were other bills, as well, some of them long-standing and for large sums of money. A pile of them, hidden in a drawer.' She dabbed at her eyes. 'The poor girl was at her wits' end, Miss Banks. She had no money to pay the rent; no money even for food.'

'How terrible,' Abigail said. 'So – what did she do?'

Sybil bit her lip hard before continuing. 'I'm ashamed to say that she tried to take her own life. Fortunately, I was already on my way to London, and I arrived and found her before it was too late. We managed to convince the authorities that it was an accident, and I nursed her back to health.'

'How long ago was this?' Abigail asked, still at a loss to know what the story had to do with her.

'Three years ago, during the war,' Sybil told her. 'Celia is still in London, working again now and earning her own living. She's as happy as she can ever be, and at least she's standing on her own two feet,' she said proudly. 'But she'll never recover from the shock and betrayal; never trust another man. He ruined her life, Miss Banks, and for that I can never forgive him.'

'That's understandable. Did she ever try to find him?' Abigail asked.

'Oh, yes. I urged her to go to the police, but they weren't very interested. I daresay they thought it was some kind of domestic dispute. He got away with it, vanished into thin air, so to speak.'

'I see.' Abigail was acutely aware of the time passing. Soon she would have to excuse herself and go. 'All this was a very long time ago, Miss Audley. It seems unlikely that the man will be found now, so how do you think I can be of help?'

'Oh dear. I'm so sorry.' Sybil shook her head, impatiently. 'Here I am, going on and on, and I know how busy you are. I just wanted you to know the full story. You see, the thing is, I believe I have found him.'

'Have you?'

'Yes, but of course I can't be sure, and supposing I've made a mistake? And even if it is him, what steps should I take? I wondered if you could advise me.'

'I'm not at all sure. What makes you think *I* can help you, Miss Audley?'

'Yes, yes, I was coming to that. You see, you know this man.'

'I do?' Abigail was beginning to wonder if the whole episode of Sybil's sister's tragedy had unhinged her mind in some way. 'How can I know him?'

'Because you took photographs of him quite recently. He was the successful candidate in the local by-election.' Sybil looked into her eyes. 'Miss Banks, I'm sorry to have to tell you, but this man is now the owner of James's timber yard. He's married to your friend, Mrs Dean.'

CHAPTER ELEVEN

Abigail was preoccupied with Sybil's disclosure for the rest of the day. There was nothing she could do alone, and she decided that she would have to confide in Andrew. He was the only person she could think of who would be able to do the necessary investigating. She telephoned him later, and as it was Sarah's evening off she asked if he would come round to the studio later that evening.

When he arrived, he seemed mystified.

'All this is very cloak and dagger,' he said, as he took off his coat in Abigail's sitting-room. 'What's it all about?'

'Something that Sybil Audley told me at lunch-time. And as it's to do with Sophie, I thought you would want to hear it.' When he was seated, she repeated Sybil's story to him. At first he looked sceptical.

'Sybil is obviously very upset by her sister's betrayal. She probably thinks she sees this man everywhere she looks, even after all this time.'

'I admit that I thought so, too, at first,' Abigail said. 'But later she described the man who married her sister. He didn't even have the same hair colour as Edwin, so I asked her what it was about him that made her so sure. She said it was everything: his build; his eyes; his voice; even the way he held his head. She's about as sure as she can be, Andrew.'

He frowned. 'All that from a newspaper photograph?'

'No. Since she first saw the photographs, she's been along to the public gallery with you to report on Council meetings.'

'Ah! That's true of course.'

'Since he's been on the Council she's seen him in person, and she's convinced that Edwin Dean is Francis Blake, her sister's husband. All she needs is proof positive.'

Andrew looked bewildered. 'Why did she never say anything to me about this? Why was it you she confided in?'

'She was afraid to make an accusation as damning as that without proof, but because I'm close to Sophie, I suppose she thinks I am in a position to find out more about Edwin's background.'

'Has Sophie ever told you how she and Edwin met? I know he isn't a local man.'

'No. I thought she might have told you.'

'Why me?'

Abigail looked at him. 'You and she seem to have become, well, quite close friends. I thought she might have said something.'

'We don't discuss her marriage,' Andrew said. 'In fact, I get the impression that it's something she prefers not to talk about.'

'Is there any way you can look into Edwin's past?' Abigail asked.

'There certainly is. I have lots of contacts in London.' Andrew took out a notebook. 'What did you say this man's name was?'

'Francis Blake. They were married about three and a half years ago in London. Caxton Hall Register Office, Sybil said.'

'That should be easy enough to trace. The problem will be in establishing that Francis Blake and Edwin Dean are one and the same man.'

'He must have bleached his hair,' Abigail said. 'Sybil says that Blake was dark-haired. If Edwin dyes his own hair, there would have to be evidence of that at Prospect House, if only we could find it.'

'I don't know how. I dread to think what would happen to Sophie if Dean ever found me on the premises. He made enough fuss over the innocent concert we attended together.'

161

'I'm forbidden to see her, too, though I have been round there once or twice when I knew he was out.' She bit her lip thoughtfully. 'We have to try somehow. It's clear now why he's so anxious for Sophie to sign away the sale of Ashford's Yard. He must be planning to abscond with the money.'

'We must do everything we can, for Sophie's sake,' Andrew said. 'If she's married to a bigamist and a confidence-trickster, he must be exposed as soon as possible.' He sighed. 'At this moment, though, I can't think how we're to do it.'

With Christmas drawing closer, Abigail's appointment book was quickly filling. It was hard to find any opportunity to visit Sophie at a time when Edwin would not be there. However, she did find time early one afternoon when she had an unexpected cancellation.

Leaving the studio in Sarah's hands, she put on her coat and went along to Prospect House on the pretext of taking Sophie her Christmas present.

'I can't stay long,' she said, as the maid withdrew from the room. 'I wanted to bring you this, and I thought I might not get another chance.' She gave Sophie the small parcel, which contained pretty embroidered handkerchiefs.

The other girl exclaimed in delight as she opened her gift.

'Oh, Abby, you really shouldn't have! You must stay for tea. It won't take a minute to make it.' Without waiting for Abigail's reply, she rang the bell for the maid.

'I shouldn't really, but maybe just for ten minutes.' Abigail sat down and looked at her friend closely. She was looking pale and drawn. 'Are you all right, Sophie?'

The other girl sighed. 'Edwin is still pressing me to sign the contract for the sale of Ashford's Yard. He gets so impatient with me sometimes.' She trailed off, and Abigail wondered whether 'impatient' meant violent, but she did not press her friend to elaborate on the subject.

There was a pause as the maid came in with the tea-tray. As she withdrew, Abigail said, 'I've often wondered how you and Edwin met. He clearly isn't local.'

'No.' Sophie began to pour the tea, her eyes downcast. 'As you know, Father had to make business trips to London occasionally. He belonged to a club. It made it easier when he had to stay overnight. He met Edwin there. They became friendly, and Father invited him to come and stay one weekend.'

'I see.' Edwin, or whatever he called himself, was obviously an opportunist, waiting to ensnare naïve businessmen up from the country. The fact that Theo James had a pretty young daughter must have played right into his hands. Abigail sipped her tea thoughtfully. 'And he met you and fell in love.'

'Yes.' Sophie flushed. 'At least, that was what he made me believe at the time. I've since had good reason to doubt it.'

'So things are no better?'

Sophie forced a smile. 'I daresay there are people worse off.' She passed Abigail a plate of biscuits. 'Maggie tells me that Annie is much better,' she said, changing the subject. 'It seems that carrying the child was a strain on her health, but now that the birth is over she is recovering quite well.'

'I know. It's good news, isn't it?' She was clearly not going to get Sophie to talk about her marital problems, and the time was ticking away. Abigail looked up. 'I'll have to go in a minute, Sophie. I have another appointment at four. I wonder, may I use your bathroom?'

'Of course.'

On the first landing, looked around her. If Edwin bleached his hair, where would he keep the bottle of bleach? Hardly in the bathroom, where Sophie might see it. It would far more likely be in his dressing-room. She knew the layout of the house well, it having been as familiar as her own home when she and Sophie were children. She knew which was Sophie's room. She also knew that Edwin slept separately. Would the large room at the front of the house that had been Theo's, now be his? She tried the door and found it unlocked, and yes, male clothing was strewn about unticily, as though the occupant had dressed hurriedly that morning.

She slipped inside and opened the door that gave on to the adjoining dressing-room. There was a washstand with shaving things. Tiptoeing across the room. she opened the small cupboard in the washstand. There were various pots of pomade and other male items, but at the back of the cupboard was a large bottle labelled 'hydrogen peroxide'. She felt a stab of triumph. So, Edwin *did* bleach his hair. She was turning away when she spotted a small desk under the window. On impulse, she opened the drawer, shuffling through the papers inside. Suddenly something caught her eye: it looked like an army pay book. She remembered having seen her father's. She flipped it open and saw the name: Private Keith Fletcher – King's Royal Rifles. There was a number and a rather blurred photograph, but before she could study it more closely, a voice made her jump.

'*What the hell do you think you're doing in here?*'

Abigail spun round, closing the drawer hurriedly behind her back. To her horror Edwin stood in the doorway, his face crimson with fury.

Feeling her own face suffuse with colour, she stammered, 'I was looking for the bathroom.'

'I would have thought it obvious even to you that this is *not* the bathroom.'

'Yes. I was just admiring the view from this window. It . . .'

'Please leave at once!' On the landing, Edwin closed the door firmly and caught her by the wrist. 'I told you not to visit my wife again,' he said, his face close to hers. 'Now that I have caught you in the act of attempting to steal from me, I see that I was more than justified.'

'I was *not* trying to steal anything!'

'Then what *were* you doing?'

'I told you. I simply opened the wrong door.'

'I am not satisfied with your explanation. I've a good mind to ask you to turn out your pockets.'

'I should be happy to,' she said defiantly, 'but perhaps it would be better if I did so in front of a policeman!'

His colour deepened. 'I shall give you the benefit of the doubt on this occasion,' he said, letting her go. 'But if I find you rifling through my private property again, I shall certainly send for the police!'

Abigail marched down the stairs in front of him, her heart thudding with humiliation and anger. By the time she reached the hall, she had regained some of her composure, and as he opened the door for her she turned to face him, her dark eyes looking straight into his.

'I don't think it would be wise to involve the police,' she said levelly. 'You probably have too much to lose.'

'I'm sorry, but I have no time for meaningless riddles.' He stared back at her without expression, but she had the satisfaction of noticing a small muscle near the corner of his mouth twitching as he closed the door in her face.

On her way back to the studio, she realized that she had been wrong to imply to Edwin that she knew more about him than he would wish. It would put him on his guard, and that was the last thing that she and Andrew wanted.

At her first opportunity, Abigail went along to the *Chronicle* office to tell Andrew about her find. He had asked Sybil to make them some coffee, and she brought it in, smiling at Abigail as she set the tray down on the desk. When Sybil had withdrawn, Abigail asked if Andrew had made any advances in tracing Sybil's brother-in-law. He shook his head.

'Nothing so far, but a friend of mine who works in Fleet Street is working on it. Of course, with Christmas coming up I'm not expecting much, but once the festive season is over, I'm hoping for some leads.'

'I went along to Prospect House to see Sophie yesterday.' Abigail could hardly contain her excitement. 'While I was there, I went upstairs to have a look round.'

Andrew looked alarmed. 'Was that wise?'

'I found a bottle of peroxide in his dressing-room.'

Andrew looked sceptical. 'Peroxide alone doesn't mean anything. He'd need ammonia as well to bleach his hair. He could always say he used it as an antiseptic. As a doctor's daughter, you must know that.'

'Yes, but it wasn't in the bathroom. It was hidden away in his washstand.'

'That doesn't prove anything, either. We'll have to do better than that.'

'I haven't told you everything, though. There was a desk in his dressing-room. I looked in the drawer and found an army pay book. The name inside it was Private Keith Fletcher of the King's Royal Rifles. There was a number and a photograph, too. Not a very good one, but unfortunately Edwin came up and caught me before I could get a good look at it.'

'My God! He *caught* you? What happened?'

'He made a bit of a fuss,' she said dismissively. 'But I just said I was looking for the bathroom and had opened the wrong door.'

Andrew took a gulp of his coffee. 'For heaven's sake, Abby, don't go taking any more risks like that. I don't want a heart attack as well as a gammy leg!'

She grinned. 'I'll try not to.'

'Unfortunately, the pay book doesn't prove anything, either. It could have belonged to anyone.'

'But you have to hand them in, don't you?' she asked. 'Why is it in his possession? You could make enquiries, couldn't you, Andrew? There must be ways of finding out who Private Keith Fletcher is, or was.' She leaned forward. 'Do you think it's him, and he's a deserter?'

'I think you're letting your imagination run away with you.' Andrew looked thoughtful. 'We're on thin ice here, Abby. Dean has a certain influence in the town. If we went off at a tangent and made a lot of wild accusations he could sue me, or even worse, the paper.'

'He wouldn't dare,' Abigail said. 'I'm pretty sure he realizes that he's got too much to lose.'

'But you don't *know* that. We need to have more proof.' He frowned, tapping his pen on the desk. 'I have to say, your timing could have been better. He might well refuse to allow you to take photographs at the timber yard now.'

'I don't think he will. It's still free publicity for him, and I get the impression that the business isn't doing too well.'

Andrew sighed. 'I only hope you're right.'

She looked at him hopefully. 'So, will you try to find out who Private Keith Fletcher is, Andrew? Edwin Dean has a lot to answer for, to so many people.' She gave him a knowing little smile. 'Not least you, Andrew. After all, it's for Sophie as well as Sybil. She's so dreadfully unhappy and I know that's important to you.'

The corners of his mouth twitched. 'Sometimes I think you are a bit of a witch, Abigail Banks. Yes, I'll make some discreet enquiries about this Private Keith Fletcher, but it might take time.' He drew towards him a folder that Sybil had brought in earlier. 'Now to business. About the local industry feature: I'd like all the photographs in house before Christmas – do you think you can manage that?'

It was to everyone's relief that Annie was making a slow but sure recovery since the birth of her baby. Abigail had offered to take a mother and baby photograph of them as a Christmas surprise for Maggie, and Annie brought the baby along to the studio one afternoon the following week.

She looked so much better that it was difficult to believe she was the same girl who had lain, white-faced on the bed, exhausted after the birth of her baby. She had put on weight, and there was a little colour now in her cheeks. Abigail complimented her.

'Doctor Maybury has been looking after me so well,' Annie said. 'He took me to the hospital in his own motor car to have some blood tests and one of those Roentgen Ray examinations because Maggie was so afraid that I had the consumption. The rays showed that my lungs were not diseased, but I did have a stubborn bronchitis that wouldn't clear up. Doctor said that carrying the baby had made things worse. He lent Maggie a steam kettle for the bedroom and gave me some medicine, and now I hardly cough at all.'

'That's such good news,' Abigail said, adjusting the camera carefully. 'And baby Rose looks wonderful.'

Annie smiled fondly down at her pretty little baby.

'Jim is so proud of her. He's promised that we'll have a place of our own as soon as we can afford it.'

As Abigail was developing the photographs that evening, her thoughts were on William and what he had done for Annie. Andrew had told her that William had attended the last planning meeting and objected to the redevelopment of Ashford's Yard, too. She decided to telephone her thanks to him. If they could postpone passing the plans for a little longer, perhaps Andrew might be able to come up with some evidence of Edwin's fraud.

William himself answered the telephone.

'Hello. Doctor Maybury speaking.'

'William, it's Abigail.'

'Abby! How nice to hear from you. You're well, I hope?'

'Very well, thank you. I've just taken photographs of Annie Johnson and her baby. I was so pleased to see how much better she looks, and she's been telling me of your kindness to her.'

'It's my job, Abby.'

'Not to take her to the hospital in your own car.'

'Well, I admit that I was a little worried about her. I wanted to reassure Maggie that it was only the baby that had taken its toll on Annie, and not TB as she feared. The woman's doubts were having a bad effect on all the family.'

'You did them all a great service,' Abigail said. 'Annie already looks so much better.'

'But with the winter on us now, and the damp in those wretched houses, I'm afraid her condition will worsen again.'

'I wanted to speak to you about that, too,' she told him. 'I heard that you raised an objection to the sale of Ashford's Yard.'

'You're right. It's disgraceful that there are no plans for the tenants to be rehoused and until there is . . .'

'Exactly. Could you keep on objecting, please, William?' she asked him 'I need the plans to be stalled for a while longer. I can't explain any more now, but I assure you it is vitally important.'

'All this is very mysterious.'

'I promise I will explain as soon as I can. Will you do it,

William?' she asked again. 'The Council will respect your objection more than anyone else's. They might even start thinking about some plan for rehousing the tenants.'

'Of course. I'll make sure I go to the next planning meeting.'

'Thank you.'

'Are you taking photographs at the Wellands' New Year party?' he enquired.

'Yes, I have been booked.'

'Then I'll see you there. Let me know if you need transport. It's good to talk to you, Abby.'

'Good to talk to you, too, and thanks again, William.'

Now that Patrick had exhausted Doctor Banks's small library of books, his Sunday evening visits had ceased. Abigail missed him more than she would have confessed. She missed the discussions they'd shared. Any other feelings she had towards him, she pushed to the back of her mind. Their paths were sure to part; Patrick himself had reminded her of that. There was no future for them, and it was foolish to pretend there was. But late at night, when she was about to fall asleep, it was always Patrick who filled her mind, and try as she would she could not deny that what she felt for him had grown to be something deeply disturbing and unsettling.

Sarah had resumed her visits to her family on Sundays. In the evenings, she usually came back to the flat to change into one of the new smart outfits she had made for herself from remnants she had bought in the market. The girl was becoming quite skilled at dressmaking. She'd had her beautiful long auburn hair cut too, much to her mother's dismay. The resulting style made her look much older and more sophisticated. Where she went on these Sunday evenings, she didn't say. Since their last talk on the subject, she had not asked Sarah any more about her older man friend, but she hoped that the girl's common sense would prevail and she would not allow things to get out of hand.

In the past, Abigail had always enjoyed her own company, cherishing the few hours she had to herself in the evenings and at weekends. But nowadays when she had finished doing the domestic chores she had no time for during the week, she often felt a new and unaccustomed restlessness. Her business was successful, and she was well on the way to achieving what she had come back to Eastmere to do, but she had begun to ask herself where her own life was going, and although she refused to admit it to herself, this new heart-searching had more than a little to do with Patrick.

One Sunday evening shortly before Christmas, she had just decided to go out for a walk when there was a ring at the street doorbell. Going down to open the dor, she found Patrick standing outside.

'Patrick! What a nice surprise. Come in.'

He took off his cap and followed her upstairs to the sitting-room.

'I wanted to come and tell you that I put in my application for the foreman's job,' he said.

She turned expectantly. 'Did you get it?'

'No.' The old glint of angry resentment was back in his eyes. 'I was turned down.'

'But why?'

'Mr Dean took me into the office and told me I was a trou-blemaker. He said I only wanted the job so that I could rabble-rouse. He also said that if I didn't keep my mouth shut and my nose clean, he'd make sure I was sorry.'

'That's intimidation!'

Patrick smiled grimly. 'That's why he said it in private.'

'It's so unfair. What are you going to do, Patrick?'

'Seems to me I have two options,' he said. 'Either I stay on and try again to get the men to take a stand for what's fair, or I cut my losses and leave now. I've been talking to Mr Jeffries. He knows people in London who'd give me a job; a better job, working in an office at party headquarters. There'd even be somewhere to live, too. Just a room, but it'd be enough for me.' He turned his cap about in his hands. 'I wish I could take up the offer. It's a job where I'd really feel I was going some-where – helping to make things better. But I can't leave Ma to cope alone, can I?'

Abigail's heart was pulled several ways at once. She ached for Patrick. He only wanted the best for everyone concerned. He really should leave Eastmere and better himself, yet deep inside she couldn't bear the thought of not seeing him again. She knew his loyalty was with his family and his fellow workers. She longed to tell him how she and Andrew were trying to expose Edwin Dean for the impostor he was, but she didn't dare. Although she trusted Patrick, a word in the wrong place now could ruin everything.

'You don't have to worry about your family, Patrick,' she said. 'They're like my own people, and I'd never see them in want. Why don't you go to London and make the best use of all you've learned? You owe it to yourself.'

'You think I should?' He looked at her with such eagerness in his eyes that her heart twisted. 'I'd miss them all.' He paused as his eyes met hers. 'I'd miss you, too.'

'And I'd miss you, Patrick.' She dropped her eyes, unable to meet his steady gaze. 'But we all have to move on in life.'

'You're right, but I think I'll stay a while longer,' he said. 'At least till after Christmas. Maybe till spring.'

A sudden thought occurred to her. She couldn't tell him about Edwin Dean's deception, but there was one thing she *could* tell him.

'I'm coming to the timber yard to take photographs soon,' she said. 'It's to go with a feature the *Chronicle* is doing on local industry.' She paused. 'Between you and me, I was hoping to come without Mr Dean being forewarned – so that I could get pictures of the abysmal lack of safety measures.'

His eyes lit up. 'That's something I can do before I leave,' he said. 'Don't worry, I'll make sure you see everything that needs showing up. Just let me know when you're coming.'

'I will! I'll be sure to let you know exactly when in plenty of time. Thank you, Patrick.'

'We have to stick together, don't we?' For a long moment they stood looking at each other, then he said, 'I wish things could be different, Abby.'

'Different?'

'I wish there was some way that you and I didn't have to lose sight of each other. I owe you so much. You've changed my life.'

'You've done that for yourself.'

'But I'd never have done any of it without your help. You've been an inspiration.'

'Oh!' She tried to laugh. 'That sounds very grand.'

'I mean it.' He paused. 'When you first came back to Eastmere, I resented you. I thought you'd come slumming, like those holier-than-thou women who visit the poor because it makes them feel virtuous. But you're not like that. You're one of us. It's going to be hard not seeing you again, Abby.'

'I'll still be here. You'll be coming home sometimes, to see your family.'

'That's not what I mean.' His voice shook. 'Oh, for God's sake! I don't really have to *tell* you I love you, do I?' He blew his breath out in a sigh. '*Damn*! I never meant to say that. I meant to go away and say nothing.'

Her heart gave a lurch. 'I had no idea, Patrick.'

'Yes, you did.' His voice was almost angry. 'You feel it, too, don't you? It's been there between us for a long time now.'

She nodded mutely.

'But we've got to be sensible, because we know it can't be, don't we? Nothing can come of it.'

'Patrick, I . . .'

'You said yourself just now that we all have to move on, and it's true,' he interrupted. 'You have your business here, and there's so much you want to do still. As for me, I've got a long way to go before I'll feel equal enough to you to ask you to share anything with me.'

'*Equal*? How can you speak of equality, Patrick? You of all people! You have a good mind, and now you have the drive and foresight to go with it. We think the same, We want the same things, for ourselves and for the world. We could . . .'

'We could ruin everything by letting our hearts rule our heads!'

172

'No!' As she opened her mouth to protest, he held up his hand.

'Don't say any more. You know what I'm saying is true. One day, perhaps,' he said. Suddenly the anger faded from his eyes and they became tender. 'If someone else hasn't snapped you up before that.'

'There'll be no one else, Patrick,' she whispered.

'Then maybe there's a chance for us; one day, when I've proved myself.'

'You don't have to prove anything to me.'

He stood very upright two feet away from her, his hands clenched tightly at his sides. She longed for him to hold her and kiss her just once, but it was clear that he would not. She stepped towards him and put her arms around his neck, reaching up to kiss him. He remained rigid, his arms at his sides, and she thought for a moment that he would push her away, but the insistent tenderness of her lips on his and the warm closeness of her body stirred him irresistibly. Suddenly, with a little moan he clasped her to him, returning her kiss passionately. They clung to each other, wrapped for a timeless moment in a place where the world outside ceased to exist. Everything in her cried out to hold him close and convince him that she would willingly sacrifice everything if only they could be together, that she would follow him anywhere and everything would surely be all right. But before she could begin to frame the words, he put her firmly from him.

'I've got to go,' he said. 'I'll wait to hear from you about your visit to the yard. Goodnight, Abby.'

'*Patrick*!' She reached out to him, but he was already walking from the room.

'Please! Don't make it even harder. It's best we leave it.'

With a heavy heart, she followed him downstairs and let him out through the street door. As he stepped out on to the pavement, he turned and looked at her, and she saw that his eyes were luminous with emotion.

'God knows, I wish things could be different,' he said quietly. 'I wish I could tell you all that I really feel. I wish we could have what we want. But the time isn't right. It wouldn't be fair. We both know it, Abby.' And before she could reply, he was walking away.

Upstairs in the sitting-room, she picked up the photograph of her father that had pride of place on her mantelpiece, and hugged it to her.

'Oh, Father,' she whispered, her throat tight and tears streaming down her cheeks. 'Daddy, please help me to understand and to bear it. Please make it stop hurting so much.'

In the last week before Christmas, Abigail had two important assignments to undertake. She had almost completed the industrial photographs; there was just the timber yard to do. She had purposely left it till last. She had already alerted Patrick that she would arrive at the yard at ten o'clock on Monday but on the Saturday before that was the Wellands' party.

William had insisted on transporting her and her equipment. She had told him that she was perfectly capable of going on her bicycle with the trailer attached, but he waved away her protests.

'My dear girl, it's too far and too cold at this time of year for any such nonsense. Besides, I'm going myself anyway. Why should I drive an empty car? It just isn't sensible.' At last she agreed.

As it happened, she had good reason to be grateful to him. The day was bitterly cold, and on the afternoon of the party it started snowing and by the time they set out a thick layer of white had covered everything.

Willow Grange was decked out with evergreens. A large Christmas tree, decorated with coloured lights and baubles, welcomed the guests in the hall and was the subject of Abigail's first photograph.

She was kept busy all evening. The hall had been cleared for dancing, and the three Welland girls were exquisitely dressed and obviously enjoying themselves. Abigail noticed that William danced with Julia throughout the evening. She was wearing a beautiful gown of red silk trimmed with velvet, and her fair hair was cut in the new shingle style with a *diamanté* band around her forehead. Abigail felt that her own dress was sadly out of date, and made up her mind to buy a new one before her next fashionable assignment. There had been little time for dressmaking since her business had taken off.

At supper-time, after she had taken all the photographs that Mrs Welland wanted, she was allowed to go below stairs as before and take supper with Mrs Carne. The cook was in a mellow mood, having partaken of more than her usual share of port. She confided in Abigail that Mrs Welland was getting quite desperate to get her eldest daughter married.

'No chance of the other two hitchin' a bloke with her eldest still on 'er 'ands.' She leaned forward, breathing alcohol fumes into Abigail's face. 'What d'you reckon then? Will the 'andsome doctor pop the question tonight?'

'I'm afraid he doesn't confide in me,' Abigail said.

Cook laughed, and refilled both their glasses.

'I reckon Mrs W'll have a seizure if he don't,' she said. 'No woman could've done more, spent more, nor dropped more 'ints. Say what you will, though, he's a fine catch for any girl, and fair's fair, she'd make a decent enough wife for a doctor. She ain't no dunce, and she's well used to entertainin', etti-ket and the like.'

On the way home, Abigail glanced once or twice at William. He was unusually quiet, and at last she asked him if he was all right.

'I'd like you to be the first to know, Abby,' he said. 'I have become engaged to Julia this evening. It's unoffcial, of course. I have to ask her father for her hand formally before I can give her my ring.'

'Congratulations! I'm sure you've made a good choice. She's a very lovely girl.'

'Yes.' He looked at her. 'You know, of course, that she wasn't my first choice.'

'William.' She shook her head. 'Julia Welland is everything

you're looking for. Everyone has been expecting you to marry her for ages. Admit it.'

'I agree. She'll make the perfect doctor's wife. I can't go on any longer as a family doctor without a wife and a family of my own. It's important to my practice. You'd be surprised how much more trust a married man inspires.'

'But you'd never commit yourself to marriage for a reason like that?' Abigail challenged.

He looked at her with a wry smile. 'What do you think?'

'I think *not*,' she said firmly. 'I believe you love Julia, and I'm sure she loves you. One look at her face when you're dancing together proves that. I'm sure you'll both be very happy.'

He smiled. 'Very perceptive, Miss Abigail Banks, photographer *extraordinaire*. Very perceptive indeed.'

William had driven back to Eastmere slowly and carefully. It was freezing hard and the roads were slippery, but as they drove into the town Abigail gasped with delight at the scene before her. It looked so pretty with the moonlight on the snow. The rooftops glistened like icing sugar, and the trees sparkled, silver against a starlit, velvet sky.

'I'd forgotten how beautiful Eastmere can look,' she said. 'As long as you can't see Ashford's Yard.'

'Aren't you glad you didn't stick to your stubborn decision to ride your bicycle this evening?' he asked.

She smiled. 'I have to admit that travelling along, snug and dry, in your motor car is much nicer.'

'So, you see I do make the right decision sometimes, don't I?' he said. 'And, unlike you, I'm capable of compromise. Sometimes we have to accept that we can't always have exactly what we want.'

Deep inside, she knew he was right, except that in her heart she was certain there would only ever be one man for her.

CHAPTER TWELVE

The Monday before Christmas dawned fine and frosty. The snow still lay thick on the ground, and Abigail wrapped herself in her thickest coat as she prepared to cross the river to the timber yard for her photographic session. Jack Bates, Edwin Dean's manager, met her when she arrived.

'Mr Dean has had to go to London today,' be told her. 'We thought you were coming tomorrow.'

Abigail shook her head. 'He must have got it wrong. My deadline is today. If I don't take the photographs this morning, the timber yard will not be included in the feature.'

The man looked uncertain. 'Well, I suppose it will be all right,' he said. 'I know Mr Dean is keen for the yard to be included.'

'I won't take too long,' Abigail assured him. 'And I'll try not to get in the way or inconvenience you.'

Bates nodded. 'Right you are, then.'

She smiled. 'If you'd like to show me the process first, I'll decide what photographs would be most effective.'

As Bates escorted her round the busy timber yard, Abigail noticed the lack of safety measures, but Jack Bates clearly thought that as a woman she was too uninformed to know about such things. For once, she was glad of his chauvinist attitude.

'I'd like to take pictures of the planks being unloaded from the barges,' she said. 'And I must get one of the big saws. They're most impressive.' She looked across to where men were carrying timber being unloaded from the dock up steeply sloping planks.

'That looks quite dangerous,' she said. 'Don't any of the men ever fall?'

Bates laughed. 'They'd better not, if they know what's good for them!'

She stood watching for a moment as the men shouldered heavy twelve-foot bundles of roughly sawn timber up the narrow springy planks to the towering stacks in the holding yard. Quickly setting up her camera on its tripod, she focused and took several photographs of the precarious exercise before moving on.

As the morning wore on, Abigail warmed to her work, fascinated by every aspect of the timber process and photographing everything she saw. She was saving the enormous circular saw till last, and when she finally arrived and set up her camera she recognized several men from Ashford's Yard working with them. One was Jim Johnson, who gave her a smile and a slight wave of his hand as she prepared her camera and looked for the most effective angle for her shots.

The roughly sawn logs were stacked at one end, ready to be sawn into planks and the men were already passing them through. The scream and buzz of the huge saw was deafening. Abigail slipped under the cloth to view her image and make any adjustments. For a moment she was preoccupied, focusing the lens and positioning the image to her satisfaction. As she squeezed the bulb to take the final shot, there was a sudden bloodcurdling cry and all hell seemed to break loose. Above the screech of the saw, someone was screaming, then, above the confusion, a man shouted:

'*Turn it off, for God's sake*! Grab him! He's passed out!'

Her heart thumping, Abigail threw off the cloth and stood for one frozen second, horror-stricken at the sight before her. A man had been caught by the massive blade of the saw. As his workmates laid him on the ground, she saw that his left arm seemed to be all but severed. A pool of blood was spreading rapidly on the ground beside him. She rushed across to break through the men who crowded round him.

'Let me through.' She fell to her knees beside the injured man. 'Have you any first aid equipment?' She looked up. 'Can someone fetch it?' She looked at the shocked faces round her. No one moved. 'Can you get the first aid box? *Now* please! We must stop the bleeding.'

The men looked helplessly at each other and someone said, 'There ain't no first aid box, miss.' Looking up, she saw that it was Bates who had spoken.

'Then you should be ashamed of yourself!' she shouted. 'This man will bleed to death if something isn't done quickly! Can someone go for Doctor Maybury? *Someone with a bicycle*. Take mine, if you have to, but for pity's sake be quick!' She stripped off the belt that she wore around her waist and fastened it round the man's upper arm, pulling it tightly in a rough tourniquet to stop the blood that pumped out from the deep wound lower down.

'Has anyone got any clean cloth? Anything will do. Please help me!' she begged the circle of stunned faces.

Someone pushed to the front of the crowd, hurriedly pulling off his shirt. It was Patrick. He gave her the shirt, which she wrapped around the arm, pressing on the wound as hard as she could. Looking up, she saw that tears stood in his eyes. Startled, she pushed the tousled hair back from the injured man's face and gasped with shock as she saw that it was young Jim Johnson.

'Oh, Patrick! I'm so sorry.'

She was still pressing on the wound when William arrived. He took one look at the amount of blood, and the young man's lifeless face, and said, 'We must get him to the hospital as quickly as we can. My car is outside. Can someone help me carry him to it?'

Two of the men quickly stepped forward. William looked at Abigail. 'Thank God you were here and knew what to do. You've probably saved his life.' He looked down at Jim again. 'I'm not so sure about the arm, though,' he added softly, under his breath.

Patrick would have gone in the car with them, but Abigail held him back. 'There's nothing more we can do for him,' she said. 'It's up to the doctors now. I think you and I should go and tell your mother and Annie.'

He stood shivering in the bitterly cold air, naked to the waist, his face pale with shock. 'Get your coat, Patrick,' she said softly. 'Put something on or you'll catch a chill.'

At Prospect House, he waited in the hall while Abigail went and explained to Sophie what had happened. She sent at once for Maggie, and together Abigail and Patrick broke the news to her in Sophie's little morning-room.

'But he's still alive?' she said, looking from one face to the other. 'You're not trying to break it gently that he's dead, are you?'

'No, Ma,' Patrick told her. 'Doctor Maybury's taken him to the hospital himself. He told Abby she'd probably saved his life.'

Maggie looked at Abigail, her mouth quivering. 'Thank you, lass,' she said.

Abigail put her arms around her. 'We'll take you home now. Sophie says you must take as much time off as you need. We still have to tell Annie. You're going to have to be strong for her and the baby.'

Later, leaving Annie weeping in Maggie's arms, Patrick came out into the back yard with Abigail.

'I can't thank you enough for all you did,' he said. 'God only knows what's going to happen to Jim now. How's he going to find work with only one arm?'

'He might not lose it.' Abigail tried to sound reassuring. 'Doctor Maybury will do his best to save it. He's a good doctor.'

'I know.' Patrick's face was working with emotion. 'God! What a thing to happen!' he said. 'You saw how dangerous conditions are at the yard. Now you've got photographic evidence. Dean *has* to pay up this time!'

'Yes. Thank you for tipping me off about Dean's movements, by the way.'

'I wish I hadn't now,' he said vehemently. 'Jim might not be lying in the hospital now, if we'd left well alone.'

'You think I was a distraction, that I might have been the cause of the accident?' Abigail remembered Jim's wave to her as she set up her camera. 'My God, if I thought that, I'd never forgive myself.'

'No, no! You're not to blame. I dread to think what would have happened if you hadn't been there. Christ! If it's the last thing I ever do, I'll fight to get him compensation, and if I can't get the men to strike after this, I'll . . .'

'Please don't do anything rash,' Abigail begged, a hand on his arm. 'Dean will get what's coming to him in the end, I'm sure of it.'

'But we can't wait that long!' Patrick said. 'We can't wait for *divine retribution*! There's a family in there needing food and clothing, and a roof over their heads!'

'I know. I know.' She put her hands on his shoulders and felt him trembling with shock and anger. 'Please, Patrick, just leave it for a little while. Everything will be all right.'

'No, it won't!' He pushed her away. 'It's all right for you. You don't understand what it is to be helpless, under the thumb of a swine like Dean who can say whether you sink or swim. This time I'll *make* him pay, if not one way, then another. Fair or foul, I don't give a damn any more.'

As she made her way back to the studio, Abigail was terribly afraid for what might happen. In this mood, Patrick was his old self, reckless and fanatical, ready to fight to the death for what he believed was right. Maybe she should have confided to him her suspicions about Edwin Dean, though, armed with the unsubstantiated knowledge they had unearthed so far, heaven only knew what he might do. He could ruin all that she and Andrew planned to do.

It was only as she entered the studio that she remembered that Sarah had yet to be told about her brother's accident. The girl looked up as she came in.

'You missed your eleven o'clock appointment,' she said. 'The woman waited for ages. I didn't know what to . . .' She

181

broke off. 'Abby, you look awful. Has something happened?'

Abigail closed the studio door and turned over the CLOSED, sign, then, as gently as she could, she told Sarah what had happened. As the news sank in, Sarah collapsed on to a chair, white-faced.

'Poor Jim,' she said. 'Poor Annie and baby Rose. Whatever will they do now?'

'If you want to go home now, you can,' Abigail said. 'I'm sure your mother would be glad to see you. And take as much time as you want.'

'How bad is he?' Sarah asked. 'Do you think he'll be all right?'

'He will, if Doctor Maybury and the surgeon at the hospital have anything to do with it. We'll just have to hope and pray.'

Somehow, she got through the afternoon, and she spent the early part of the evening developing the day's photographs. But as soon as she had finished, she telephoned William.

'William, it's Abby. How is Jim?'

'We saved his arm,' he told her. 'Although I'm not sure how much use it will be to him. The tendons and nerves were in a mess. The bone was broken, of course, but not too badly damaged. The worst part was that the renal artery had been severed, which was why it was so important to stop the bleed-ing quickly. Kidney failure can be alarmingly rapid after such an injury. Then there was the shock to contend with. Shock of that magnitude can be overwhelming. But he has youth on his side, and so far he's come through it well.'

'Thank God. Thanks for everything, William.'

'It's thanks to you that he's alive at all. He could have bled to death if you hadn't acted so quickly.'

'I'm a doctor's daughter,' she reminded him. 'I remembered my first aid.'

'And that young man owes you his life because of it. What about you, Abby?' he asked. 'Are you all right? It can't have been a pleasant experience.'

'I was more concerned for the family,' she told him. 'The Johnsons are good people. It's hit them all very hard.'

'Well, if there's anything I can do, just tell them they only have to ask.'

Although she had assured William that she was all right, she was feeling the strain now that the day was over. Knowing that the Johnsons would be needing time together to recover, she made herself a hot drink and went to bed early.

Next morning, the telephone rang as she was getting up.

'Abby, it's Andrew. I hear you were a heroine yesterday.'

She sighed wearily. 'Bad news travels fast. I just happened to be there,' she said. 'Luckily, I knew what to do.'

'Well, it's going on Saturday's front page,' he told her. 'Did you get the photographs?'

'Yes. The accident would not have happened if proper guards had been in place. The photograph I took shows that very clearly.'

'Good girl! All right if my head reporter interviews you as an eyewitness?'

'Andrew, I'd rather not,' she said. 'It was a horrible experience. I expect you know that it was Maggie Johnson's son, Jim, who was injured. His wife has just had a baby. It was awful, and I'd rather not dwell on it. And please don't make me out to be a heroine. I just did what anyone would have done.'

'All right, just as you wish, but I'd still like your account of it.'

'I'll tell you all I saw.'

'You're coming in to the office this morning?'

'I'll come when I can,' she told him. 'I'll get the pictures to you as soon as possible. Obviously I had to send Sarah home to be with her family, so I'll have to close the studio and come between appointments.'

'That's fine.' He paused. 'Abby, are you all right?'

'Not really, Andrew,' she said. 'It was so awful, and it's only just sinking in.'

It was lunch-time before Abigail managed to go round to the *Chronicle* office with her photographs of the timber yard. Andrew looked through them approvingly.

'Good work. These are just the ticket, and there's still time to rush the feature through for publication on Saturday. We're going to press this afternoon,' he said. 'Will you give an interview about the accident now, before you go?' He saw her reluctance, and added, 'It will all add to the evidence of malpractice on Dean's part, remember.'

She nodded. 'I know. Of course I'll do it.'

During the afternoon, Sarah dropped in to the studio.

'I thought I'd come and get a few of my things.' She sighed. 'I wish I could come back, but Ma insists on going back to work at Prospect House. You know what she's like. She has to keep herself busy. But poor Annie is so shaken up, I don't like leaving her on her own.'

'You might as well stay on,' Abigail said. 'You'd be going home for Christmas tomorrow anyway. How is Jim?'

'That's why I'm here. Ma said to come because she knew you'd be wondering about him. She went with Annie and Pat to see him last night. She said he was still a bit sleepy from the operation, but he didn't seem too bad. The doctor says he won't lose his arm, but he'll be in hospital for a while.'

'I'm so relieved he didn't lose it.'

'He can't remember much about it at all,' Sarah went on. 'But he's ever so grateful to you for what you did for him. Pat told him all about how brave you were. Oh, and Ma says are you coming to us for Christmas Day?'

Abigail smiled. 'That would be lovely. Of course I'll come. What about the rest of you? Are you all right?'

'Ma's worried about what Pat might do,' Sarah said. 'He says he's going to see Mr Dean and tell him he's got to pay our Jim some compensation for the accident. He says those saws should have proper guards on them. Mr Dean took them off because he says it slows down production. Ma reckons Pat'll lose his job before he's done, and where will we all be then, what with Jim laid up as well?'

Christmas Day at Ashford's Yard was a sombre affair. Maggie tried her best to make things cheerful. The mantelpiece was decorated with holly, and Patrick had bought baby Rose a little Christmas tree in the market and decorated it with sugar mice and little glass baubles.

Abigail had provided a plump capon, and Sophie had sent Maggie home with a plum pudding, one of half a dozen she had made several weeks before. Sarah and Abigail cooked the dinner, and afterwards Maggie and Annie went to the hospital to visit Jim. Sarah and Ted took baby Rose out for a walk, leaving Abigail and Patrick alone.

She looked at him. 'Have you seen Dean yet?'

He shook his head. 'I couldn't trust myself to speak to him while I was still so angry. But we're back to work on Saturday, and I mean to see him then. He's not getting away with it this time.'

'When the *Chronicle* comes out on Saturday, the feature will be in,' she told him. 'Andrew means to put in a frank comment about the lack of safety guards.'

'Good! About time folks knew what went on at that place.'

'There will also be an eyewitness account of Jim's accident,' she told him. 'Mine. At first I didn't want my name mentioned, then I thought that one of the men might be blamed for speaking out if it went in anonymously, so I agreed to be named.'

'That was good of you.' He put a hand on her shoulder. 'Especially as Mrs Dean is your friend.'

'What are you going to do, Patrick?'

He heaved a sigh. 'First, I mean to get compensation for Jim,' he said. 'That's the main thing. I'll probably lose my job for my pains, but that can't be helped.'

'There's a job for you in London, remember.'

He looked at her. 'I can't leave now, can I? There'd only be Ma's pittance coming in, and how would the four of them live on that?'

'But you *must* go,' she said. 'It's your chance, Patrick. You might not get another. Besides, if Dean does sack you . . .'

'He'll make sure I don't get another here in Eastmere,' he finished for her. 'I'll be labelled a troublemaker – if I'm not already. You think I haven't thought of that?'

She sighed. 'So, what good will you do in staying? What will you do?'

'I don't know. I'll have to take it one step at a time. We have to face the fact that we're in a hole, Abby.'

'You know I'll help as much as I can.'

'I know you will.' He moved to sit beside her, and took both her hands in his. 'You know how much I wish things could be different, don't you, Abby?'

She looked into his eyes. 'They could be. If you asked me to, I'd come to London with you. You know I would.'

He shook his head. 'No. It wouldn't work. You'd end up hating me for the sacrifices you'd made. I couldn't bear that, or for us to start life like Jim and Annie. I want so much more for us.'

'At least they're together,' Abigail said. 'At this rate, we might never be.'

'They're together, but at what price? I love you too much to risk that. You mean too much to me.' He leaned forward and kissed her gently. 'You're special, Abby. If I can't give you what you deserve, I'd rather . . .'

He was interrupted by the street door flying open with a rush of cold air as Ted wheeled the pram in. His young face was rosy from the frosty air, and he gave an exaggerated shiver as he closed the door quickly behind him.

'Brrr-rrr! It's freezing out there. Wouldn't surprise me if we had more snow.' He rubbed his hands together and looked from one to the other. 'What's up? Nothing's happened, has it?'

'No.' Patrick smiled wryly at Abigail. 'Not likely to, either, with you bursting in like a whirlwind!'

'Is Sarah not with you?' Abigail asked.

Ted shook his head. 'No, she said she had to see someone and she'd be back later, though who she had to see on Christmas Day, I can't think.'

Abigail could, but she said nothing.

Maggie and Annie returned from the hospital, looking more cheerful.

'He looks much better,' Maggie said. 'He can't move his arm yet, but that's to be expected with it being all stitched up and everything. But he's got a bit of colour back in his cheeks and he looks more like his old self.'

While Maggie busied herself filling the kettle and setting it on the range for tea, Annie moved to sit beside Abigail.

'He put on a brave face for his ma,' she said. 'But he's still in a lot of pain. I'm so worried about what's going to happen. Mr Dean won't give him his job back if he doesn't regain the full use of his arm, and Doctor Maybury warned us that he might not.'

'Don't worry about that yet,' Abigail told her. 'He's alive and recovering. That's the most important thing.'

On Saturday, the day after Boxing Day, Abigail opened the studio just for the morning. Because she did not expect much business, she had told Sarah to stay on with her family till Monday.

When she went downstairs, the *Chronicle* had been delivered and she picked it up eagerly. The front page carried the dramatic story of Jim's accident, highlighting Abigail's part in saving his life. She was annoyed with Andrew for making so much of it when she had specifically asked him not to, but when she opened the paper and saw the centre-page spread given to the feature on local industry, she was even more apprehensive.

There were glowing reports on most of the town's factories, but James's timber yard was not among them. Attention was drawn to the lack of safety guards, as clearly shown in her photographs, and it was even reported that no first aid measures were in place.

Abigail closed the paper with mixed feelings. It could go either way. If Edwin Dean had any conscience or human feeling he would hastily change the way things worked at the yard. But she had no confidence that he had either of these attributes.

It was still bitterly cold, and after lunch there were few

people about in the streets, so Abigail closed the studio and went upstairs. Joe Tarrant and his wife had gone to their daughter's for the holiday, and the house seemed unusually quiet. She made herself a meal and sat by the fire, trying to relax with a book. An hour later she was dozing when suddenly she was alerted by a noise. Distant at first, it gradually grew louder, and she recognized it as men's voices raised in anger.

Soon it became obvious that they were coming closer, and she got up and went to look out of the window. From her living-room, high up on the second floor, she could see the rooftops of the town spread out before her. To her left was the town bridge that spanned the river, and as she watched she saw a crowd of men crossing it. They were shouting something, but she couldn't make out the words. They reached the town side and turned in a body towards the right. Then suddenly her blood chilled as she realized they were making for Prospect House.

With a loud shout, one of the men threw a stone and she heard the tinkle of glass as a window smashed. A man's voice shouted stridently:

'Come out, Dean! Come out, you bloody coward, and face the music! How many more men have to be maimed so that you can live in luxury?'

The other men joined in, and more stones were hurled towards the house. Abigail feared for Sophie and wondered if she should telephone for the police. Then she thought of Patrick. What was his part in this? Was he among the crowd? If the police came, would they arrest him?

The shouts grew louder and angrier as more stones were thrown and windows were broken. She opened the window and leaned out in an attempt to see more. Other windows in the street were open now, and anxious faces peered out, wondering apprehensively what the disturbance was about. She was still wondering what to do when she spotted a black police van trundling across the bridge. The rear doors opened and half a dozen policemen jumped out, truncheons at the ready. Ploughing into the crowd of men and striking left and right, they soon had the disturbance under control. Several men were bundled into the van, but Abigail could not see whether Patrick was one of them.

Finally, grumbling vociferously and still resentful, the men dispersed in small groups. Abigail closed the window again and stood biting her lip. Poor Sophie must be terrified. The irony was that she had probably been in the house alone. Edwin spent very little time with her. Had Patrick managed at last to rouse the men to strike? If he had, would it do any good, or just make matters worse?

Abigail was in bed later that night and almost asleep when something wakened her suddenly. The house was quiet and the night was very still, any sound hushed by the thick layer of snow that lay over everything. For a moment she thought she must have been dreaming, and turned over to sleep again. Then she heard it again: a loud thumping; scuffling feet and muffled voices, then what sounded like a groan.

Slipping out of bed and pulling on her dressing-gown, she pushed up the window and leaned out.

'Is anyone there?' she called. There was silence.

Her heart thudding in her breast, she crept down the stairs and stood by the street door in the studio, listening. For a moment all was quiet, then she heard the scrape of boot studs and the sound of running feet; more than one pair, emerging from the alleyway at the side of the building.

Hurrying through to the kitchen, she unlocked the back door and peered out into the yard. There was no sound, then just as she was about to close the door she heard the moaning sound again.

Her heart in her mouth, she went out into the yard and called tremulously, 'Is anyone there?'

The groan came again. Someone was hurt – in the alleyway between the buildings. There was no moon, and it was pitch dark. Stepping back into the kitchen, she took a box of matches from the dresser drawer and slipped it into her pocket. She was afraid, but someone out there needed help and she couldn't ignore it. In the entrance to the alleyway, she struck a match. For a moment she could see nothing, dazzled by the sudden flare, then as the flame died she saw a man huddled against the wall. As he looked up at her, she was shocked to see that it was Patrick; an almost unrecognizable Patrick, his hair and face caked in blood. When he raised one hand to her in a helpless attempt at reassurance, she saw that that also was bloodied.

'*Patrick*!' She sank to her knees beside him. 'Can you stand? Let me get you inside.'

She helped him to his feet and managed with difficulty to get him into the house. Inside with the light on, he looked even worse. Both eyes were rapidly closing; his face was battered and bruised, and one hand looked as though it had been stamped on. Abigail poured water into a bowl and fetched clean cloths and iodine.

'They set on me,' Patrick said, his voice muffled through swollen lips. 'I'd just left a meeting with the men. There were three of them – didn't recognize any – just took it in turns to punch and kick – thought my number was up.'

She bathed his face as gently as she could, wincing in sympathy with him as she applied the iodine to the broken skin.

'Who did this to you, Patrick?' she asked.

'Your guess is as good as mine. I went to see Dean this morning and asked him for compensation for Jim. I showed him the article in the *Chronicle*. He laughed in my face, Abby. Said Jim should have taken more care – that it was his fault and he must live with the consequences.'

'The riot this afternoon,' she said. 'Did you incite the men?'

He shook his head. 'No. I had nothing to do with that. I'd never have encouraged them to do things that way. It was the article in the paper that set them off. They realized that other bosses took more care of their workers. True, I'd been on at them for months, but Jim's accident and then the report in the paper was the last straw. Now there'll be more men out of work.'

He gave a sudden gasp of pain and she asked, 'Are you hurt

anywhere else?'

He put a hand to his left side and grimaced. 'Ribs. Hurt like hell.'

She helped him off with his shirt, and found livid bruises and abrasions on his chest and back.

'I'm going to telephone for William,' she said. He held up his hand in protest, but she was firm. 'You don't know what damage those thugs might have caused. Better have a doctor look at you. Do you think you can get up the stairs? I can make you more comfortable there.'

William came promptly. He examined Patrick in Abigail's living-room, and diagnosed cracked ribs. He took bandages from his bag and proceeded to strap Patrick's chest tightly.

'Keep the strapping on,' he instructed. 'They'll take a few weeks, but they'll be as good as new.' He glanced at Abigail. 'The Johnson brothers have had a rough time this week,' he remarked. 'Any idea how it happened?'

'He was attacked,' Abigail said.

William looked at Patrick. 'Were you robbed?'

Patrick shook his head, his teeth clenched against the pain. 'Nothing for them to take,' he said. 'I can guess who probably arranged it, though. Call it punishment – rough justice.'

'Patrick tried to get compensation from Edwin Dean for his brother's injury,' Abigail said. 'I think he believes that Dean paid someone to thrash him.'

William looked shocked. 'I see.'

Downstairs, as he took his leave, he turned to Abigail. 'Get him to rest for a couple of days, if you can. Can you manage to get him home, or shall I take him?'

She shook her head. 'I don't want Maggie to see him like this. She's had more than her share of worry over the past months. I'll keep him here.'

William raised an eyebrow at her. 'Is that wise?'

'Let's say it's necessary,' she said.

Abigail made Patrick as comfortable as she could on the sofa in the living-room. Next morning, the swelling to his face had reduced and he looked a little better.

'You should get away as soon as you can, Patrick,' she told him. 'Take up Mr Jeffries's offer and go to London as soon as you're better.'

'You talk as if you can't wait to get rid of me,' he said.

She dropped down beside him. 'You know that's not true. I'm telling you to go because I love you and I want you to take this chance. Surely what happened last night proves that there's only one choice left to you?'

He cupped her face in his bruised hands. 'If you knew how hard it is just *thinking* of leaving you.'

'Then let me come with you.'

He shook his head impatiently and got up to pace the floor. 'You know that's not possible. We've been through this before. You have every reason to stay; I have none.'

She made him rest, and he slept on and off throughout the day. Late in the afternoon she made a meal, and took it upstairs on a tray to the living-room, where they shared it in front of the fire, Patrick seated on the sofa, and Abigail sitting on the rug at his feet.

'It's a good thing Sarah stayed at home today,' she said. 'The fewer people who know what happened to you, the better.' She looked up at him. 'I've been thinking, and I have a plan. I want you to do as I say. Will you?'

He smiled. 'Maybe you'd better tell me what it is first.'

'I want you to let me go and see Mr Jeffries,' she told him. 'I'll tell him what happened to you, and that you want to accept his offer and go to London. Let him help you, Patrick.'

He looked doubtful. 'It's a hell of a step.'

'But one you have to take before you can move forward.' She took his hand. 'This is the big turning-point in your life, Patrick, and I believe you have to find the courage to take it.'

'With two black eyes and broken ribs, I won't look a very appealing prospect to an employer, will I?'

'I agree it's not the ideal time, but it can't be helped. The swelling has already gone down a lot. In a week from now, you'll be almost back to normal,' she urged. 'Maybe Mr

Jeffries knows somewhere where you could stay and rest until you're healed.'

'I don't know.'

'Don't you see, Patrick? If you're going, it has to be soon; it's urgent now. You can't go home looking like that, and if you stay on here, people will be sure to see you and ask questions. Sarah will be back at work tomorrow morning.'

'I need things, though,' he said. 'More clothes, and shaving stuff.'

'I've washed your shirt and done the best I could with your jacket, but they're still tattered. Mr Jeffries could probably lend you some things to wear and a spare razor, so that you needn't go home. Will you let me go and talk to him for you?'

He shook his head. 'I don't know. What about Ma?'

'I'll explain to her. I'll make her see that it was the right thing for you. And you can write to her when you get settled.'

He looked down into her eyes. 'You really want me to go, don't you?'

'The thought of not seeing you again tears me apart,' she said, her eyes filling with tears. 'But I know that if you stay on here now, after this, you'll never achieve any of the things you want.'

Finally he agreed, and he scribbled the Jeffries's address down for her. She put on her coat and went out into the evening dusk.

The Jeffrieses lived in a house on the fringe of the park, quite near to where Andrew Naylor lived. A light was on in the hall, and she knocked on the door. Presently a man answered it. He was tall and slightly stooped, and she recognized him as Malcolm Jeffries from Patrick's description. She introduced herself and he invited her to step inside. As briefly as she could, she explained to him what had happened and that Patrick wanted to take up his offer of help. He nodded understandingly.

'Come into my study,' he invited, opening a door. 'I'll write a letter for him and make a couple of telephone calls. I have a sister in Bloomsbury who will be happy to put him up, and as soon as he's fit enough he can take this letter to a friend of mine who will help him find work.'

Abigail waited while he made the calls and wrote the letter. At last he gave her the envelope and a map he had drawn to help Patrick find the way.

'There's one more thing,' Abigail said. 'He can't go home to pack. His clothes were torn in the attack and he needs a razor. I wonder . . .'

Malcolm Jeffries smiled. 'Of course. I'm sure I can find him something. Wait here.' He went upstairs, returning a few minutes later with a brown paper parcel.

'I hope these will tide him over,' he said. 'Now, the mail train leaves at four o'clock tomorrow morning. Can you see that he gets on it?' He pushed another envelope into her hand. 'There's enough in there for his fare, and a little over for something to eat. Wish him luck for me, will you?'

Abigail nodded. 'Thank you so much, Mr Jeffries. Patrick won't forget your kindness, and I know he'll pay you back as soon as he can.'

'No need,' he said. 'That young man has a lot of potential. Just tell him to fulfil it. That's repayment enough for me.'

Patrick was moved by Malcolm Jeffries's generosity. The clothes he had sent fitted well enough, and Patrick looked and felt much better after a shave. Abigail found him a small case in which to pack his few belongings.

'Did Sarah come in?' she asked.

'No.'

'She's obviously staying with your mother till tomorrow. I was hoping she would. The train leaves at four. You'll be gone by the time she comes in for work at half-past eight. No one need know about the beating.' She took both his hands. 'Patrick, sit down. There's something I have to tell you before you go.'

When he was seated, she told him about Sophie being the owner of Ashford's Yard and the way Edwin had forced her to put up the rents.

'She feels so bad about it,' she said. 'But there was nothing she could do. Now he's pressing her to sell the land to a property dealer and evict the tenants.'

Patrick's face darkened. 'And you expect me to leave? With all that going on?'

'Andrew and I have been working hard to make sure it doesn't happen,' she told him. 'There is strong suspicion that Edwin Dean is not who he says he is. He may be a bigamist or an army deserter – possibly both. Andrew is waiting for a friend in London to make some investigations for him. Once we have proof, we'll report him to the police, and Eastmere will have seen the last of him.'

'Why didn't you tell me any of this before?'

'I was afraid to. Andrew and I agreed that the fewer people who knew about it, the better. After all, until we have proof, there's nothing we can do.'

'So why are you telling me now?'

'It's only right that you should know before you leave.'

He put the last of his belongings into the case and snapped it shut.

'Well, that's that. I'm ready.'

For a long moment they stood looking at each other.

'I suppose this is it, then,' he said, with a sigh. 'This is the last time we shall be together for God knows how long.'

She nodded, swallowing hard. 'We don't seem to have had much time together, do we? Just a handful of hours.'

'Long enough for me to know I love you.' He stepped towards her and drew her into his arms. 'This could be good-bye, Abby,' he said. 'I can't see any future for us, and you deserve a future. It's better you forget me and all that I am.'

'Never.' She lifted her face for his kiss. 'You're what I want; you and all that you stand for.'

'You could have anyone – Doctor Maybury.'

'I don't love William Maybury; I love *you*.' Her heart quickened as she looked up at him. 'We still have tonight, Patrick,' she whispered. 'For our last few hours, I want us to be together – *really* together.'

He drew back his head to look down at her.

195

'Do you know what you're saying?'

'Of course I do. It's what I want.'

'Are you sure?'

'I've never been more certain of anything in my life.'

'No, Abby. You're not thinking straight.'

'If we don't make the most of this time, we'll regret it for ever.'

'We may regret it if we do.'

'*I* won't! Can you look at me and honestly tell me *you* will?'

He pulled her close with a groan.

'Oh, Abby, if you only knew how much I want you.'

'Then why are we wasting time?'

Taking his hand, she led him out of the room and along the corridor to her own room. Inside, she closed the door and held out her arms to him.

'Just for a few hours we can pretend it's for ever,' she said, holding him close. 'For tonight, we exist only for each other.'

CHAPTER THIRTEEN

The station was dark and bleak, the gas lamps flickering in the wind that howled along the line, flinging gusts of icy sleet before it.

Abigail and Patrick shivered as they waited on the platform, their hands tightly clasped. Since the moment they had left Castle Terrace to walk through the darkened empty streets, neither had spoken, each too painfully aware that there was no knowing when they would see each other again.

At last the signal changed with a clatter, and Patrick looked at her and sighed. Saying goodbye could be put off no longer. A moment later the train appeared, puffing round the bend in the line. The station staff stood by with the heavy mailbags as it pulled in alongside the platform with a squeal of brakes and a hiss of steam.

Patrick clasped her to him one last time and climbed aboard as the mailbags were loaded into the guard's van.

Abigail frantically searched her mind for something to say, something momentous that he would remember, but all she could think of was that he had never looked lonelier or more vulnerable. As he leaned out of the open window, his face still bruised and his coppery hair falling over his forehead, her heart quickened with sudden doubt and apprehension. Had she been wrong to urge him to go? London was so far away from his family and friends, from all that was dear and familiar to him and, worst of all, so far away from her.

'This is goodbye, then,' she said, swallowing hard at the lump in her throat.

'Not goodbye,' he said. 'We'll be together again soon.'

Suddenly she remembered the sandwiches she had hastily made for him while he was getting dressed.

'I almost forgot. I made these for the journey.' She pushed them into his hand. 'You won't forget to eat them, will you?'

He smiled. 'Thanks. I won't.'

The doors slammed and the guard blew his whistle.

'I'll miss you,' she said, standing on tiptoe to kiss him one more time. 'I'll miss you so much, Patrick.'

'Not as much as I'll miss you, sweetheart.'

As the train began to move, she walked along the platform, her hand still clinging to his.

'You'll write?'

'When there's some news.'

'Please – whether or not. Let me know you're safe.' The train gathered speed and she was forced to let his hand go. She began to run until she reached the end of the platform, where she stood waving until Patrick faded from view. Even then she stood there, her eyes fixed on the train's red tail-light until it disappeared into the gloom of the early winter morning. Then she slowly turned to walk out of the station and back through the empty streets, alone.

It was almost five when she got back to the studio, but she didn't dare go to bed. If she slept now, she would never waken in time to open the studio. She made herself some strong black coffee and stirred the smouldering embers of the fire in the living-room. Gazing into the flames, she thought over the events of the past week, and in particular the last few hours that she and Patrick had spent together, knowing that if she lived to be a hundred she would never forget the closeness and the sweet tenderness they had shared.

She dozed on and off, half dreaming that he was still with her. Once again she could sense the warm, sweet scent of him, and feel the gentle touch of his hands that had made her heart race and set her body alight with desire. The tingling magic of his skin against hers was breathtaking, and the final rapture of their lovemaking had taken her to heights she could never have imagined. Closing her eyes, she could see his face, young and tender, all the bitterness and anger that had become so much a part of him smoothed out by love. She would never forget the sweet things he had murmured to her as they lay in each other's arms, his voice soft and husky with passion: '*My girl, my darling. I love you. I'll always love you.*'

The little clock on the mantel struck eight, rousing her from her drowsiness and reminding her cruelly that Patrick had gone. She knew that with every minute that passed, he was travelling further and further away from her. She had sent him away, and she had no idea when she would see him again. And now it was time to go downstairs and open the studio, just as though it was an ordinary day.

Looking at her reflection in the mirror, she was aware that she looked terrible. There were dark circles under her eyes, and her face was deathly pale from lack of sleep. She pinched her cheeks and bit her lips to bring up the colour, then she combed her hair neatly and hoped that no one would notice anything else. By 9.30 she was beginning to wonder where Sarah was. True, she had told the girl to take as much time off as she needed, but she had expected her to appear for work this morning.

At ten o'clock, Andrew telephoned. He sounded excited. 'Abby, I thought you would want to know. I've had a wire from my friend in London. I don't want to talk about it on the phone, so can you come in?'

'It's difficult,' she told him. 'Sarah's not back, and I'm on my own.'

'It's quite important.'

'Well, I've no appointments this morning. I suppose I could ask Mrs Tarrant to come down and look after things for me for an hour.'

'Good. I'll expect you soon, then.'

When she arrived at the *Chronicle* office, Abigail found Andrew in a state of exhilaration.

'I think Sybil should be in on this,' he said. 'She'll be joining us in a minute.'

The moment Sybil came in, Andrew rose and closed the door.

'Sit down, Sybil,' he said. 'I have news that I think will interest both you and Abigail.' He returned to his desk and opened a notebook. 'My colleague in London is head reporter on the *Daily Messenger,* and he has kindly made some enquiries for me. First, about that pay book you saw, Abby. It appears that Private Keith Fletcher of the King's Royal Rifles went absent without leave in April 1915; during the battle of Ypres, to be exact. No trace has been found of him since.' He glanced up at Sybil. 'Francis Blake, who seems to bear a strong physical resemblance to Private Fletcher, is wanted by the police for embezzlement.' Sybil gasped, one hand flying to her mouth and Andrew went on: 'It seems he was working for an insurance firm in south London, and again he went missing, this time with quite a lot of the clients' cash in his pocket. You say that he stole money from your sister, too? Did she report it to the police when he went missing?'

Sybil shook her head. 'I begged her to, but she was too ashamed. The silly girl felt that it must somehow be her fault.'

'According to the register of marriages at Somerset House, he married a Miss Celia Audley in August 1916.' Andrew closed the notebook. 'It seems certain that Edwin Dean is Fletcher's current alias. It looks very much as though he is in the habit of playing on the affections of vulnerable women, and later robbing them.'

Abigail and Sybil looked at each other. 'What should we do about it?' they asked.

Andrew smiled. 'I've already done it,' he said triumphantly. 'I notified the police yesterday. They've been to see me this morning to tell me that they have notified both the military police and the Metropolitan Police. They're on his track at last. Ironically enough, Dean asked the local police for protection yesterday when the men from the timber yard rioted, but when they called at Prospect House later to take a statement from him, he had already left.'

'So, once again he's escaped?' Abigail asked.

'For the time being, but he can't have gone far. It's only a matter of time before they catch up with him. His description has been circulated, and they'll be watching railway stations and ports in case he tries to go abroad. Every bobby in the country will be looking for him shortly. I've also syndicated a current photograph of him to all the national papers. By the end of the week, everyone in the country will know what he looks like. The net is closing.'

Abigail gave a sigh of relief. 'Thank goodness Sophie didn't let him persuade her to sell Ashford's Yard. Does she have any idea where he might have gone?'

Andrew shook his head. 'I daresay the police have questioned her, but I haven't had time to contact her yet.'

Abigail looked at him 'You won't make too much of this in the paper, will you? It will be so humiliating for her.'

'I'll have to report it,' Andrew said. 'The owner of the *Chronicle* would be up in arms if I didn't. It's the biggest story Eastmere has had for years! But don't worry, obviously I'll treat Sophie's part in it as sympathetically as I can.'

She stood up. 'I must go and see her. She must be devastated.'

'Tell her I'll be along as soon as I can,' Andrew said. 'And Abby . . .'

She turned in the doorway. 'Yes?'

'I do have her interests at heart. You know that, don't you? Please tell her that.'

She nodded. 'I will.'

When she left the *Chronicle* office, it had started to rain, turning the snow on the pavements to slush. Abigail turned up the collar of her coat and hurried along as fast as she could, her feet slipping perilously on the wet cobbles.

At Prospect House, the maid opened the door.

'Mrs Dean is unwell. She has said that she doesn't want to see anyone this morning.'

'I think she'll see me,' Abigail told her. 'Please tell her I have important news.'

The girl went away, to reappear a few minutes later and beckon her in. Sophie was huddled in her chair by the window, a shawl around her shoulders. She looked deathly pale, and her eyes were red and puffy from crying. She looked up as Abigail came in.

'Edwin has gone, Abby. I woke up this morning and found he'd left. He's taken all his things, all the money that was in the house and every bit of my jewellery. He's even taken my only bank book, the account where I keep the Ashford's Yard rents – all I have for housekeeping money.' She gave a stifled sob. 'The police have been here, too, asking so many questions that I can't answer. I feel like a criminal. I'm sure they believe I'm lying, that I'm a collaborator in whatever it is he's supposed to have done.'

'I'm sure they don't think that.'

'What *has* he done, Abby? No one will tell me.'

Abigail sank to her knees beside her friend. 'It seems that he's been wanted by the police for some time,' she said gently. 'He's done a lot of bad things, deserted from the army, embezzled money from a firm he worked for in London. But . . .' She bit her lip, wondering if Sophie was in a fit state to hear the rest. The other girl looked at her.

'Can there be worse?'

'I'm sorry, darling, but I'm afraid there is.'

'Then please tell me. I'll have to hear it all sometime, and I'd rather it came from you.'

Abigail took a deep breath. 'When he met you, he was already married, Sophie,' she said. 'He left her, too, and ran off with everything she possessed. He must have known then that the police were on to him so he changed his name again.'

'He is a *bigamist*!' Sophie gave a shuddering sigh. 'That means that we were never legally married.' Her tears began again. 'If he gets away again this time I'll have lost everything. My dignity and self-respect, as well as everything Father worked for all his life. I'll have to sell the house. Thank God he didn't live to see it! He trusted all he had to Edwin's keeping.'

Abigail put her arms around the trembling girl. 'They'll catch him this time,' she said. 'Andrew is determined. By a quirk of fate, it was Sybil Audley's sister he married in London. Sybil recognized him from the newspaper photographs I took when Edwin was elected to the council. Andrew asked a colleague who works on a national newspaper to make enquiries, and he discovered the truth.'

Sophie's eyes widened as a thought struck her. 'The *papers*! It will be in all the papers. I'll never live down the shame. Who will want to know me, after a scandal like this?'

'None of this is your fault. You are the victim, and if your so-called friends desert you, then they can't be real friends. You still have Andrew and me. We shan't abandon you.'

Sophie clung to her gratefully, and begged her to stay longer, but when she looked at the clock, Abigail realized that she had been away from the studio almost all of the morning.

'I'm sorry, but I can't stay now,' she said. 'I'll come back as soon as I can, and Andrew said to tell you he'd be round to see you as early as he could.'

Sarah was on Abigail's mind as she walked home, and she found herself walking towards Ashford's Yard. If Sarah were there, perhaps she would return to the studio with her. Annie answered the door of number ten to her knock, and looked puzzled when Abigail asked for Sarah.

'Isn't she with you? She came with me to see Jim in the hospital yesterday afternoon. When we left, I thought she was coming back to Castle Terrace.'

Abigail shrugged. 'Oh, she must have stayed with a friend last night. I've been out all morning. I daresay she's back by now.'

She had deliberately played the situation down, but now she was seriously worried. Where could Sarah be? As she hurried back to the studio, she hoped desperately that she would find the girl's smiling face waiting to greet her there.

But there was no Sarah waiting. Only Mrs Tarrant, who said that she had not seen the girl. Thanking the woman for standing in for her, Abigail closed the studio for the lunch-hour and went upstairs. In the flat, she stood hesitantly in the doorway of Sarah's room. A horrible thought was haunting her. Suppose the girl had run off with this man she had been meeting in secret? Searching her room felt like an intrusion, but she had to assure herself that her fears were groundless.

To her relief, there seemed to be nothing missing, as far as she could tell. All Sarah's clothes appeared to be there. But on opening the top drawer of the dressing-table, she found a small leather box tucked underneath a pile of clean handkerchiefs. Inside, a small pendant nestled on white velvet. It was gold, and formed in the shape of a clover-leaf, each of the three leaves set with a different stone: a blue sapphire, a green emerald and a red jasper.

Her heart gave a lurch as something in her memory stirred. The first letter of each of the gems stood for the owner's initials: S.E.J. Yes it fitted. *Sarah Emily Johnson.*

For a moment it was as though she was paralysed, unable to move as the truth sank in. She recognized the pendant. In fact, the initials stood for *Sophia Elizabeth James*. Sophie's father had given it to her for her fifteenth birthday. Abigail had been with her when she received it. It was purest coincidence that the initials were the same as Sarah's. It was clear now; the situation was even worse than she had feared. *Sarah's secret lover was Edwin Dean!*

Abigail stood for a long moment, staring down at the trinket. The police were looking for a single man, not a couple, so could he have taken Sarah with him to act as a cover? Or could it be that he had seduced and eloped with her as a cruel and cynical revenge on Patrick? Either way, she was sickened at the thought. What was she to tell Maggie? Worse, what would become of poor love-struck, naïve little Sarah?

She made herself eat some bread and cheese, realizing suddenly that she had eaten nothing all day and was beginning to feel light-headed. Sarah's disappearance should be reported at once, she knew it, but she could not make herself go round to Ashford's Yard with more bad news for Maggie. She felt so helpless. If only there were something positive she could do.

All afternoon she was acutely aware of the time passing. Edwin and Sarah could be anywhere by now, though he could not take her abroad without a passport. She longed to tell someone, share the awful responsibility. But the only person she could confide in was Andrew. She decided that if Sarah didn't come home before morning, she would have to tell him. Sarah had been brought up to have strong morals, and a sense of what was right and wrong. But she herself knew all too well that sense flew out of the window when it came to affairs of the heart. The possible consequences of the delay she was planning frightened her. If anything happened to Sarah and she had not reported her missing, it would be her fault.

She spent the rest of the afternoon in the studio, sorting out photographs that had been left for framing. Joe had taken a week off for Christmas, but he would be starting work again tomorrow. When the shop closed, she gathered the photographs together in their protective envelopes, marking each with the style of framing required, then she locked up and went across the yard to the workshop to leave them ready for him in the morning.

It was still raining, and there was no moon to light the way across the cobbled yard. She opened the door of the workshop, but the moment she stepped inside, the fine hairs on the back of her neck stood up. She sensed that someone was there. It was an almost tangible feeling, a presence. She stood quite still on the threshold, her heart thumping in her chest, then she heard it, a whimper, almost like an animal in pain.

'Is someone there?' she called, trying not to let her voice tremble. At first there was no reply, but she heard a rustling sound as though someone or something was moving among the shadows. She strained her eyes to see, then she heard it:

'Abby.' It was little more than a whisper. 'Abby, it's me. Sarah.'

From the gloom, a dishevelled figure emerged. Sarah was wet and bedraggled. Her pretty hair hung around her face in rat-tails, and she was shivering violently.

'Sarah! Where have you been? What have you done to yourself?' Abigail reached out her arms, and the girl ran into them, sobbing.

'Oh, Abby, I've been such a fool. I'm sorry. I'm so, *so* sorry.'

She was weeping so much that she couldn't speak, and Abigail held her close, feeling every muscle in the girl's slender body trembling.

'There, you're safe now,' she said. 'Come indoors and get warm. Don't try to say any more now. You're home, and that's all that matters.'

Upstairs, Abigail stirred the fire and helped Sarah out of the wet clothes and into dry ones. Then she wrapped her in a blanket and went downstairs to make her a hot drink and something to eat. Once the girl was calmer, Abigail managed to coax the story out of her.

'We'd arranged to meet yesterday evening,' she began haltingly. 'When he said he was going away and asked me to go with him, I knew it was wrong, but he said he wasn't ever coming back and if I didn't go with him we'd never see each other again.' Sarah raised despairing eyes to Abigail's. 'I loved him so much, Abby. I couldn't bear the thought of never seeing him again.'

'When was this?'

'Last night, after I'd been to see Jim at the hospital. I wanted to come back and get my things, but he said no. No one had to know we were going until we'd had a chance to get as far away as we could.'

Abigail reached out her hand. 'Didn't you ask him why he was going?'

'It was because of me,' Sarah whispered. 'He said he couldn't stand keeping our love secret any more. He was going to get a divorce and marry me.'

Abigail sighed. 'It was Edwin Dean, wasn't it, Sarah?'

Sarah's eyes widened. 'How did you know?'

'When you didn't come back, I was worried. I looked in your room to see if you'd taken your things. And I found the pendant he gave you. I recognized it. I knew it belonged to Sophie.'

Sarah hung her head. 'She's your friend. You must hate me.'

'You've been silly,' Abigail said. 'You've been taken in by a man who's had a lot of practice.'

'It was exciting at first,' Sarah said. 'Going away with him in the motor car. He said he would buy me new clothes when we got to London. After that, he said we'd go to Paris and have a wonderful new life together. We drove all night, then when it got light Edwin said we should leave the car and catch a train. We stopped at this railway station, and I went to the ladies' room to wash, but when I came back on to the platform I couldn't find him. He'd gone!'

'Gone? You mean he'd caught a train?'

'No. There were a lot of people waiting, and a train came in. I was frantic. I ran up and down, looking and looking for him. I kept asking people if they had seen him, but no one had. When the train had gone, I asked the ticket-collector and he told me that two policemen had come and taken him away in handcuffs. I couldn't believe it. I thought it must have been some terrible mistake; that they'd soon let him go and he'd come back for me. But I waited and waited. Hours and hours, I waited, and he didn't come. It was like a nightmare. I didn't know where to go or what to do.'

'What *did* you do?'

Sarah took a deep shuddering breath. 'In the end, the ticket-collector came and spoke to me. He was a kind man. He said he'd got a daughter my age and that I should get home to my family. I felt so stupid, Abby; so ashamed.' She began to cry again. 'I had some money in my bag. Not much, but enough to get a ticket as far as Halesby. I – I walked the rest.'

'Halesby! But that's at least twelve miles away. You walked all that way?'

'Yes. It was raining and I thought I'd never get here.'

Abigail held her while she cried. 'Never mind. You're here, and it's all over now.'

'You won't tell anyone, will you, Abby?'

'No. I won't tell.'

'Does anyone know I didn't come home last night?'

'I saw Annie this morning, and naturally I asked her where you were. But we both assumed that you stayed with a friend last night.'

'Promise me you won't tell Ma, Abby! She'd kill me if she knew I tried to run away with her precious Miss Sophie's husband!'

'If you promise me that you'll never do anything so foolish again, Sarah.'

'I promise,' Sarah said fervently. 'I've learned my lesson.' She looked at Abigail. 'I still don't know why he was arrested. What had he done?'

'There's a whole catalogue. He deserted from the army during the war. He stole money. He even committed bigamy. Yes, he was already married before he came to Eastmere. He's an utter scoundrel, Sarah. You had a lucky escape.'

When Andrew telephoned the following morning to tell her that Edwin Dean had been arrested, Abigail had to pretend she didn't already know. He told her that he had been to Prospect House the previous evening to give Sophie the news, and that she was relieved.

When she went round to see Sophie herself a few days later, Abigail was surprised to see how well she had recovered from Edwin's betrayal, and how positive she had become.

'The business account at the bank is frozen,' she said. 'The ownership of the timber yard and everything else that Edwin had fraudulently inherited will revert to me. I've already consulted a solicitor about it. Andrew helped me. I don't know what I would have done without him. I've discussed everything with the solicitor, and I've decided to sell the timber yard. I shall sell Ashford's Yard, too. I'll accept the offer Edwin had already had, after the buyer's credentials have been checked, of course. Also, he'll have to agree to wait for the new houses to be built for the tenants before he goes ahead with the demolition.'

'Do you think he will?' Abigail asked.

'He wants that land very much, and as it will make more

work for him I doubt if he will refuse,' Sophie told her. 'I shall use some of the money I get for the timber yard to pay for the houses. I already have my eye on the perfect site.' She smiled. 'It's just a little way up river. Not too far from town. There are trees, an old apple orchard. It's almost like the countryside. I want so much to make it up to Maggie and her family, and all the other tenants. When we get planning permission, I shall insist on proper drainage and running water in each house.'

'This is such good news, Sophie.' Abigail was amazed by the change in her friend. Her eyes were bright, and she was more animated than she had seen her since her return to Eastmere. 'I had no idea you could be such a good business-woman.'

'It's what your father and mine always dreamed of, isn't it?' Sophie said, clasping her hands together. 'It was all your idea, so a lot of the credit must go to you. None of it would have happened if you hadn't come back to Eastmere.'

It was a week later that the first postcard came from Patrick. On one side was a view of Westminster Abbey. On the other he had written that he had a job at the office where Mr Jeffries's friend worked.

'*I'm only a glorified errand boy at the moment,*' he wrote, '*but there will be a vacancy for a clerk at the office soon, and if I'm lucky I'll get that. I have a nice room with Mr Jeffries's sister in Wandsworth, and I'm gradually finding my way round London. I wish you were here with me. I miss you. Love, Patrick.*'

He had added a postscript: '*I've written to Ma. I hope she'll forgive me for not saying goodbye.*'

When Abigail had read it several times, she put it into her pocket and carried it around with her all day. She was happy to know that Patrick was safe and well, and that he had work, but deep inside was the desolate feeling that she would not see him again. She had come back to Eastmere with only one aim: to carry through her father's plan to rid the town of its slum area. Now the fulfilment of that aim was within sight. What she hadn't bargained for was that she would fall in love, and lose the man she loved in the process.

CHAPTER FOURTEEN

The spring of 1920 was memorable. Sophie sold the timber yard and Ashford's Yard to property developer Alfred Winfield, who readily agreed to undertake the building of a new estate of houses for the working people of Eastmere. There were to be fifty houses on the new estate, which would more than accommodate the tenants of Ashford's Yard and, after discussing it with Abigail, Sophie had decided that it was to be named James Banks Gardens, after its two founders.

As the year progressed, Abigail found herself busier than ever. In the summer there was a crop of weddings, perhaps the smartest of these being the marriage of Doctor William Maybury and Miss Julia Welland. The ceremony took place at the parish church, and the reception was held at Willow Grange. The hundred or so guests were made up of the cream of county society, and Abigail took dozens of photographs, some of which, with the permission of the bride and groom, she later sold to the county magazine. Soon afterwards, the editor approached her, asking if she would work for him regularly on a freelance basis, an offer she was delighted to accept. Driving lessons quickly followed, and the purchase of a smart little van with enough room to take all her equipment. It was a big outlay, but an investment she knew she had to make. If she was to accept the new work that was coming in, she had to be able to travel much further afield than was possible on her old bicycle and trailer.

Edwin Dean's court martial took place in the late summer.

211

He was tried for the crime of desertion, found guilty, and sentenced to life imprisonment. Sarah wept at the news. For months, Abigail had been worried about her. She was quiet and subdued. Edwin's betrayal seemed to have killed all her youthful zest and enthusiasm. She went about her work as diligently as ever, but her pleasure in it was missing. But with his conviction, she seemed to find a kind of release and threw herself into her work with renewed enthusiasm, determined, as she told Abigail, to make herself independent and self-supporting. Soon Abigail felt confident enough to trust her with some of the studio work, which left her free to carry out her new assignments. She was rapidly making a name and a reputation for herself, and drew great satisfaction from the fact.

The first twelve houses of James Banks Gardens were completed in late autumn. The tenants of Ashford's Yard were to have priority so that the demolition work could go ahead. During the planning process, Sophie had relentlessly pestered the Council to subsidize the rents so that she could incorporate more amenities into the project. At last, shamed by the fact that they had allowed the slum of Ashford's Yard to remain for so long, and afraid of the adverse publicity, they agreed.

On the completion of the first dozen houses, there was a ceremony officially opening the new estate for habitation. Sophie performed the symbolic cutting of a ribbon, Andrew sent along a reporter and Abigail took photographs for the *Chronicle*. Soon after that, the tenants of Ashford's Yard began to move in.

Maggie was delighted with her new home. Upstairs, there were two bedrooms, a bathroom and a tiny room for baby Rose. On the ground floor were two rooms and a kitchen with a cooking range that also had a back boiler for heating the water. Maggie could hardly believe this wonderful new convenience; for the first time in her life she had a bathroom with hot water coming out of the taps, and windows that looked out on to a view of trees instead of grimy brick walls.

Although Jim had recovered well from his accident, and the doctors had saved his arm, he remained disabled. He had limited use of the injured arm and it was several months before he was fit for work. Instead, he stayed at home and cared for baby Rose while Annie went back to her previous job at the laundry. To Ted's great pride, he had been made second under-gardener on Lord Branford's estate, and he still lodged with the head gardener and his wife.

Abigail received regular letters from Patrick. He now had a job as a clerk at Labour Party Headquarters. His free time seemed to be spent attending meetings and taking part in debates. Towards the end of the year, she received an excited letter telling her that he had been invited to speak at a trade union meeting in Wales. There was unrest among the miners, with a threatened strike. In October, the threat became a reality when all of the coal mines in the country closed down. Chaos followed when the transport workers joined in. Trains, apart from those carrying workers, were stopped, and a state of emergency was announced.

Maggie was angry.

'They should be ashamed of themselves,' she announced. 'It's making hardship for all those families. And to think that my Patrick is one of them standing up for it.'

'They're campaigning for a higher minimum wage,' Abigail explained. 'What they have to live on is scandalous. He's only helping to get better conditions for them. It's all he's ever tried to do. He's on the side of the workers, just as he's always been.'

Maggie looked at her askance. 'Troublemaking, I call it! You mark my words, no good'll come of it. We were put on this earth to know our place, that's what I always say, and we should be satisfied with what we get.' She looked at Abigail. 'You always take his part, don't you?' she said. 'If I didn't know better, I'd almost think you were sweet on him!'

Christmas came once more. Abigail had hoped that Patrick might make the effort to come home for the holiday, but along with Maggie she was to be disappointed. He wrote to say that

213

he had only two days off for the holiday and that he was to speak at a miners' meeting in Yorkshire in early January.

'I doubt we'll ever see him again,' Maggie said bitterly. 'All this getting himself involved in politics. He's in his element, I bet. No more time for the likes of us.'

'He'll come home when he's achieved something to be proud of,' Abigail told her. 'And he does write and send you money, doesn't he?'

Grudgingly, Maggie had to agree. Patrick had sent her as much money as he could spare every week from the moment he was earning a decent wage.

'I want to *see* him, though. I want to be sure he's all right.' Maggie's face crumpled, and suddenly Abigail saw her vulnerability under the bitterness. 'I never thought he'd forget he had a mother and a family,' Maggie went on. 'After all, he's my first-born, and he always used to care so much for us.'

Abigail put her arms round Maggie.

'I'm sure he hasn't changed,' she said. 'He still cares. I know he does.'

She wanted to see Patrick, too. Sometimes her longing for him was almost too much to bear. In her letters to him, she told him all the news of Eastmere; of the new estate and Sophie's part in it, of Edwin Dean's trial and conviction. She congratulated him on his promotion and the success he was having with the party, and took great care not to reproach him for not coming home. But with each letter that passed between them, it seemed to her that they grew further and further apart. Not wanting to put any pressure on him, she never wrote about the things she felt in her heart, and although he always wrote that he missed her, his letters gave no hint of passion or longing. London was not the other side of the world, but with the gulf that was widening between them, she felt that it might as well be.

In the early spring of 1921, Sophie and Andrew announced their engagement. Abigail was delighted for both her friends. No two people deserved happiness more. Andrew's sister, Anne, had wanted for some time to return to London to care for their elderly mother, and Mary, now a bright little girl of six, was overjoyed to know that Sophie was to become her stepmother and that they would all be living at Prospect House together. The wedding was planned for early May, and Sophie asked Abigail to be a bridesmaid. She declined, planning to take the photographs instead. They were to be her wedding present to the couple. It would be the most enjoyable job she had ever undertaken.

She became happily involved in helping Sophie with the preparations; choosing fabric for the wedding dress, and menus for the reception; discussing the merits of roses over lilies for the bridal bouquet. She watched Sophie blossom from the pale and fragile wraith Edwin had made of her, into a beautiful young woman again. Her happiness surrounded her like an aura, and there were times when Abigail had to make herself swallow a sharp little pang of envy.

She was in town one day when she ran into Malcolm Jeffries. She hadn't seen him since the night she went to his house to ask him to help Patrick, but he recognized her at once.

'Miss Banks! I expect you've heard about Patrick,' he said.

'He writes quite regularly,' she told him 'He seems to be happy.'

'I always knew he had potential as a politician,' Malcolm said.

'A politician?' She raised an eyebrow.

'You haven't heard, then? There's to be a by-election here shortly,' he explained. 'I'm sure you know that Sir John Hartley, the present MP, is retiring. He has represented Eastmere as a Liberal for the past thirty years. We think the time is right for a change, so for the first time ever we've decided to put up a Labour candidate. I've put Patrick's name forward to the committee.'

She stared at him 'Patrick, a Member of Parliament?'

'Eventually, maybe.' He smiled. 'I've been hearing good things about him from my colleagues in London. He seems to have developed quite a talent as a speaker. He has yet to be selected, of course,' he told her, 'but he's been summoned for an interview.'

'How exciting.'

'Of course, nothing is cut and dried. If he *is* selected, he'll need to work extremely hard to persuade the voters, but he's a local man, and I believe that if anyone can stir the people of Eastmere into voting Labour, Patrick can.'

Abigail was shaking her head, hardly able to take in the news. 'When is he to be interviewed?'

'Quite soon, and if he is successful, Patrick will have a lot of groundwork to put in before the election. He's hinted to me in his letters that he's thinking of getting married, and I approve. A prospective candidate needs the support of a good wife.'

Abigail's heart missed a beat. Surely he wouldn't get married without even mentioning it to her?

Malcolm was looking at her. 'Would you like me to let you know the date of his interview?'

'No. And please don't mention to him that you've spoken to me,' she said. 'I daresay Patrick would prefer to tell me his good news himself.'

He smiled. 'Naturally.'

She walked on with her mind in a whirl. Patrick, a parliamentary candidate, and engaged to be married! He had made no hint of these things in his letters. But at least when – *if* – he came to tell her, she would be forewarned. If he did not come, she would know it was over anyway.

A week passed, then another, with no word from Patrick. Then, almost before she knew it, the week of Sophie's wedding had arrived. There was much to do, and little time to brood. The heaviness in her heart lightened a little with the anticipation of the wedding. She was determined that it would be the best of days. The wedding of her two best friends. Nothing must mar their joy.

The seventh of May was a bright, sunny day. Bluebells nodded and danced in the churchyard, and Abigail was there bright and early to set up her camera. Sophie was to be given away by a cousin who had travelled down from Yorkshire, and as she stepped out of the car at the church gate, Abigail caught her breath, Sophie looked beautiful and ethereal in her gown of ivory satin. Under her veil, her fair hair gleamed golden in its smooth chignon, crowned by a circlet of lilies of the valley. Anne, her matron of honour, and Mary, her pretty little bridesmaid, waited for her in the porch, both in dresses of lilac silk. Abigail took photographs of them all, then slipped in to sit at the back of the church for the ceremony.

Afterwards, there was much bustle and banter as the group photographs were taken, then the newly wed couple made a dash for their car amid a shower of confetti. The guests then drifted away in groups, bound for the reception at Prospect House.

At the reception, she took many more photographs, of the bride and groom cutting the cake, the guests, the speeches. At last, everyone came out on to the steps to wish the newly-weds every happiness as they drove away for their honeymoon. Sophie hugged her friend with tears in her eyes.

'If it hadn't been for you, none of this would have happened,' she whispered.

Abigail shook her head. 'We did it together, just as our fathers would have wished,' she said. 'Be happy, darling. You deserve it.'

At last the day that had taken months of planning was over, and there was nothing more for Abigail to do but pack up and go home. She felt a painful sense of anticlimax as she stowed everything carefully inside the van.

She was just closing the doors when a voice behind her made her spin round, her heart in her mouth.

'My goodness! *Abigail Banks. Photographer.*'

He stood by the wall, reading the inscription on the side of the van and smiling.

'Well, I must say, it's an improvement on the bike and trailer.'

'*Patrick!*' She longed to throw herself into his arms, but checked herself. 'It's good to see you. Why didn't you let me know you were coming home?'

'It's a flying visit,' he said. 'I have to be back on Monday.'

She smiled wryly. 'I might have guessed.'

'Whose wedding was it?'

'Sophie and Andrew Naylor's.'

'I wasn't surprised to hear about Edwin Dean's court martial. We always knew he was a wrong 'un, didn't we?'

She looked at him. 'Have you been to see your mother?'

'I went to the new house and saw Jim and Annie. They said Ma and Sarah were working.'

'That's right. They served at the wedding reception. Sarah has gone home with Maggie for the weekend, so you'll catch them all together. Can I give you a lift there?'

'Not at the moment.' His eyebrows rose slightly, but he said nothing more, looking at her steadily for a moment. 'I thought I might get more of a welcome from you, Abby, after all this time,' he said at last.

'*All this time*. Exactly!' She opened the van door and looked at him enquiringly. 'Well, are you coming, or is it goodbye again?'

Shaking his head, he walked round to the passenger side and got into the van.

'Where to?' she asked him.

'Where are you going?'

'Back to the studio.'

'That'll do me, too.'

At the studio, he helped her unpack and carry the camera and equipment indoors. She watched him out of the corners of her eyes as he worked, noticing the change in him. He had put on a little weight and he looked well. His clothes were smart, and his hair neatly cut. With a little pang she realized how handsome he was, and once again she checked herself. Closing the cupboard where she kept the photographic plates, she turned to him.

'Thank you for helping. I mustn't keep you.'

He looked puzzled. 'What's wrong, Abby?'

'I haven't seen you for a year and a half, and you ask me

that!'

'I've written. I know I'm not good at putting my thoughts on paper, but . . .'

'What about *facts* – important facts, like being interviewed for selection as a Labour candidate?'

'I wanted to tell you in person. It was to be a surprise.'

'And what about your forthcoming marriage? Was that to be a surprise, too?'

He frowned. 'Who have you been talking to?'

She turned away. 'It doesn't matter.'

'Yes, it *does*!' He grasped her by the shoulders and turned her round. 'Abby, look at me.'

But she couldn't meet the fiery green eyes that looked so intently into hers.

He gave her a little shake. 'I said, *look at me*!' When she raised her eyes to his, he said, 'Do you really believe I would marry without telling you?'

'I don't know.' Her throat tightened, and she could feel tears about to erupt. In desperation that he would see, she pushed him away. 'Let me go, Patrick.'

'No, I will not!' He looked down at her. 'Did Malcolm Jeffries tell you this?'

'Y-yes.'

'But you know it's *you* I love. There's never been anyone else. How could you even think it?'

'How was I to know that, when you never said anything?' she said, her voice shaking. 'Your letters were so cool. You never used the word love once.'

He shook his head impatiently. 'Because written down it looks so – I don't know – *inadequate*. Of course I love you, Abby. I told you so that night – that wonderful night before I went away. Everything I've done has been for you. You were the first person to have faith in me – to believe in what I could do. Do you think I could ever forget that? Do you think I could ever let you down?'

'So, you're *grateful*. But you don't have to be, Patrick. You don't owe me anything. I—' Her words were cut short as his mouth came down hard on hers. For a moment she struggled, her hands pushing at his shoulders, but he held her fast and the kiss went on, became deeper and more passionate, until she could resist it no longer. Giving in, she relaxed against him with a little moan, her arms closing around him, At last he released her.

'Now can you doubt me?' he asked, looking down at her.

She shook her head, unable to stop the tears flowing now.

'I missed you so much,' she said, hiding her face against his chest. 'There were times when I wished I hadn't encouraged you to go. Do you think I wanted to send you away? I thought so many times that I'd lost you.'

He laughed softly and pulled her close again.

'You're never going to lose me, Abby. I only hope you don't live to regret it.' He cupped her face in his hands, smoothing the tears from her cheeks with his thumbs. 'Last month we failed to get what we wanted for the miners. All the courage they put into the strike was for nothing. But they're good, strong men, and they haven't given up. It's only a matter of time before a Labour government is elected, and then we'll see.' He kissed her and looked into her eyes. 'Listen. This afternoon, I was selected by the committee as Eastmere's first Labour candidate in the coming by-election.'

She caught her breath. 'Patrick! That's wonderful.'

'It means I've achieved something at last. I have something to offer you. We can meet on equal terms.'

'You know that isn't important to me.'

'But it is to me. This will be my constituency, and I'm going to be around a lot, canvassing, speaking at meetings, holding surgeries. I mean to be successful, Abby. I'm determined to convince people that I can truly represent them, and I want you at my side while I do it, because if it wasn't for you none of this would be possible.' He smiled down at her. 'How do you fancy being the wife of an MP?'

She gave him a wry smile. 'Am I to take that as a proposal?'

He drew her closer. 'I want your help and support,' he said. 'I want your encouragement and faith and, if luck is against us and things don't go our way, I'll want your strength and confidence. But more important than any of that, Abby, I *need* your love. I can offer you all that I am and all I intend to be, but my whole future depends on your answer. So, will you marry me – please?'

Deeply moved, she swallowed the lump in her throat and reached up to kiss him.

'They said you were a good speaker,' she said, laughing. 'How can the people of Eastmere not vote for you?'

'And do I get *your* vote, Abigail Banks?' His eyes were serious as they looked searchingly into hers. 'Because I'm no good to anyone without it.'

'You get more than my vote,' she told him. 'You get my love and all that it stands for – for always and always.'